CERN

Satan's Playground

NICK HUNTLEY

First Edition

PAGE PUBLISHING, INC.
Conneaut Lake, PA

First originally published by Page Publishing 2020

ISBN 978-1-64701-516-9 (pbk)
ISBN 978-1-64701-517-6 (digital)

Printed in the United States of America

To My beautiful daughter Nicole Huntley,

I originally wrote this book for everyone, but I came to realize that you, Nicole Huntley, were my loudest cheerleader, my motivational speaker and you helped me press on. You continue to believe in me as a new author and you helped me finish a big challenge. One that I was unsure I could complete myself.

As a result, you helped me achieve my goal and finish a three year project, this amazing book, and by the time it is printed you will be forever remembered and some day you will be truly wise enough to rule the world.

CHAPTER 1

In the very beginning, the big bang happened, and this was about 13.8 billion years ago. Everything came into existence. The universe was suddenly born out of nothing, and this was truly the beginning of everything and all matter—the big bang!

Up until about the middle of the twentieth century, most of the world's scientist believed the universe as infinite and even ageless. Well, at least until Albert Einstein's theory of relativity gave us better understanding of gravity. In the year 1964, cosmic background radiation was discovered, not by experiments, but by accident. This is a relic of the early universe that, together with other observational evidence in and the rest of it, made the big bang the accepted theory in science. Since that time, there has been a great advancement in technology.

The Hubble telescope has given us a really good picture of the big bang and the structure of the cosmos. Recent observations even seem to suggest that the expansion of the universe is accelerating.

We must then ask this question: How can something come from nothing?

Over the years, our space telescopes have allowed us to look further and further back in time. We can now observe the faintest lights of the universe that formed just three hundred thousand years after the big bang. After this cosmic explosion, the main agenda of the cosmos was expansion, ever diluting the concentration of energy that filled space. After this, with even passing movement the universe became somewhat bigger; it became a little bit cooler and even somewhat dimmer.

For thirty-eight thousand years, energy and matter coinhabited a kind of opaque soup in which free-range electrons continually scattered the photons every which way. Photons didn't travel far in this early epoch before encountering an electron. At that time, if the goal was to simply see across the universe, you could not. Any photon that could be detected had careened off an electron only nano- and picoseconds earlier. Since this is the largest distance that information can travel before reaching one's eyes, the entire universe was simply a glowing opaque fog. The sun and all the other stars behave the same way as well.

As the temperature decreased, particles began to move more slowly, then even slower. It was at this time that the universe first experienced a temperature of below three thousand degrees Kelvin. Electrons actually slowed down just enough to be captured by passing protons, bringing real-deal atoms into the worlds in which we now live.

Imagine this: only one microsecond after the big bang, all that existed was soup. This was a primordial broth of subatomic particles known as quarks and gluons that will eventually make up every neutron, proton, and atom ever. This really is the hottest soup that has ever existed. This soup is about 250 times hotter than the center of the sun we know and love. Yes, that is really hot. With the help of some of the most complex machines ever built, this quark soup can be cooked up in tiny portions.

First, we will need a collider of atom smasher. Anything that can take a fundamental building block of nature and accelerate it to high energy and smash it into smoothing else. So at this time, there are only two colliders in the whole wide world, although the country of China plans construction very soon, to begin building the biggest particle collider ever known to man.

For now, we have two colliders. One is called RCIC, which stands for Relativistic Heavy Ion Collider. It is located at Brookhaven Nation Laboratory, and it's made of two counterrotating rings, and the reason that is done is that particles can be accelerated and they can be looped around, over and over, and passed through one another so that they collide over and over.

Next, the collider is chilled out (-459.67/-273.15 degrees Celsius). The beams that are going to collide with each other are contained inside these pipes essentially made up of a superconducting magnet. They are cooled down to a few degrees above absolute zero, and the reason this is done is that certain kinds of metals, when cooled down that much, can pass current through them, and without any resistance at all, which means no overheating and much faster acceleration.

Now, let's add just little bit, a pinch of heavy ions, to accelerators. The physicists at Brookhaven prefer gold (AU), and it's made up of a bunch of protons and neutrons. Next, they accelerate those, and they are sped up to very close to the speed of light.

The more energy that can be put into the collision between these things, the more it allows you to break things into smaller pieces.

The next step is to collide ions until data emerges. When the collision occurs, all the protons and neutrons melt so that all you have left are quarks and gluons, and that thing is expanding rapidly.

As it is expanding, it starts to cool down, and as it cools down, it goes through the same phase transitions that occurred in the early universe, where you go from a quark-gluon plasma into things like protons and neutrons, the very same stuff that we are all made of.

This momentous act of destructions and creations, or hot quark soup, only lasts for about ten to minus twenty-three seconds, which is an extremely short amount of time. These little bangs are infinitely small, about one millionth of one billionth of a meter across.

Now, what scientists really would like to do is take a microscope and look to see what was really there, but it is too small and it cannot be done, so all one can do is look at what came out.

Basically, they cannot see the "soup"; they can only see what is known as the splatter, which is caused by the collision. Unless you are a physicist, you may look at all this, the abstract image they have, and think, *Wow, this is way too complicated!* For a really complex problem, you need an equally complex solution.

At positions where those collision will occur, scientists have built huge detectors; they are gigantic three-dimensional digital cameras. They do have spectacular title names, like PHENIX and STAR. These detectors are feats of superengineering, and they provide clear snapshots of collisions.

The line coming out of the collision each represents a particle that went flying through a detector. How much the particle bends tells us whether they are matter or antimatter, whether they are positively charged or negatively charged, and it also tells us how much energy they actually have.

So now we are looking at how the particles are moving together, and by looking at this, you can look at the source that created them, and as physicists and scientists piece together the soup from the splatter, they can examine its consistency and quality. It behaves very collectively, so they all know about each other and they are all moving together in concert with each other, being what many call nearly perfect fluid.

That scientists are able to recreate the primordial soup that farmed all matter is really just the beginning. It's not just that it has been done and that we can still do it, but what is important about all this is that scientists can tell you a lot about what they have created, but they don't have a really good idea of why. Why does it become like this? In order to understand that, we need to want to vary the size of the thing.

Brilliant minds ask what happens if they are to use smaller ions, like copper, for example, or larger ones, like uranium. They would next vary the initial temperature, and also, it would need to be studied by looking at different scales inside, and from that they can figure out basically the answer to a very fundamental question.

At what point do you transition from just a whole bunch of quarks and gluons to something that becomes a perfect fluid?

This is a lot like cooks or chefs testing ingredients, techniques, and temperatures; the physicists, scientists, and engineers at Brookhaven continue to refine their experiments.

Deep down below the ground near Geneva, Switzerland, lies CERN's Large Hadron Collider (LHC). CERN, which is also known as the European Organization for Nuclear Research, was established on September 29, 1954. The CERN facility was built on the Franco-Swiss border.

CERN has at least twenty-two different countries inside its membership and is home to the world's largest known particle collision machine, or particle collider, the world has come to know as the Large Hadron Collider. On September 10, 2008, the largest and most complex machine ever devised by man was flipped on, turned on, and brought to life. The Large Hadron Collider is a seventeen-mile-long circle of superconducting electromagnets buried approximately one hundred meters, or about three hundred feet, below the ground level near the city of Geneva on the Franco-Swiss border, where CERN conducts many physics experiments and in particles acceleration.

Chilled to temperatures colder than the void of outer space and generating a magnetic field more than one hundred thousand times than of the Earth's, this machine accelerator beams proton particles to a velocity just under the speed of light and next smashes them together inside the particle chamber detector in order to break apart the nuclei and unloose the subatomic secrets of matter. At full power, the LHC produces roughly six hundred million collisions per second, creating fleeting atomic explosions up to a million times hotter than the interior of the sun. The data collected from these collisions is processed by the world's wide LHC computing grid, one of the most expensive and powerful computing grids on the planet.

The Grid, as it is known, builds on the technology of the World Wide Web, which was invented at CERN in 1989. The Large Hadron Collider is the primary research instrument of the European Organization for Nuclear Research, otherwise known as CERN.

After the devasting detonations of the Little Boy and Fat Man over Nagasaki and Hiroshima at the end of the of World War II, mankind was thrust into the atomic age. In accordance with the inevitability thesis, once technology is introduced into society, what follows is the inevitable development of that technology.

It is known in many circles that the scientific community, impelled by military interests around the globe, became totally obsessed with the idea of harnessing the power of the almighty atom, unraveling the very fabric of physical reality at the subatomic level. In the year 2010, CERN accomplished smashing two particles together in the Large Hadron Collider, a task that has been described as similar to "firing two needles across the Atlantic Ocean and getting them to hit each other" by the LHC engineer Stephen Myers. Physicists have been searching for Higgs boson, an elementary particle and the only missing piece in the standard model of particle physics for over forty years, until it was discovered by CERN in the year 2012, then confirmed to be the so-called God particle in 2013. As a side note, if the universe is the answer, what is the question? Now, in reality, the Higgs boson is a quantum exaltation of the Higgs field, which is a field that is believed to exist everywhere in the universe and gives all particles mass through a process known as the Higgs effect.

The Higgs effect is the transference of mass energy passing through the Higgs field via the Higgs boson, which contains the relative mass in the form of energy.

As particles begin to take on mass, they become heavier, slowing down and allowing an attraction between particles to occur. The Higgs boson holds matter together and therefore also has the very potential to tear matter apart; with that side, it really does seem fitting that CERN has a statue of the Hindu god Shiva, the creator, destroyer, and regenerator, on display in front of their laboratory. CERN said that this deity was chosen because of a metaphor that was drawn between the cosmic dance of the Nataraja and the modern study of the cosmic dance of subatomic particles. In Hinduism, Shiva's dance has two forms, one of which is gentle and associated with creation, while the other dance is very violent and even dangerous, associated with destruction. In another dance, Shiva dances in symmetries to remind us that the dance of life is not perfect, and he dances just as much in mystery and death as in life and relation. And this has to be accepted, because it is only on the left foot that we can accept it. There is a plaque on the Shiva statue at CERN, and it reads, "In our time, physicists have used the most advanced technology to portray the patterns of the cosmic dance. This unifies the ancient's mythology."

However, there are many who fear that this statue is actually symbolic of CERN's intentions to rule the world like gods controlling the dance of life from creation to destruction and through to regeneration.

Some have speculated that CERN is the engine behind a satanic new world order agenda, but can an institution as reputable as CERN be associated with such dark intentions? This bronze Shiva statue in front of CERN stands within a great circle, a sort a halo that has flames going out. This is the circle of mass, energy, space, and time. In the all-embracing material world. Within this Shiva dance, the lord of the dance is everywhere in the universe. The manifestation of the world is called his play. He sends his rain onto the just and the unjust. He is beyond good and evil. It's all an immense manifestation of play. It has been told that Shiva has very long hair that streams out to the limits of the universe, and his knowledge includes everything.

He has four arms, and the upper right arm is holding a drum, which is the drum that summons things into creation. When this drum is beaten, things come into existence.

In Shiva's left arm he holds a fire, which is what destroys everything, as he both creates and destroys. His lower right hand is held up, which means not to be afraid in spite of everything, that it is all right. The other hand points down at his feet, and one foot is planted squarely on the back of a dwarf. This infinitely powerful dwarf is called Malacca. Shiva's other foot is raised; it is raised against gravitation and is the symbol of spiritual contemplation. The whole thing is there. The world is space, time, matter, and energy, the world of creation and destruction and the worlds of physiology.

CHAPTER 2

In front of the CERN nuclear research facility, right in plain site is a statue of the goddess of destruction, a statue of the Lord Shiva. Shiva is known as the destroyer within the Trimurti, the Hindu trinity, which includes Brahma and Vishnu. Also known as Mahadeva (literally the great god) is one of the principal deities of Hinduism. He is one of the supreme beings within Shaivism, one of the major traditions within contemporary Hinduism.

In Shaivism tradition, Shiva is one of the supreme beings who create, protect, and transform the universe. In the Shaktism traditions, the goddess, or devil, is described as one of the supreme, yet Shiva is revered along with Vishnu and Brahma. A goddess is stated to be the energy and creative power (Shakti) of each, with Parvati (Sati) the equal, complementary partner of Shiva. He is one of the five equivale. According to the Shaivism sect, the highest form of Ishvara is a formless, limitless, transcendent, and unchanging and absolute Brahman and the primal atman (soul, self) of the universe.

There are many both benevolent and fearsome depictions of Shiva. In benevolent aspects, he is depicted as an omniscient yogi who lives an ascetic life on Mount Kailash, as well as a householder with his wife, Parvati, and his two children, Ganesha and Kartikeya. In his fierce aspects, he is often depicted slaying demons. Shiva is also known as Adiyogi Shiva, regarded as the patron god of Yoga, meditation, and arts.

Ent deities in panchayatana puja of the Smarta tradition of Hinduism. The iconographical attributes of Shiva are the serpent around his neck, the adorning crescent moon, the whole Ganga River flowing from his matted hair, the third eye on his forehead, the trishula or trident as his weapon, and the damaru drum. He is usually worshipped in the aniconic form of lingam. Shiva is a pan-Hindu deity revered widely by Hindus, in India, Nepal, and Sri Lanka.

Shiva is also called as Brahman, which can also be said as Para Brahman. *Shiva* means "nothingness." The word *Shivoham* means the consciousness of one individual. The lord says he is omnipotent, omnipresent, as he is present in the form of one's consciousness.

In Tamil, he was called by different names other than Siva: Nataraja (dance form of Shiva), Rudra (enraged form of Shiva), and Dakshinamurthy (Yoga form of Shiva). Nataraja is the only form of Shiva worshipped in a human figure. Elsewhere, he is worshipped in lingam figure.

Pancha Bootha temples are located in South India. Pancha Bootha Stalam refers to five temples dedicated to Shiva. Tamil literature is enriched by Shiva devotees, called sixty-three Nayanars (Navanars).

The Sanskrit word *Siva* (Devanagari: शिव, transliterated as Shiva or Siva), states Monier Monier-Williams, means "auspicious, propitious, gracious, benign, kind, benevolent, friendly." The roots of Siva in folk etymology are *Si*, which means "in whom all things lie, pervasiveness," and *va*, which means "embodiment of grace."

The word *Shiva* is used as an adjective in the Rig Veda (approximately 1700–1100 BC) as an epithet for several Rig Vedic deities, including Rudra. The term *Shiva* also connotes "liberation, final emancipation" and "the auspicious one." This adjective sense of usage is addressed to many deities in Vedic layers of literature. The term evolved from the Vedic *Rudra-Shiva* to the noun *Shiva* in the epics and Puranas as an auspicious deity who is the "creator, producer, and dissolver."

Sarabha, or Sharabha, presents another etymology with the Sanskrit root *sarv*, which means "to injure" or "to kill," with the name interpreted to connote "one who can kill the forces of darkness." The Sanskrit work *Saiva* means "relating to the god Shiva," and this term is the Sanskrit name both for one of the principal sects of Hinduism and for a member of that sec. It is used as an adjective to characterize certain beliefs and practices, such as Shaivism.

Some authors associate the name with the Tamil word *Sivppu*, meaning "red," noting that Shiva is linked to the sun (Sivan, "the red one," in Tamil) and that Rudra is also called Babhru (brown, or red) in the Rig Veda. The Vishnu Shurangama interprets Shiva to have multiple meanings: "the pure one" and "the one who is not affected by three gunas of Prakriti (sattva, rajas, and tamas)."

Shiva is known in many names, such as Viswanatha (lord of the universe), Mahadeva, Mahandeo, Mahasu, Maheshvara, Shankara, Shambhu, Rudra, Hara, Trilochana, Devendra (chief of the gods), Neelakanta, Subhankara, Trilokinatha (lord of the three realms), and Ghrneshwar (lord of compassion).

The highest reverence for Shiva in Shaivism is reflected in his epithets *Mahādeva* ("great god"; *maha* "great," and *deva* "god"), Maheśvara ("great lord"; *maha* "great," and *isvara* "lord"), and Parameśvara ("supreme lord").

The Sahasranama are medieval Indian texts that list a thousand names derived from aspect and epithets of a deity. There are at least eight different versions of the *Shiva Sahasranama*, devotional hymn (stotras) listing many names of Shiva. The version appearing in book 13 (*Anuśāsanaparvan*) of the Mahabharata provides one such list. Shiva also has Dasha-Sahasranamas (ten thousand names) that are found in the *Mahanyasa*. The *Shri Rudram Chamakam*, also known as the Śatarudriya, is a devotional hymn to Shiva hailing him by many names.

The Shiva-related tradition is a major part of Hinduism found all over the Indianan subcontinent, such as India, Nepal, and Sri Lanka, and in Southeast Asia, such as Bailli, Indonesia. Scholars have interpreted early prehistoric painting at the Bhimbetka rock shelters, carbon-dated to be from pre-10,000 BCE period, as Shiva dancing, Shiva trident, and his mount, Nandi. Rock paintings from Bhimbetka, depicting a figure with a trishul, have been described as Nataraja by Erwin Neumayer, who dates them to the Mesolithic period.

Of several Indus Valley seals that show animals, one seal that has attracted attention shows a large central figure, either horned or wearing a horned headdress and possibly ithyphallic, seated in a posture reminiscent of the lotus position, surrounded by animals. This figure was named by early excavators of Mohenjo Daro as Pashupati ("lord of animals," Sanskrit paśupati), an epithet of the later Hindu deities Shiva and Rudra.

Sir John Marshall and others suggested that this figure is a prototype of Shiva, with three faces, seated in a "yoga posture," with the knees out and feet joined. The semicircular shapes on the head were interpreted as two horns. Scholars such as Gavin Flood, John Keay, and Doris Meth Srinivasan expressed doubts about this suggestion, however.

Gavin Flood states that it is not clear from the seal that the figure has three faces, is seated in a yoga posture, or even that the shape is intended to represent a human figure. He characterizes these views as "speculative" but adds that it is nevertheless possible that there are echoes of Shaiva iconographic themes, such as half-moon shapes resembling the horns of bull. John Keay writes that "he may indeed be an early manifestation of Lord Shiva as Pashupati," but a couple of his specialties of this figure do not match with Rudra. Writing in 1997, Srinivasan interprets what John Marshall interpreted as facial as not human but more bovine, possibly a divine buffalo-man.

The interpretation of the seal continues to be disputed. McEvilley, for example, states that it is not possible to "account for this posture outside the yogic account." Asko Parpola states that other archaeological finds such as the early Elamite seals dated to 3000–2750 BCE show similar figures, and these have been interpreted as "seated bull" and not yogi, and the bovine interpretation is likely more accurate. Gregory L. Possehl, in 2002, associated it with the water buffalo and concluded that while it would be appropriate to recognize the figure as a deity, and its posture as one of a ritual discipline, regarding it as a proto-Shiva would "go too far."

The Vedic literature refers to a minor atmospheric deity with fear dedicated to Rudra, and he finds occasional mention in other hymns of the same text. The term *Shiva* also appears in the Rig Veda, but simply as an epithet that means "kind, auspicious," one of the adjectives used to describe many different Vedic deities.

While a fierce, ruthless natural phenomenon and storm-related Rudra is feared in the hymns of the Rig Veda, the beneficial rains he brings are welcomed as Shiva aspect of him.

This healing, nurturing, life-enabling aspect emerges in the Vedas as Rudra-Shiva and, in post-Vedic literature, ultimately as Shiva, who combines the destructive and constructive powers, the terrific and gentle, as the ultimate recycler and rejuvenator of all existence.

The similarities between the iconography and theologies of Shiva with Greek and European deities have led to proposals for an Indo-European link for Shiva or lateral exchanges with ancient Central Asian cultures.

His contrasting aspects, such as being terrifying or blissful, depending on the situation, are similar to those of the Greek god Dionysus, as are their iconic associations with bull, snakes, anger, bravery, dancing, and carefree life. The ancient Greek texts of the time of Alexander the Great call Shiva as Indian Dionysus, or alternatively called Dionysus as god of the Orient. Similarly, the use phallic symbol as an icon for Shiva is also found for Irish, Nordic, Greek (Dionysus), and Roman deities, as was the idea of this aniconic column linking heaven and earth among early Indo-Aryans, states Roger Woodward. Others contest such proposals and suggest Shiva to have emerged from indigenous pre-Aryan tribal origin.

Shiva as we know him today shares many features with the Vedic god Rudra, and both Shiva and Rudra are viewed as the same personality in Hindu scriptures. The two names are used synonymously. Rudra, the god of the roaring storm, is usually portrayed in accordance with the element he represents as a fierce, destructive deity.

The oldest surviving text of Hinduism is the Rig Veda, which is dated to have been written between 1700 and 1100 BC based on linguistic and philological evidence. A God named Rudra is mentioned in the Rig Veda. The name *Rudra* is still used as a name for Shiva. In RV 2.33, he is described as the "father of the Rudras," a group of storm gods.

The hymn 10.92 of the Rig Veda states that the deity Rudra has two natures, one wild and cruel (Rudra), and another that is kind and tranquil (Shiva). The Vedic texts do not mention bull or any animal as the transport vehicle (vahana) of Rudra or other deities. However, post-Vedic texts, such as the Mahabharata and the Purana, state the Nandi bull, the Indian zebu, in particular, as the vehicle of Rudra and of Shiva, thereby unmistakably linking them as the same.

In the Smarta tradition of Hinduism, Shiva is a part of its panchayat a puja. This practice consists of the use of icons or anicons of five deities considered equivalent, set in a quincunx pattern. Siva is one of the five deities, others being Vishnu, Devi (such as Parvati), Surya, and Ganesha or Skanda, or any personal god of the devotees' preference (Ishta Devata).

Philosophically, the Smarta tradition emphasizes that all idols (murti) are icons, to help focus on and visualize aspects of Brahman, rather than distinct beings. The ultimate goal in this practice is to transition past the use of icons, recognize the absolute symbolized by the icons, on the path to realizing the nondual identity of one's atman (soul, self) and the Brahman. Popularized by Adi Shankara, many Panchayatana mandalas and temples have been uncovered that are from the Gupta Empire period.

Adiyogi Shiva statue, recognized by the Guinness World Records as the "largest bust sculpture" in the world, is for inspiring and promoting Yoga and is named Adiyogi, which means "the first yogi," because Shiva is known as the originator of Yoga.

Shiva is considered the great yogi who is totally absorbed in himself—the transcendental reality. He is the lord of Yogis and the teacher of Yoga to sages. As Shiva Dakshinamurthi, states Stella Kramrisch, he is the supreme guru who "teaches in silence the oneness of one's innermost self (atman) with the ultimate reality." The theory of practice of yoga, in different styles, has been a part of all major traditions of Hinduism, and Shiva has been the patron of spokespersons in numerous Hindu Yoga texts (Brahman). These contain the philosophy and techniques for yoga. These ideas are estimated to be from or after the late centuries of the first millennium CE and have survived as yoga texts, such as the Isvara Gita (literally, "Shiva's song"), which, Andrew Nicholson, a professor of Hinduism and Indian intellectual history, states, have had "a profound and lasting influence on the development of Hinduism."

Lord Shiva has been described and called both destroyer and benefactor. In Yajurveda, two contrary sets of attributes for both malignant or terrifying (Sanskrit: *rudra*) and benign or auspicious (Sanskrit: *śiva*) forms can be found, leading Chakravarty to conclude that "all the basic elements which created the complex Rudra-Śiva sect of later ages are to be found here." In the Mahabharata, Shiva is depicted as "the standard of invincibility, might, and terror," as well as a figure of honor, delight, and brilliance.

The duality of Shiva, fearful and auspicious, attributes in a contrasted name. The name Rudra reflects Shiva's fearsome aspect. According to the traditional etymologies, the Sanskrit name *Rudra* is derived from the root *rud*, which means "to cry, howl." Stella Kramrisch notes a different etymology connected with the adjectival form *raudra*, which means "wild, of Rudra's nature," and translate the name Rudra as "the wild one" or "the fierce god." R. K.

Sharma follows this alternate etymology and translates the name as "terrible." Hara is an important name that occurs three times in the Anushasanaparvan version of the Shiva sahasranama, where it is translated in different ways each time it occurs, following a commentarial tradition of not repeating an interpretation. Sharma translate the three as "one who captivates," "one who consolidates," and "one who destroys." Kramrisch translates it as "the ravisher."

Another of Shiva's fearsome form is as Kāla, "time," and Mahākāla, "great time," which ultimately destroys all things. The name *Kāla* appears in the *Shiva Sahasranama*, where it is translated by Ram Karan Sharma as the "supreme lord of time." Bhairava, "terrible" or "frightful," is a fierce form associated with annihilation. In contrast, the name Śankara, "beneficent" or "conferring happiness," reflects his benign form. This name was adopted by the great Vedanta philosopher Adi Shankara (c. 788–820), who is also known as Shankaracharya.

The depiction of Shiva as Nataraja (Sanskrit: *natarāja*, "lord of dance") is popular. The names Nartaka ("dancer") and Nityanarta ("eternal dancer") appear in the Shiva Sahasranama. His association with dance and also with music is prominent in the Puranic period. In addition to the specific iconographic form known as Nataraja, various other types of dancing forms (Sanskrit: nrtyamūrti) are found in all parts of India, with many well-defined varieties in Tamil Nadu in particular.

The two most common forms of dance are the Tandava, which later came to denote the powerfully named masculine dance as Kala-Mahakala, associated with the destruction of the world. When it requires the world or universe to be destroyed, Shiva does it by Tandava.

CHAPTER 3

A great deal of funding for CERN comes from taxpayers in various Western countries. It is very possible that you and your neighbor or a family member has even helped to finance CERN simply by paying taxes. Before I discuss the Rockefellers and their large contributions of money to CERN, I want to start off with some basic background information.

It is true that many people have covered various aspects about CERN, and to date, I have yet to see a report or even a news story of who is funding CERN.

Now, here we are. We have an entire world so addicted to the delusion it has created. Now you have a world immersed into the matrix. The very truth is, CERN already controls us; it controls you. Just look at your cell phone, open up your favorite app, and you become entrenched in an abyss with billions of different directions, sometimes impossibly difficult to navigate. They want you inside the matrix, trapped there forever.

So who is funding CERN and its Large Hadron Collider, which has led to depression, anxiety, mental illness, and mental enslavement? Who has funded this endless pornography machine? Who would ever want millions of people to fall into a "spider's web," a willing victim of a kill? The answer may not come as a surprise when you hear who is behind this.

They don't just want you trapped; they want you enslaved inside a matrix of images, numbers, infinite data to overstimulate your mind. It is then that they can control you and all of us, because they control everything inside the "spider's web." The end goal of the matrix is really quite simple: it is to keep you inside of it.

CERN scientists have received hundreds of grants and endowments from governments all across the world totaling hundreds of millions of dollars. The price of CERN's annual operation is unknown, but the entire construction of machines and their upkeep total billions and billions of dollars, so one must be assisting in funding CERN and its LHC. There have been many private donors involved as well. CERN is constantly having to raise money in order to continue operating its experiments, as they appear to be looking for the "dark universe," and this requires many billions of dollars.

CERN has a fundraising arm that collects private donations from very wealthy contributors all across the whole entire world. Not surprisingly, CERN is heavily supported by the Rockefeller family, not just financially, but also through a scientist who works for Rockefeller University, which is owned by Rockefeller family. Many know for a fact that the Rockefellers are actually sending scientists over to work at CERN.

Two of these scientists are Sebastian White and Robert Ciesielski, CERN physicists. Ciesielski's bio is very impressive and states he is hunting for "super symmetry and the dark universe." Robert Ciesielski is a CERN research associate. He is an experimental high-energy physicist, a member of the Compact Muon Solenoid (CMS)experiment at the Large Hadron Collider in Geneva, Switzerland. His focus is on QCD studies and searches for beyond standard model physics. He has contributed to activities of the forward and small-x QCD (FSQ) group. He also served as a convener of the diffractive and exclusive processes subgroup, where some study processes with large rapid gaps in the final state, mediated by photons or objects carrying the quantum numbers of vacuum. Robert Ciesielski is also a convener of the CMS+TOTEM Combined Analysis group, which investigates diffractive interactions in a uniquely wide kinematic range, by combining information from the CMS and TOTEM experiments.

Within the hadronic calorimeter (HCAL) calibration group, he coordinates the work of the gains and RadDam team, which monitors gains stability and radiation damage of the hadron endcap (HE) and hadron forward (HF) calorimeters. He has also contributed to activities of the supersymmetry (SUSY) physics group by studying the QCD contribution to events with jets and missing transverse energy signature.

The other scientist sent to CERN from the Rockefeller University is Sebastian White. He is a physicist participating in the LHC experiment at CERN and is currently living in Geneva, Switzerland. He has done much of the research at CERN, starting with his thesis experiment as a PhD student of Leon Lederman (who first came up with the name "the God particle"). For part of the year, he was at the Center for Studies in Physics and Biology at the Rockefeller University. Dr. White is also the great-grandson for Stanford White.

CERN has been instrumental in the CMS experiments that have discovered several new subatomic particles. Sebastian White studied under a man named Leon Lederman, who wrote the book *The God Particle* in the year 1993. This was long before the particle was even discovered, so wrap your mind around that. It really should be noted that one of the books written by Leon Letterman appears to be a piece of predictive programming, found in music videos, movies, and many of what Hollywood does, but very few people talk about predictive programming found in books.

Let's begin to uncover the secrets that are contained inside books. Speaking of books, two books document the intimate involvement of the Rockefeller Institute in CERN's experiments. One book is called *Core Structure Matter*, and another is called *The History of CERN Part 3*. Both of these books suggest Rockefeller scientists have played major roles in the discovery of subatomic particles at CERN. More importantly, the Rockefellers control the massive amount of money transferred at CERN. In fact, the Rockefellers control all the money that is being transferred to CERN.

A nonprofit charity called the King Baudouin Foundation, which is based at 10 Rockefeller Plaza in New York City, funnels all donations to CERN that are made by private donors within the United States. The founder of this charity, King Baudouin of Belgium, was a personal friend of David Rockefeller, who runs the

Nelson Rockefeller Brothers Fund, which is nonprofit charity that contributes huge amount of money directly to the King Baudouin Foundation, totaling millions in donations. There is an absolute connection between the money behind CERN and the Rockefeller family.

We know CERN is looking for something. They have said publicly that they are looking for the "dark universe," though many have doubted their claims and say they are looking for something else. It costs lots of money to do research. Is an investment in science the path to future economic prosperity? What role can science and innovation play in encouraging economic growth? Does CERN have a dark agenda? More questions, as with science.

Some believe the term *dark universe* may be a dark-cloak phrase with alternative meaning. According to CERN, it is believed that the universe is mapped out like a cosmic tree. The universe is shaped out like a tree, and much of that is made up of "dark matter." Only the buttes of the tree are lit up as light matter. CERN is really trying to find the contours of this cosmic tree; many even believe they are looking for the tree of life.

Brian Cox, Royal Society University Research fellow at the University of Manchester, discusses the benefits of funding scientific research even when it does not appear to have immediate practical application. He highlights the examples of CERN, which was instrumental in helping Tim Berners-Lee launch the World Wide Web.

CHAPTER 4

CERN is a European research organization that operates the largest particle physics laboratory in the world. Established in 1954, the organization is based in a northwest suburb of Geneva, on the Franco-Swiss border, and has twenty-three member-states. Israel is the only non-European country granted full membership. CERN is known to be an official United Nations observer.

The nuclear research facility's main function is to provide the particle accelerators and other infrastructure needed for high-energy physics research. As a result, numerous experiments have been conducted at CERN through international collaborations. The main site at Meyrin hosts a large computing facility that is primarily used to store and analyze data from experiments as well as simulate events. Researchers need remote access to these facilities, so the lab has historically been a major wide area network hub. CERN is also the birthplace of the World Wide Web.

The enormous contribution of CERN to the international economy in terms of the World Wide Web has led to trillions of dollars in the world's economy.

It all started in March of 1989. CERN is where the web was born, and from the year 1991 and onward, the team at CERN developed the World Wide Web, all to do with accessing documents.

April 30, 1993, is the date on the document with which CERN gave up the rights to charge royalties for World Wide Web technology. This is a very important date and an important document, as it allowed the web to take off. In the year 1994, people were able to break off from CERN and develop the World Wide Web properly, and the rest is history. Jumping ahead, web technology has become very exciting. There is voice browser technology, which is coming along very well and will completely change the things we can do with human interface. Web services technology and semantic web technology allow machines to talk to one another and perform electronic commerce and so many other things, allowing machines to solve problems for humans instead of bringing us problems in the form of web pages or emails. There are many exciting things happening with technology, and for the very same reason, these must be released in the public domain, or they must be made available, so the basic infrastructure and the web standards are available and free of royalties.

When great things come out of research labs, whether they are government or corporate funded, then, in the case of web technology, the investment must be plowed in, as it is very important for new things to grow, that infrastructure be royalty-free. The web is open; anybody can talk to anybody.

We have this wonderful right to free speech; however, part of using the web is our concern about privacy, and could Big Brother be watching us? Lots of things are clearly visible, and lots are not visible at all. We now know that surveillance is happening, by people that may even abuse the data collected.

Edward Snowden has enlightened the world to the power and access given to the employees at the NSA. The National Security Agency is a national-level agency of the United States Department of Defense, under the direct authority of the National Intelligence. The NSA is responsible for global monitoring, collection, and processing of information and data for foreign and domestic intelligence and counterintelligence purposes, specializing in a discipline known as signals intelligence (SIGINT).

Several countries have banned their citizen from accessing the web and have even blocked Twitter. Some believe protesting is necessary to make sure that censorship is cut down so that the web is opened up where there is censorship. Again, the web is open and everyone can communicate with anyone all around the globe. CERN did bring the web to life, and this is only the beginning of technology to come. The sky and the universe are the limit. The future is exciting.

Many people and companies love to join these gigantic social networking companies, which, in fact, have very effectively built these silos where it is so much easier to talk to people inside the same social networks than it is to talk with somebody in a different one.

The founder of the World Wide Web is Tim Berners-Lee. He is the inventor of the web. His work continues today as in the privacy that is now involved and the talk of where we go in terms of transparency in the World Wide Web.

When the WWW first started, there were just a few people using it and it was looked upon as a luxury. The number of people using the web has now risen to about 20 percent of the entire planet.

Tim Berners-Lee realized that there are really two pieces to this. If there are 20 percent of the world using the web, what about the other 80 percent of the world that are not using the web? The scientists at CERN asked himself, Does he have a duty and foundation to do just that?

The end of the twentieth century has seen many extraordinary developments in telecommunications and networking technologies, with applications dramatically improving the collaboration between people, and sometimes in very unexpected ways. In the early 1990s, the World Wide Web was created at CERN to help the exchange of documents between particle physicists collaborating in experiments from all over the world. Not long after, the web exploded and seemed to cover almost every aspect of our lives.

CHAPTER 5

Scientists today have many problems to solve, and added to the list for many is limited computing power. Biologists, physicists, and meteorologists need to run very heavy calculations that involve heavy amounts of data. Although computers are becoming more and more powerful, the real needs of breakthrough scientific research still exceed the technological progress. To solve this problem, scientists are developing a new tool, the grid.

As the web allows sharing of information over the internet, the grid will allow sharing of computing power and resource, like disk storage, databases, and software applications. While one computer may take days or weeks to complete a complex scientific calculation, the grid will make available hundreds, or even thousands, of collaborative computers and get the same result faster and much more efficiently.

Once connected to the grid, the user will see it as one large computer system providing almost-infinite computer power. How does the grid work? you may ask. By entering the grid using a software interface that runs on your computer. After clearing security validation, your computer will be able to talk to the core of the grid, known as the resource broker. The resource brokers will query the information service to know which hardware and software are available to process your program at that moment and the replica catalog to know the locations of all existing data.

Once the appropriate resource has been located, the resource broker assigns the job to a computing element where it is executed. Most countries have already started significant developmental activities. At the European level, data grid is the largest software development project, with two hundred researchers. The project will be set as a production grid using data and application coming from high-energy physics, environmental science, and informatics, building the base of a stable resource that scientists from all over Europe will be able to plug in to and use. Many other grid-enabled applications are under study in fields much closer to everyday life, like simulation and visualization for surgical procedures, flooding crisis, and weather forecasts. The grid will make it possible for scientific collaboration to share resource beyond belief.

CERN performs many experiments each year, with enough data that could be stored on four hundred thousand compact discs, storing the interesting stuff. Their scientists are analyzing this data if they are to understand antimatter better, but to do so with a normal computer would be impossible. It cannot even be analyzed with all ten thousand computers in CERN's computing center.

Instead, particle physicists worldwide have connected their computer resources together to form the grid, a worldwide supercomputer that is powerful enough to do the job for us.

The huge amounts of data collected from the experiments have to be analyzed on this supercomputer, on this grid, and these calibrations are formed from scientists all over the world with different cultures, different religions, and even different political ideas, but still, in LHCb, like with any other CERN experiment, these scientists share their knowledge, experience, and efforts, and it is with one common aim, to discover and better understand nature.

The Large Hadron Collider started production, colliding protons forty million times per second, and at an energy of 7 TeV. This was three and a half times higher than anything seen before. Each proton collision produces the matter and antimatter particles. LHCb will study how these particles and antiparticles behave and try to understand why there is a difference between them.

Sometimes, the more we discover, the less we actually know, and the less we know, the more there is to find out. It is this endless quest to understand more about the universe around us, this desire to journey into the unknown, that has driven CERN to be what they are today.

Having a massive computerlike grid really comes in handy on a day like March 30, 2010, at CERN. It was on that day, inside the LHCb control room, when scientists attempted to increase the energy of the Large Hadron Collider to 7 TeV. This was there very first attempt in history.

Let's go back in time even further, to the 1970s, when the CERN data center was built. Today, CERN's computers are busy at work, and when standing near this data center, you can hear the many, many fans that cool the computers. It also has an extension, located in Budapest in Hungary, but together they form a single data center. But what exactly are they doing in there, and what does it look like inside? It looks like a computer land. Full of computers just like you would have at home, but one of the computer systems area, however, has two hundred thousand processor cores—two hundred thousand computer brains, if you prefer.

This is where all the LHC data is stored on magnetic tapes and on disks. CERN uses a robot to move all the tapes and discs around.

In the year 2015, over forty million gigabytes alone were stored, which is the equivalent of almost ten million DVDs. All this data can be accessed by physicists from all over the world for their research. They can access it via the high-speed network installed at CERN. In addition, the whole region benefits as this is one of the connection nodes for the internet and for the whole region. But the data center is also the starting point for the computing grid. CERN is basically doing grid computing and using a planet-size computer with computing and storage power that spread across 170 centers and in about forty-two countries worldwide. Over two million calculations are carried out every day. This is what is needed to properly analyze and store the data produced by CERN's particle accelerator, the Large Hadron Collider.

Only 20 percent of that computing power is located in Geneva at CERN. The grid is all about sharing. The scientists and physicists at CERN all opted for an easy communication structure, which was, in essence, a precursor of computing that we all know today as the grid. Scientists are able to share resources, computing, and storage resources; they are able to share all this information with a lot of computers all connected together and be able to use them as one huge "single big computer."

The grid at CERN, the computer center, operates as just one part of the Large Hadron Collider's computer grid, which is a worldwide organization or federation of data centers that provides data that is produced by detectors around the LHC, of which there are around 150 computing centers in the area. At CERN, there is a tier 0 and a tier 1 data center. Tier 1 has eleven computing centers. All the data collected ends up at the tier 0 data center, then it's massaged a little bit, processed, and then sent off to tier 1 data center for further processing. There are different LHC detectors that are connected to the same computing center. In Europe, it's called center, with a deliciated network of ten gigabytes per second, as it is a very powerful network. This data is then stored permanently in paper storage. Then CERN is also connected to the dedicated links of ten gigabytes per second to eleven computing centers all around the world. This data is then transferred, depending on the experiment, to a proper scientist or physicist.

There are literally hundreds of computing centers that are part of the Large Hadron Collider computing grid. Maybe a scientist far away from the LHC is researching an experiment and wants to know what happened in a specific detector or in a specific subdetector of a detector; then a file can be requested that could reflect a recording of what happened at that last time.

This file may be stored at the requestor's storage center, or it may be stored at a data center that is completely in a different part of the world, or it could be retrieved from the tier 0 data center at CERN. In many cases, the scientists can have the file in a fraction of a second.

CHAPTER 6

It has been called the biggest jigsaw puzzle ever attempted, and it is all happening in Switzerland, at the European Organization for Nuclear Research. Better known as CERN, it is the largest scientific research project on the entire world. More than seven thousand scientists or the world's particle physicists use its facilities.

CERN was established near the French-Swiss border, outside Geneva, in 1951 to study the building blocks of matter, the component of everything in the known universe. CERN has not discovered all the answer, but in the process, CERN has given us the World Wide Web and highly advanced medical scanners. CERN is described as a place where people from all over the world, some of the brightest minds from all over the world, can share conversation and information about new thoughts of dark matter or how the universe could have begun.

The Large Hadron Collider has been called the most ambitious scientific experiment ever attempted. A twenty-seven-kilometer enclosed ring, punctuated by four enormous camera-like detectors, mimics and records events, seconds right after the big bang, in the hope of finding the answers to the universe, life, and everything. ATLAS and CMS are the largest of these detectors.

They are so large that each has their very own two-thousand-person construction team. Creating a home for these enormous machines calls for world-class engineering to get the infrastructure into place. Project engineers must construct the caverns to house these gigantic machines. In one particular site, the workers had excavated 220,000 meters of rock and gravel to form these two new caverns. These caverns are two of the biggest underground areas ever constructed or created by man.

Physicists from both Argon National Laboratories outside Chicago and from UK's Oxford University are behind the team responsible for building ATLAS. This is one of the biggest experiments in the world, the ATLAS detector, and it's really just an enormous camera that takes pictures four hundred million times a second. At CMS, physicists and doctors from CERN are at the helm. CMS was started not for the sake of building something complicated but for the sake of doing experiments in physics. CMS is just the start of an adventure, and the physics are earth-shattering. CMS and ATLAS won't be just talking any old pictures; they will be capturing the very birth of our universe.

To achieve this, particles are accelerated along the collider's twenty-seven-kilometer ring so fast that it will reach close to the speed of light, covering over billion kilometers in ten hours—that is enough to get to Neptune and back.

About eight hundred times every second, the particles will smash together right inside the center of the CMS and ATLAS, mimicking the big bang. CMS and ATLAS are not identical, but they are built to parallel each other, so both can capture the results of these catastrophic collision. It means the scientists can compare and check any results. They will snap away up to forty million times per second, capturing data that scientists hope will provide answers to the elements of our universe that we still do not understand. This groundbreaking collaboration of hearts and minds has taken many years to mature.

While the scientists scratch their heads, the engineering teams press on, finding the final resting place for the "mega machines." ATLAS and CMS are on opposite sides of the collider. They are much too massive to be lowered into the caverns in one piece; they are built in segments on the surface and then dropped down and then bolted into place a section at a time.

CHAPTER 7

At CERN in Switzerland and France, one of two huge particle physics detectors in operation is CMS, also known as the Compact Muon Solenoid. This is a general-purpose detector built on the Large Hadron Collider at CERN. The CMS experiment is to look deep into a very wide range of physics, and this does include any particles that could possibly make up dark matter, extra dimensions, and searching for Higgs boson.

The construction of this detector is mind-blowing. The Compact Muon Solenoid is 15 meters in diameter, and it is 21.6 meters long, weighing an amazing fourteen thousand tons. It represents about two hundred scientific institutes, at least forty-three countries, and 3,800 people have all come together to form what has been called the CMS collaboration. These are the people, the physicists and the scientists, who built and operate the detector, which is located in an underground cavern at Cessy in France, which is right across the border from Geneva. Scientific history was made at CERN in July of 2012 when, along with the detector ATLAS, CMS discovered the Higgs boson. Its existence was confirmed in March of the year 2013.

There have been many, many experiments at CERN, and one of the recent collider experiments like the Large Electron-Positron Collider and the renovated Large Hadron Collider (LHC) at CERN. Back in October of 2011, Tevatron at Fermilab, which has been closed, have really provided fantastic insights into the standard model of particle physics in our world and universe. When it comes to the Large Hadron Collider, one of the greatest achievements is the discovery of a particle that is known to be consistent with the standard-model Higgs boson. This is the particle that provides an explanation for the masses of what is called elementary particles, the particles resulting from the Higgs mechanism. The Compact Muon Solenoid was created and designed as a Higgs mechanism. The Compact Muon Solenoid was created and designed as a general-purpose detector, and it also studied the unlimited number of aspects of proton collision at the center of mass energy of the Large Hadron Collider.

The collision occurs at a center of mass energy of 8 TeV, and at full luminosity, each of the collisions has the potential to produce an average of twenty proton interactions. In September 2008, the first test run was expected to operate at a much lower collision energy, but this was all prevented by the September 2008 shutdown. The momentum of particles is extremely crucial in helping to build up what has been called a picture of events at the heart of collision.

The CMS tracker is capable of recording the path taken by particles that have been charged by finding their positrons at a number of key points. One way this is done to calculate the momentum of a particle is to track its path through a magnetic field. The more curved the path, then the less momentum the particle has—it's all math, science, and physics.

The tracker has a remarkable job. It can reconstruct the paths of high-energy muon, electrons, and even hadrons, which are known to some as particles made up of quarks. To record particle paths accurately, the tracker needs to be lightweight, so as to disturb the particle path as little as possible. By taking the position measurement perfectly accurate, so accurate that tracks can be reconstructed by using just a few measurement points, it is true that each measurement is accurate to a fraction of the width of a hair.

As particles travel through the tracker, the pixels and microscripts and microstrips produce tiny electric signals that are detected and amplified. The CMS tracker is made completely of silicon, and it employs sensors covering an area the size of competition-size tennis court, incorporating at least seventy-five million electronic readout channels. In the pixel detector, there are six thousand connections per square centimeter.

To increase the radiation tolerance and the overall performance of the tracker, an upgrade is planned; this part of the detector has been called the entire world's largest silicon detector.

The CMS silicon tracker is one of a kind and consists of fourteen layers in the endcaps and thirteen layers in the central region. The innermost three-layer layers consist of 100×150 micrometer pixel, about sixty-six million. During full-luminosity collisions, the occupancy of the pixel layers per event is expected to be about 0.1 percent and 1–2 percent in the strip layers. Scientists believe the expected HL-LHC upgrade will increase the number of interactions greatly, and even to point of where overoccupancy would greatly reduce track-finding effectiveness at record levels.

The electromagnetic calorimeter (ECAL) may sound like something from the future one would use to measure calories when on a diet, but this device is used to measure with very high accuracy the energies of electrons and photons. ECAL is actually constructed from the crystals of lead tungstate. Crystal is made mostly of metal and is much heavier than stainless steel, for example.

With just a wee bit, a very small amount of oxygen in this crystalline form, it is highly transparent and scintillates when photons and electrons begin to pass through it. This means that it has begun to produce light that is in perfect proportion to the particle energy. The high-density crystals can produce light in short, fast, well-designed photon bursts that allow for a precise compact detector.

The hadronic calorimeter (HCAL) measures the energy of hadrons, particles made of quarks and gluons. One example that comes to mind are phonons, neutrons, pions, and kaons, uncharged particles such as neutrinos.

The HCAL is made up of layers of dense material, such as steel or brass, interleaved with tiles of plastic scintillators, readout wavelength-shifting fibers, by hybrid photodiodes. This is the allowed maximum amount of absorbing material inside the magnetic coil.

CHAPTER 8

Particle Fever is a 2013 American documentary film tracking the first round of experiments at the Large Hadron Collider (LHC) in Switzerland. The film follows the experimental physicists at CERN who run the experiments, as well as the theoretical physicists, who attempt to provide a conceptual framework for the LHC's results. The film begins in 2008, with the first firing of the LHC, and concludes in 2012, with the successful identification of the Higgs boson.

The Communication Awards of the National Academies of Sciences, Engineering, and Medicine awarded a $20,000 prize for excellence in communicating science to the general public in film/radio/TV to David Kaplan and Mark Levinson for *Particle Fever* on October 14, 2015. The awards are given to individuals for four categories (books; film, radio, and TV; magazine and newspaper; and online) and are supported by the W. M. Keck Foundation.

The film is composed of two narrative threads. One follows the large team of experimental physicists at CERN as they try to get the LHC running properly. After a promising initial test run, the LHC suffers a liquid helium leak in 2007 that damages its electromagnets.

Fabiola Gianotti, Martin Aleksa, and Monica Dunford are all shown discussing how to handle the negative publicity surrounding the accident and how to proceed. After repairs in 2009, the LHC begins to run experiments again at half-power.

The other thread follows the competing theories of Nima Arkani-Hamed and his mentor, Savas Dimopoulos. In the film, Arkani-Hamed advocates for the "multiverse" theory, which predicts the mass of the Higgs boson to be approximately 140 GeV. Dimopoulos argues for the more established supersymmetry theory, which predicts the mass of the Higgs boson to be approximately 115 GeV.

The narrative threads combine at the end of the film, when CERN announces the confirmed existence of a Higgs-like particle, with a mass of approximately 125 GeV. The discovery of the particle is met with a standing ovation, and Peter Higgs is shown wiping away tears. However, neither of the competing theories of the universe is definitively supported by the finding. Later, Kaplan is shown admitting that none of his theoretical models are supported by this finding and that the long-term implications of the discovery are unclear.

The film was shot over a period of seven years. It was directed by Mark Levinson, a former theoretical physicist with a doctorate from UC-Berkeley. Levinson produced the film along with David Kaplan, a professor of physics at Johns Hopkins University and producers Andrea Miller, Carla Solomon, and Wendy Sax.

The team gathered nearly five hundred hours of footage from both professional camera crews and amateur video self-recordings shot by the physicists themselves. This footage was then edited by Walter Murch, who has previously won Academy Awards for his work on *Apocalypse Now* and *The English Patient.* Kaplan worked with MK12 to create the animated sequences that are used throughout the film.

The film received critical acclaim, with reviewers praising the film for making theoretical arguments seem comprehensible, for making scientific experiments seem thrilling, for making particle physicists seem human, and for promoting physics outreach.

Physics outreach encompasses facets of science outreach and physics education and is an umbrella term for a variety of activities by schools, research institutes, universities, clubs, and institutions such as science museums aimed at broadening the audience for and awareness and understanding of physics.

While the general public may sometimes be the focus of such activities, physics outreach often centers on developing and providing resources and making a presentation to students, educators in other discipline, and in some cases, researchers within different areas of physics.

Particle Fever is alive and well. The documentary is very good, and several reviewers singled out Murch's editing for praise.

On his blog, theoretical physicist and string theory critic Peter Woit called the film "fantastically good" but cautioned that Arkani-Hamed's linking of the Higgs boson to multiverse theory was a tenuous proposition, as this theory did not currently make testable predictions.

Review aggregate website Rotten Tomatoes reports the film as holding an overall 96 percent positive approval rating based on forty-eight reviews, and a rating average of 7.9 out of 10. The site's consensus states, "The concepts behind its heady subject matter may fly over the heads of most viewers, but Particle Fever presents it in such a way that even the least science-inclined viewers will find themselves enraptured." On Metacritic, the film has an 87 out of 100 rating, based on eighteen critics, indicating universal acclaim.

CHAPTER 9

On July 4, 2012, CERN made history, very big history. A new particle was discovered, the Higgs boson. The finding began to make news all around the world. For the scientists who discovered this for themselves, this was particularly momentous. Now that this particle has been discovered, what's left to do? Our current understanding of the universe is based on the modestly named standard model, a theory of all fundamental matter particles and their interactions. Virtually all the standard model has been verified, apart from one crucial element. What gives a matter its mass?

HIGGS BOSON

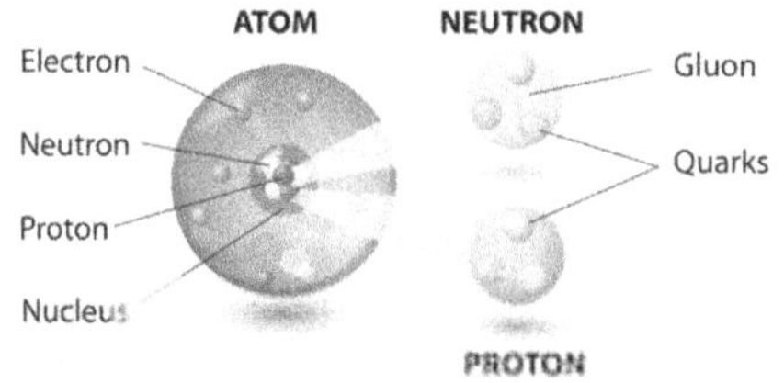

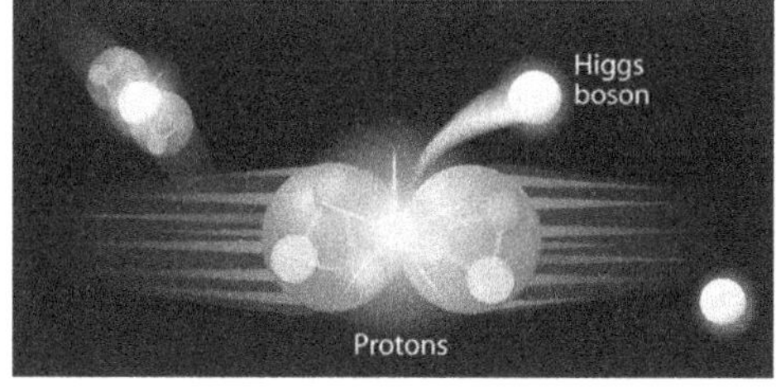

What is critical, even to our daily existence, is, if an electron could be massless, it could not be bound to a proton. You could not have an atom, all the stars, the planets, chemistry, and life couldn't exist because instead of electrons bound to protons in hydrogen atoms and also in larger atoms, you would just have electrons shooting off into infinity.

In the standard model, mass is explained by the Higgs mechanism, of which the Higgs boson is only one part. For example, researchers have heard that the Higgs boson gives mass to the other subatomic particles, and if this is true, shouldn't there be Higgs boson everywhere? Why would it be so difficult to recreate and detect them?

In truth, it is not the particle itself that gives mass to the other particles; it is the Higgs field. One could think of or imagine the Higgs field has a huge "sea of honey" that fills all space. Some particles are able to travel through it, unimpeded, while others interact with it, slowing down in the process, and that translates into mass. When enough high energy is added to the field, fleeting Higgs boson are created.

Using powerful magnets, the Large Hadron Collider wizzes two beams of protons in two opposite directions, around a twenty-seven-kilometer circular tunnel. When the protons collide, their energy can be converted into the mass of new particles, like the Higgs boson. Short-lived, these particles decay quickly; it is their decayed products that are then analyzed by massive detectors. The CMS detector is a giant apparatus. It is one of two major detectors on the beamline, where the protons collide. There is a life-size picture of the CMS detector located there. It is big.

When standing above the beamline, scientists have protons whizzing around underneath their feet, ninety meters under the ground and at speeds that are basically the speed of light, 99.9999999 the speed of light. The other big experiment that examines the proton collisions is called ATLAS. The teams at ATLAS and CMS, each made up of about three thousand scientists, work independently in a sort of friendly rivalry.

It is essential that if there is a major discovery that is made, it is confirmed ultimately by the two experiments and independently.

One of the newest discoveries announced in the year 2012 was very dramatic; both detectors saw the same results more or less simultaneously.

Protons are bags of other particles. When they smash together, a mass of new particles is created, and it is the pattern of the debris that provides the answers. CERN has found new evidence of a new particle with a mass of 125 and 125 GeV.

The LHC will conduct many more collisions, and this should allow scientists to determine the properties of the new particle. If it is not the standard model Higgs, scientists may still be able to determine that. The reason for doing science is, we all want answers, but generating more questions is most likely what happens.

CHAPTER 10

The first particle collisions in the Large Hadron Collider (LHC) were recorded on November 23, 2009. These collisions were called the LHCb experiments. This is a really big deal. CERN begins to buzz with excitement and celebration, and it is at that point where the real adventure begins, now that they have beams colliding at almost the speed of light. The scientists and physicists are ecstatic.

The beautiful minds of CERN are in a state of happiness as the experiments at the nuclear research facility go on, and each one of these experiments is looking for something with a different method, a different strategy; each one is trying to understand a different aspect of our universe. We will look at one of these in particular, the one on the quest to study antimatter, LHCb, the beauty experiment. It has taken at least twenty years to build and design the CERN facility. It's taken thousands of scientists and engineers to build the machine the Large Hadron Collider.

Toward the beginning of time, things were very, very different from what they are now. It is the structure of reality itself that has changed. The universe was very different when it had just been born. Way back then, there were no stars, no planets, no water, and no gases. There was no matter and no light in the way that we are familiar with today, just a massive explosion of pure radiation, the big bang.

When matter and antimatter met, in the early universe, they annihilated to release pure energy, and this energy in turn could make new pairs of matter and antimatter particles that could also meet and annihilate, and this process continued as the universe expanded. However, as the universe expanded, it was also cooled, so after about one minute, there was no longer enough energy to make new pairs of matter and antimatter particles and the process stopped, and what remains now in the universe is a coincidence of a very tiny difference, no more than one part in a billion, between the amount of matter and antimatter that existed at that time. CERN and antimatter, and here we go.

We don't really know why there was a difference, but we would not be here right now if there wasn't one. This difference is indeed a mystery, but it has given birth to everything we see around us. So to really understand the universe and why it looks the way it does, we need to understand antimatter, except that everything has the opposite charge. For example, the electrical charge is opposite. Now, if you look at antiatoms, they are made out like a mirror image of yourself, with opposite charges. The tricky thing is that if matter and antimatter meet, they would annihilate, disappearing in a flash of energy. In 1928, a young physicist, by the name of Paul Dirac, wrote an equation that revolutionized our understanding of the universe.

This equation, which was written on a chalkboard, consisted of four collations. The first two clearly refer to the electron; the other two, identical particles, are twins, but opposite. This equation stated that each particle has an antiparticle twin—that is, another particle exactly identical, but with opposite charge. So for protons, there are antiprotons; for neutrons, antineutrons; and so on. The positron is symmetric and opposite the electron. It is like its mirror image, and the levels of physics would work in exactly the same way as they would for electrons; in other words, matter and antimatter should behave in a perfectly symmetrical pattern. It took thirty years to find out that this assumption was wrong. In 1964, an American physicist, James Cronin, discovered, by examining the decay of a particle called a kaon, that its matter and antimatter versions do not always behave in the same way.

For the first time, the symmetry between matter and antimatter seemed to be broken. Fast-forward forty years later, we have built an instrument that can help us understand this, and this instrument is right here; it's in a cavern, one hundred meters underneath the ground, and it's the combination of years of planning and construction by an international collaboration called LHCb. Now, *b* stands for *beauty*, or the "beauty quark," because if this instrument can study the beauty quark and its antimatter twin, this can help us understand much more about the difference between them.

Below is the instrument of science breakthroughs at CERN, the LHCb. Scientists believe that the difference between matter and antimatter will be easiest to see in these particular particles. To see how all this works at CERN, let's go down one hundred meters underground, where the Large Hadron Collider and the first experiment in the cavern of the LHCb project are. This is really where the LHC collaboration peers back at the early universe. Now, you would think that this is best done with telescopes, but in fact, at CERN, it is done by recreating the whole conditions of the absolute first moments after the big bang. So how does all this really work? The protons circulate in a collider, via a beam pipe, meeting up with the opposite beam, inside a component box.

Now, very much like the heat you feel when you clap your hands, CERN recrates the hot conditions after the big bang by smashing these particles together at the highest energy ever achieved in a lab, in any lab. Very often, they may be achieved with temperatures that are hot—say, the heat's a billion times the temperature in the center of the sun—and this takes us back to a fraction of a second after the birth of the entire universe. Now, with the help of a collider, CERN can do this, forty million times per second, hours at length. These collisions are studied by registering them with a four-and-a-half-thousand-ton LHCb detector. Forty million times per second it registers information about the particle coming out of the little big bangs.

This detector is composed of many small parts, over a length of twenty meters, and is responsible for performing many different tasks. Scientist are very interested in learning and knowing the shapes of the collision by using so-called particle-tracking detectors. They also measure the individual energies of each particle, and of course, they want to know the identities, so there are special detectors dedicated to that. All the information from the particle detector is first collected way down in the LHCb and sent up, onto the surface, to the computers, a mere one hundred meters above the collider. Later on, this information is distributed all around the great big world, to many hundreds of physicists, for analyses.

CHAPTER 11

When I talk about CERN, one of the first things people ask me is, How do the physicists collide particles, and what is a particle accelerator? A *particle accelerator* is a machine designed to take either atom with the electron stripped off (which are called ions) or the particles inside the atoms themselves, either electrons or protons, and give them energy and increase their fields to accelerate, and magnetic fields to bend and control the particles.

An electric field surrounds an electric change, and experts force on other charges in the field, attracting or repelling them. Electric field is sometimes abbreviated as e-field. A magnetic field is a vector field that describes the magnetic influence of electric charges in relative motion and magnetized materials. Magnetic fields are observed in a wide range of size scales, from subatomic particles to galaxies.

The effects of magnetic fields are commonly seen in permanent magnets, which pull on magnetic materials (such as iron) and attract or repel other magnets. The Earth has a magnetic field, and coming from the sun are charged particles. The only reason those particles do not eradicate us is that the Earth's magnetic field uses the very exact same principle and bends them away from us and actually protects us, kind of like a magnetic shield around the entire Earth. This same principle in physics is called Lorentz force.

In physics (specifically in electromagnetism), the Lorentz force (or electromagnetic force) is the combination of electric and magnetic forces on a point charge due to electromagnetic fields. A particle of charge (q) moving with a velocity (v) in an electric field (E) and a magnetic field (B) experiences a force.

A charged particle in a magnetic field gets bent, and we are using that exact same principle, but to bend particles around inside a particle collider. If you take an electric field or electrical potential and you sit a charged particle within that, it will field the electrical force, which will move it from one side to the other—so like charges repel, and opposite charges attract. Using just that basic principle to give the particle a small kick or a push. And if it does that enough times, over and over, more and more energy is produced.

There is somewhat of a creative process that people will go through when they are tasked with designing an accelerator. Often, the design of an accelerator starts with the thoughts of one person and their concept. Most particle accelerators really get those from where you make them.

There is something giving the particles energy, there is some sort of acceleration mechanism, there is control, and that's usually a magnet system. So that's how you control and organize the beams of particles and there is collision.

But not all accelerators are colliders, as in a beam is usually used with a fixed target or even into a person's body or just onto some kind of sample or screen. There is also detection. Obviously, there is no point in doing all that unless you can actually measure what's going on with the beam at the end of the physics day. There are lots of different types of particle accelerators, but we can classify them into three main categories. The first one is a linear accelerator, and as the name suggests, it's a straight line. Most commonly, they are used for radiotherapy in hospitals to accelerate electrons, using those to generate x-rays, and then the x-rays are used for a cancer patient's treatment.

The other type of accelerator is circular, probably the most common one. In the term of numbers, it's called a cyclotron. It's a compact, sort of a reversion of the old-style accelerator, in which the particle starts in the center, and as they gain energy, they spiral outward. A cyclotron is a type of particle accelerator invented by Ernest O. Lawrence in 1929–1930 at the University of California-Berkeley and patented in August 1932, the most powerful accelerator in the world at that time. A cyclotron accelerates charged particles outward from the center along a spiral path. It was one of the largest machines made in that day.

To reach higher energies, CERN physicists use a machine called synchrotron, and a synchrotron has to keep both electric and magnetic fields perfectly synchronized with the particles as they increase in energy, and that is actually where it gets its name from. Maybe this is a part of the reason CERN is obsessed with symmetry. A synchrotron is a particular type of cyclic particle accelerator, descended from the cyclotron, in which the accelerating particle beam travels around a fixed, closed-loop path. The magnetic field that bends the particle beam into its closed path increases with time during the accelerating process, being synchronized to the increasing kenotic energy of the particles. The synchrotron facilities, since the bending, beam focusing, and acceleration, can be separated into different components.

The LHC, or Large Hadron Collider, the world's biggest accelerator, is also a synchrotron, since bending, beam focusing, and acceleration can be separated into different components. The most powerful modern particle accelerators use versions of the synchrotron design. The largest synchrotron-type accelerator, also the largest particle accelerator in the world, is the twenty-seven-kilometer-circumference (seventeen miles) Large Hadron Collider (LHC) near Geneva, Switzerland, built in 2008 by the European Organization for Nuclear Research (CERN). It can accelerate beams of protons to an energy of 6.5 TeV (tera-electron volts).

The synchrotron principle was invented by Vladimir Veksler in 1944. Edwin McMillian constructed the first electron synchrotron in 1945, arriving at the idea independently, having missed Vekster's publication (which was only available in a Soviet journal, although in English). The first proton synchrotron was designed by Sir Marcus Oliphant and built in 1952. Several specialized types of synchrotron machines are used today. A storage ring is a special type of synchrotron light source that usually contains a linear accelerator (Linac) and another synchrotron that is sometimes called a booster in this context. The Linac and the booster are usually to successively accelerate the electrons to their final energy before they are magnetically "kicked" into the storage ring.

Synchrotron light sources, in their entirety, are sometimes called synchrotrons, although this is technically incorrect. A cyclic collider is also a combination of different accelerator types, including two interesting storage rings and the respective preaccelerator. The synchrotron evolved from the cyclotron, the first cyclic particle accelerator. While a classical cyclotron uses both a constant guiding magnetic field and a constant-frequency etic field (and is working in classical approximation), its successor, the isochronous cyclotron, works by local variations of the guiding magnetic field, adapting the increasing relativistic mass of particles during acceleration.

In a synchrotron, this adaption is done by variations of the magnetic field strength in time rather than in space. For particles that are not close to the speed of light, the frequency of the applied electromagnetic field may also change to follow their nonconstant circulation time. By increasing these parameters accordingly as the particles gain energy, their circulation path can be held constant as they are accelerated. This allows the vacuum chamber for the particles to be a large thin torus rather than a disk, as in previous compact accelerator designs. Also, the thin profile of the vacuum chamber allows for a more efficient use of magnetic fields than in a cyclotron, enabling the cost-effective construction of larger synchrotrons.

While the first synchrotrons and storage rings like cosmotron and ADA strictly used the toroid shape, the strong focusing principle independently discovered by Ernest Courant et al. and Nicholas Christalilos allowed the complete separation of the accelerator into components with specialized functions along the particle path, shaping the path into a round-cornered polygon. Some important components are given by the radio frequency cavities for direct acceleration, dipole magnets (bending magnets) for deflection of particle (to close the oath), and quadrupole/sextupole magnets for beam focusing.

The combination of time-dependent guiding magnetic fields and the strong focusing principle enabled the design, and separation of modern large-scale accelerator facilities is required not only for radio frequency cavities but also for particle detectors (in colliders) and photon-generation devices, such as wigglers and undulators (in third-generation synchrotron light sources). The maximum energy that a cyclic accelerator can impact is typically limited by the maximum strength of the magnetic fields and the minimum radius (maximum curvature) of the particle path. It's just science and physics.

CHAPTER 12

China has big ambitions and wants to make a very powerful collider. The Chinese Institute of High Energy Physics has big plans to begin construction of a massive particle accelerator over the next decade and plans for it to be situated east of Beijing. The Chinese claim that their project will be five times more powerful than the Large Hadron Collider (LHC) in Europe. It will be located in a one-hundred-kilometer underground tunnel. This amazing construction feat will be a double-ring collider complete with "electron and positron beams" inside sperate pipes, which will circulate beams in opposite direction. Chinese researchers also plan to build a super proton-proton collider and use it to collide electrons with positrons.

Scientists behind the project expect the collider could potentially generate more than a million Higgs particles and others such as W and Z bosons. A prototype is planned before the actual Chinese collider is built. This eight-year monster project is set to begin in the year 2022. Meanwhile, a Russian scientist is trying to learn more about the universe. The Russians have the superconductive cryocentric neucleotron, which is simply a series of pipes used to propel atomic particles at tremendous speed. In a few years' times, this Russian project will be in full gear and will have an amazing staff on board; even some of the physicists are from the CERN facility.

The Russians collider will consist of several accelerators. Gold molecules will be accelerated and collided, and the result recorded.

The collisions are expected to help the hunt for the origins of the universe and even the mysterious nature of dark matter. So if somebody asked me, "What is dark matter?" my answer would be that it's basically a form of matter that is thought to account for approximately 85 percent of the matter in the universe and about a quarter of total energy density. The majority of dark matter is thought to be nonbaryonic in nature, possibly being composed of some as-yet undiscovered subatomic particles. Its presence is implied in the variety of astrophysical observations, including gravitational effects that cannot be explained by accepted theories of gravity unless more matter is present than can be seen. For this reason, most experts think dark matter to be abundant in the universe and to have had a strong influence on its structure and evolution.

Dark matter is called *dark* because it does not appear to interact with observable electromagnetic radiation, such as light, and this is invisible to the entire electromagnetic spectrum, making it extremely difficult to detect using usual astronomical equipment, and in addition, the world is building particle colliders for what seems like a very long time now. Early accelerators all use single beams with fixed targets. They tended to have very briefly run, inexpensive, and unnamed experiments. Cyclotrons, way back then:

Accelerator	Locations	Years of Operation	Shape	Accelerated Particle	Kinetic Energy	Notes and Discoveries Made
9-inch cyclotron	University of California-Berkeley	1931	circular	H+	1.0 MeV	Proof of concept
11-inch cyclotron	University of California-Berkeley	1932	circular	proton	1.2 MeV	
27-inch cyclotron	University of California-Berkeley	1932–1936	circular	deuteron	4.8 MeV	Investigated deuteron-nucleus interactions
37-inch cyclotron	University of California-Berkeley	1937–1938	circular	deuteron	8 MeV	Discovered many isotopes
60-inch cyclotron	University of California-Berkeley	1939–1962	circular	deuteron	16 MeV	Discovered many isotopes

88-inch cyclotron	Berkeley Rad Lab, Now Lawrence Berkeley National Laboratory	1961–present	circular (isochronous)	hydrogen through uranium	MeV to several GeV	Discovered many isotopes, verified two element discoveries, performed the world's first single-event effects of radiation testing in 1979, and tested parts and materials for most US spacecraft since then
184-inch cyclotron	Berkeley Rad Lab	1942	circular	various	MeV to GeV	Research on uranium isotope separation
Calutrons	Oak Ridge National Laboratory	1943	horseshoe	uranium nuclei		Used to separate isotopes for the Manhattan project
95-inch cyclotron	Harvard Cyclotron Laboratory	1949–2002	circular	proton	160 MeV	Used for nuclear physics (1949–1961) and the development of clinical proton therapy until 2002
Forschungszentrum Jülich	Jülich, Germany	1967–present	circular	proton, deuteron	75 MeV	Now used as a pre-accelerator for COSY and irradiation purposes

Fermi National Accelerator Laboratory (Fermilab), located just outside Batavia, Illinois, near Chicago, is a United States Department of Energy notional laboratory specializing in high-energy particle physics. Since 2007, Fermilab has been operated by the Fermi Research Alliance, a joint venture of the University of Chicago and the Universities Research Association (URA). Fermilab is a part of the Illinois Technology and Research Corridor.

Fermilab's Bevatron was a landmark particle accelerator; until the startup in 2008 of the Large Hadron Collider (LHC) near

Geneva, Switzerland, it was the most powerful particle accelerator in the world, accelerating antiprotons to energies of 500 GeV and producing proton-proton collision with energies of up to 1.6 TeV, the first accelerator to reach one "tera-electron volt" energy. In addition to high-energy collider physics, Fermilab hosts fixed-target and neutrino experiments, such as MicroBooNE (Micro Booster Neutrino Experiments), including MINOS (main injector neutrino oscillation search), MINOS+, MiniBooNE, and SCIBooNE (SciBar Booster Neutrino Experiment).

The MiniBooNE detector was a forty-foot-diameter (twelve-meter-diameter) sphere containing eight hundred tons of mineral oil lined with 1,520 photos-tube detectors.

An estimated one million neutrino events are recorded each year. SCIBooNE sat in the same neutrino beam as MiniBooNE but has fine-grained tracking capabilities. The NOvA experiment uses, and the MINOS experiment used, beams of neutrinos that travel 455 miles (732 kilometers) through the Earth to the Soudan Mine in Minnesota and the Ash River, Minnesota, site of the NOvA Far Detector.

In the public realm, Fermilab is home to a native prairie ecosystem restoration project and hosts many cultural events: public science lectures and symposia, classical and contemporary music concerts, folk dancing, and arts galleries. The site is of Weston, Illinois, was a community next to Batavia voted out of existence by its village board in 1966 to provide a site for Fermilab.

The laboratory was founded in 1967 as the National Accelerator Laboratory; it was renamed in honor of Enrico Fermi in 1974. The laboratory's first director was Robert Rathbun Wilson, under whom the laboratory opened ahead of time and underbudget. Many of the sculptures on the sites are of his creation. He is the namesake of the symbol for Fermilab and which is the center of activity of the campus.

After Wilson stepped down in 1978 to protest the lack of funding for the lab, Leon M. Lederman took on the job. It was under his guidance that the original accelerator was replaced with the Tevatron, an accelerator capable of colliding protons and antiprotons at a combined energy of 1.96 TeV. Lederman stepped down in 1989 and remains director emeritus. The science education center at the site was named in his honor, which is open from dawn to dusk to visitors who present a valid photo ID.

As of 2014, the first stage in the acceleration process (preaccelerator infector) takes place in two ion sources that turn hydrogen gas into H-ions. The hydrogen ion is introduced into a container lined with molybdenum electrodes, each a matchbox-size, oval-shaped cathode and a surrounding anode, separated by one millimeter and held in place by glass ceramic insulators. A magnetron generates a plasma to form the ions near the metal surface. The ions are accelerated by the source to 35 KeV and matched by low-energy beam transport (LEBT) into the radio frequency quadrupole (RFQ), which applies a 750 KeV electrostatic field, giving the ions their second acceleration. At the exit of RFQ, the beam is matched by medium-energy beam transport (MEBT) into the entrance of the linear accelerator (Linac).

The next stage of acceleration is a linear particle accelerator (Linac). This stage consists of two segments.

The first segment has five vacuum vessels for drift tubes, operating at 201 MHz. The second stage has seven-side coupled cavities, operating at 805 MHz. At the end of Linac, the particles are accelerated to 400 MeV, or about 70 percent of the speed of light, immediately before entering the next accelerator. The H-ions pass through a carbon foil, becoming H+ ions (protons).

The resulting protons then enter the booster ring, a 468-meter (1,535-feet) circumference of circular accelerator whose magnets bend beams of protons around a circular path. The protons travel around the booster about twenty thousand times in thirty-three milliseconds, adding energy with each revolution until they leave the booster accelerated to 8 GeV.

The final acceleration is applied by the main injector (circumference 3,319.4 meters, or 10,890 feet), which is the smaller of the two rings in the last picture below (foreground). Completed in 1999, it has become Fermilab's "particle switchyard" in that it can route protons to any of the experiments installed along the beamlines after accelerating them to 120 GeV. Until 2011, the main injector provided protons to the antiprotons ring (circumference 6,283.2 meters, or 20,614 feet) and the Tevatron for further acceleration but now provides the last push before the particles reach the beamline experiments.

The overall goal of PIP is to increase the repetition rate of the booster beam from 7 Hz to 15 Hz and replace old hardware to increase reliability of the operation.

Before the start of the PIP project, a replacement of the preaccelerator injector was underway. The replacement of almost forty-year-old Walton generators to RFQ started in 2009 and was completed in 2012. At the Linac stage, the analog beam position monitor (BPM) modules were replaced with digital boards in 2013. A replacement of Linac vacuum pumps and related hardware was expected to be completed in 2015.

A study on the replacement of 201-MHz drifts tubes is still ongoing. At the boosting stage, a major component of the PIP is to upgrade the booster ring to a 15-Hz operation. The booster has nineteen radio frequency stations. Originally, the booster stations were operating without solid-state drive system, which was acceptable for 7- but not 15-Hz operation. A demonstration project in 2004 converted one of the stations to solid-state drive before the PIP project. As part of the project, the remaining stations were converted to a solid state in 2013.

Another major part of the PIP project is to refurbish and replace forty-year-old booster cavities. Many cavities have been refurbished and tested to operate at 15 Hz. The completion of cavity refurbishment was expected in 2015, after which the repetition rate can be gradually increased to a 15-Hz operation. A longer-term upgrade is to replace the booster cavities with a new design. The research and development of the new cavities is underway, with replacement expected in 2018.

The goals of PIP-II include a plan to deliver 1.2 MW of proton beam power from the main injector to the Deep Underground Neutrino Experiment target at 120 GeV and the power near 1 MW at 60 GeV, with a possibility to extend the power to 2 MW in the future. The plan should also support the current 8-GeV experiments, including Mu2e, g-2, and other short-baseline neutrino experiments. These require an upgrade to the Linac to inject to the booster with 800 MeV. The first option is to add 400-MeV "afterburner" superconducting Linac at the tail end of the existing 400 MeV. This requires moving the existing Linac up fifty meters (160 feet). However, there are many technical issues with this approach. The preferred option is to build a new 800-MeV superconducting Linac to inject to the booster ring. The new Linac site will be located on top of small portions of Tevatron near the booster ring in order to take advantage of existing electrical and water and cryogenic infrastructure.

The PIP-II Linac will have low-energy beam transport line (LEVT), radio frequency quadrupole (RFQ), and medium-energy beam transport line (MEVT) operated at the room temperature with 162.5 MHz and energy increasing from 0.03 MeV. The first segment of Linac will be operated at 162.5 MHz and energy increased up to 11 MeV. The second segments of Linac will be operated at 325 MHz and energy increased up to 177 MeV. The last segment of Linac will be operated at 650 MHz and will have the final energy level of 800 MeV.

Fermilab, as of 2016, stands to become the world leader in neutrino physics through the Deep Underground Neutrino Experiment at the Long-Baseline Neutrino Facility. Other leaders are CERN, which leads in accelerator physics with the Large Hadron Collider (LHC), and Japan, which has been approved to build and lead the International Linear Collider (ILC).

Fermilab will be the site of LBNF's future beamline, and the Sanford Underground Research Facility (SURF), in Lead, South Dakota, is the site selected to house the massive far detector. The term *baseline* refers to the distance between the neutrino source and the detector. The far detector's current design is for four modules of instrumented liquid argon with a fiducial volume of ten kilotons each. The first two modules are expected to be completed in 2024, with the beam operational in 2026. The final module is planned to be operational in 2027.

LBNF/DUNE program in neutrino physics plans to measure fundamental physical parameters with high precision and to explore physics beyond the standard model. The measurements DUNE will make are expected to greatly increase the physics community's understanding of neutrino beam to be near detector on the Fermilab site and far detector eight hundred miles (1,300 kilometers) away at SURF.

Muon *g*-2 (pronounced "gee minus two") is a particle physics experiment to measure the anomaly of the magnetic moment of a muon to a precision of 0.14 ppm, which will be a sensitive test of the standard model. Fermilab is continuing an experiment conducted at Brookhaven National Laboratory to measure the anomalous magnetic moment of the muon. The magnetic dipole moment (*g*) of a charged lepton (electron muon, or tau) is very nearly 2. The difference from 2 (the "anomalous" part) depends on the lepton and can be computed quite exactly based on the current standard model of the particle physics.

The standard model of particle physics is the theory describing three of the four known fundamental forces (electromagnetic, weak, and strong interactions, and not including the gravitational force) in the universe, as well as classifying all known elementary particles.

It was developed in stages throughout the latter half of the twentieth century, through the work of many scientists around the world, with the current formulation being finalized in the mid-1972 upon experimental confirmation of the existence of quarks.

Since then, confirmation of the top quark (1995), the tau neutrino (200), and the Higgs boson (2012) has added further credence to the standard model. In addition, the standard model has predicted various properties of weak neutral currents and W and Z bosons with great accuracy.

CHAPTER 13

Scientists are building particle detectors all around the world, and one of them happens to be located in an abandoned gold mine, buried 4,850 feet underground. This facility is just one of many where scientists are attempting to solve some of the biggest mysteries in the universe. The search is one, and it is for something that is so elusive that scientists must construct and build massive detectors that are literally the size of Olympic swimming pools just to catch them, and if all goes according to their plan, this gigantic science experiments could answer some of the deepest questions in the cosmos and maybe even explain why we are all here.

The scientists are looking for time-traveling particles called neutrinos. So what is a neutrino, anyways? you may ask. A *neutrino* (denoted by the Greek letter *v*) is a fermion (an elementary particle with half-integer spin) that interacts only via the weak subatomic force and gravity. The neutrino is so named because it is electrically neutral and because its rest mass is so small that it was long thought to be zero. The mass of neutrino is much smaller than that of the other known elementary particles. The weak force has a very short range, the gravitational interaction is extremely weak, and neutrinos, as leptons, do not participate in the strong interaction. Thus, neutrinos typically pass through normal matter unimpeded and undetected.

Thousands of scientists from around the world are studying neutrinos, but still they need a neutrino hunter. Neutrinos are supersmall, tiny particles in the electron family; they are extremely light, and they don't interact. They do not hit much at all, and for the most part, neutrinos pass right through our bodies and are very, very abundant.

Neutrinos are so abundant that right now there are approximately sixty-five billion neutrinos passing through all of us. They are considered fundamental building blocks of matter in what is called the standard model. The standard model of particle physics is the theory describing three of the four unknown fundamental forces. Although the standard model is believed to be theoretically self-consistent and has demonstrated huge successes in providing experimental predictions, it leaves some phenomena unexplained and falls short of being a complete theory of fundamental interaction. It does not fully explain baryon asymmetry, incorporate the full gravitation as describe by general relativity, or account for the acceleration expansion of the universe as possibly described by dark energy. The model does not contain any viable dark matter particle that possesses all the incorporated neutrino oscillations and their nonzero masses. The development of the standard model has driven theoretical and experimental particle physicists alike. For theorists, the standard model is a paradigm of quantum field theory, which exhibits a wide range of physics, including spontaneous symmetry break, anomalies, and nonperturbative behavior.

It is used as a basis for building more exotic models that incorporate hypothetical particles, extra dimensions, and elaborate symmetries (such as supersymmetry) in an attempt to explain experimental results at variance with the standard model, such as the existence of dark matter and neutrino oscillations. The standard model is comprised of these twelve blocks of matter and particles that help those building blocks of matter communicate or talk with one another through the fundamental forces of nature.

In 1954, Chen Ning Yang and Robert Mills extended the concept of gauge theory for abelian groups (e.g., quantum electrodynamics) to nonabelian groups to provide an explanation for strong interactions. In 1961, Sheldon Glashow combined the electromagnetic and weak interactions. In 1967, Steven Weinberg and Abdus Salam incorporated the Higgs mechanism, which is believed to give rise to the masses of all the elementary particles in the standard model. This includes the masses of the W and Z boson and the masses of the fermion, i.e., the quarks and leptons.

After the neutral weak currents caused by Z boson exchange were discovered at CERN in 1973, the electroweak theory became widely accepted and Glashow, Salam, and Weinberg shared the 1979 Nobel Prize in Physics for discovering it.

The W and Z bosons were discovered experimentally in 1983, and the ratio of their masses was found to be as the standard model predicted. The theory of the interaction (i.e., quantum chromodynamics, QCD), to which many contributed, acquired its modern form in 1973–1974, when asymptotic freedom was proposed (a development in which the QCD are the main focus of the theoretical research), and experiments confirmed that the hadrons were composed of fractionally charged quarks. The term *standard model* was first coined by Abraham Pais and Sam Treiman in 1975, with reference to the electroweak theory for quarks. Many scientists are at the very heart of one of the greatest mysteries in physics today, which is why, after the big bang, we came into existence.

The big bang theory is the prevailing cosmological model for the observable universe from the earliest known periods through its subsequent large-scale evolution. The model describes how the universe expanded from a very high-density and high-temperature state and offers a compressive explanation for a broad range of phenomena, including the abundance of light elements, the cosmetic microwave background (CMB), large-scale structure, and Hubble's law (the farther away galaxies are, the faster they are moving away from Earth).

The big bang was basically what would be like a huge bath of energy, and as it cooled, and as the universe expanded, particles were formed. When they meet, they annihilate again into a puff of energy. This is really a good thing to many, as it conserves all the laws of nature. In those moments after the big bang, matter actually won over antimatter, so something very unusual happened. There appeared to have been some process where there was an imbalance between how matter and antimatter were formed that left us with a tiny bit of matter that is seen in the universe. Many physicists and scientists believe that neutrinos might be the culprit. Physicists are looking to see that if neutrinos somehow behave differently, would that cause this imbalance in the universe? Are neutrinos the reason we exist in the universe?

The field of neutrino detection is having a major moment. Physicists are constructing ambitious experiments in very exotic locations to up their odds (so to speak) of catching them from multiple sources, such as cosmic ray showers that are produced in the upper atmosphere. They can be made in nuclear reactors, and they can be made in particle accelerators on Earth. These neutrino detectors are considered marvels of extreme engineering.

A neutrino detector is a physics apparatus that is designed to study neutrinos. Because neutrinos only weakly interact with other particles of matter, neutrino detectors must be very large to detect a significant number of neutrinos.

Neutrino detectors are often built underground, to isolate the detector from cosmic rays and other background radiation. The field of neutrino astronomy is still very much in its infancy; the only confirmed extraterrestrial sources so far as of 2018 are the sun and the supernova 1987A in the nearby Large Magellenic Cloud. Another likely source (three standard deviations) is the blazar TXS 0506+056, about 3.7 billion light-years away. Neutrino observatories will "give astronomers fresh eyes with which to study the universe."

Various detection methods have been used. Super-Kamiokande is a large volume of water surrounded by phototubes that watch for the Cherenkov radiation, emitted when an incoming neutrino observatory is similar, but uses heavy water as the detecting medium. Other detectors have consisted of large volumes of chlorine or gallium, respectively, which are created by neutrinos interacting with the original substance. MINOS uses a solid plastic scintillator also watched by phototubes, Borexino uses a liquid pseudocumene scintillator also watched by phototubes, and the NOvA detector uses a liquid scintillator watched by avalanche photodiodes. The proposed acoustic detection of neutrinos via the thermoacoustic effect is the subject of dedicated studied done by ANTARES, IceCube, and KM3NeT collaborations.

IceCube is a neutrino detector that is buried well over two thousand meters underground in the South Pole. The IceCube Neutrino Observatory (or simply IceCube) is a neutrino observatory constructed at the Amundsen-Scott South Pole Station in Antarctica. Its thousands of sensors are located under the Antarctic ice, distributed over a cubic kilometer.

Similar to its predecessor, the Antarctic Muon and Neutrino Detector Array (AMANDA), IceCube consists of spherical optical sensors called digital optical modules (DOMs), each with a photomultiplier tube (PMT) and a single-board data acquisition computer that sends digital data to the counting house on the surface above the array. IceCube was completed on December 18, 2010. DOMs are deployed on strings of sixty modules each at depths between 1,450 and 2,450 meters into holes melted in the ice using a hot water drill. IceCube is designed to look for point sources of neutrinos in the TeV range to explore the highest-energy astrophysical processes. In November 2013, it was announced that IceCube had detected twenty-eight neutrinos that likely originated outside of the solar system.

Next, there is Super-Kamiokande in Japan, a neutrino detector with an amazing fifty thousand tons ultrapure water sitting underneath a mountain.

Super-Kamiokande (semiabbreviation of full name Super-Kamioka Neutrino Detection Experiment, also abbreviated to Super-K or SK) is a neutrino observatory located under Mount Ikeno near the city of Hina, Gifu Prefecture, Japan. It is located one thousand meters (3,300 feet) underground in the Mozumi Mine in Hida's Kamioka area. The observatory was designed to detect high-energy neutrinos to search for a proton decay, study solar and atmospheric neutrinos, and keep watch for supernovae in the Milky Way galaxy. It consists of a cylindrical steel tank about forty meters (131 feet) in height and diameter holding fifty thousand tons of ultrapure water. Mounted on an inside superstructure are about thirteen thousand photomultiplier tubes that detect light from Cherenkov radiation. A neutrino interaction with the electrons and nuclei of water can produce an electron or positron that moves faster than the speed of light in water (not to be confused with exceeding the speed of light in a vacuum).

There is SNOLAB, located in an active nickel mine in Canada, and there is the great KM3NeT. The Cubic Kilometre Neutrino Telescope, or KM3NeT, is a future European research infrastructure that will be located at the bottom of the Mediterranean Sea. It will host the next-generation neutrino telescope in the form of a water Cherenkov detector with an instrumented volume of about five cubic kilometers distributed over three locations in the Mediterranean: KM3NeT-Fr (off Toulon, France), KM3NeT-It (off Portopalo di Capo Passero, Sicily, Italy), and KM3NeT-Gr (off Pylos, Peloponnese, Greece).

The KM3NeT project continues work done under the ANTARES (telescope built off the coast of France), NEMO (planned telescope off the coast of Italy), and NESTOR (planned telescope off the coast of Greece) neutrino telescope projects. KM3NeT will search for neutrinos from distant astrophysical sources like supernovae remnants, gamma-ray burst, supernovae, or colliding stars and will be a powerful tool in the search for dark matter in the universe. Its prime objective is to detect neutrinos from sources in our galaxy.

Now, let's talk about the latest detector to make news and that has just broken ground, DUNE, the Deep Underground Neutrino Experiment. DUNE is by far the biggest neutrino experiment that's ever been undertaken in the world. It is considered to be the biggest because they are using a particle beam from Fermilab in Chicago, Illinois, to shoot neutrinos and antineutrinos on what some may call a wild eight-hundred-mile ride through the Earth to South Dakota, where they will be detected.

The Deep Underground Neutrino Experiment (DUNE) is a neutrino experiment under construction, with a near detector at Fermilab and a far detector at the Sanford Underground Research Facility, that will observe neutrinos produced at Fermilab. It will fire an intense beam of trillions of neutrinos from a production facility at Fermilab (in Illinois) over a distance of 1,300 kilometers (810 miles) to an instrumented forty-kiloton volume of liquid argon located deep underground at the Sanford lab in South Dakota.

The neutrinos will travel in a straight line through the Earth, reaching about 30 kilometers (nineteen miles) underground near the midpoint; the far detector itself will be 1.5 kilometers (4,850 feet) under the surface. About 870,000 tons of rock will be excavated to create the caverns for the far detectors. More than one thousand collaborators work on the project.

The far detector's current design is for four modules of instrumented liquid argon with a fiducial volume of ten kilotons each. The first two modules are expected to be completed in 2024, with the beam operational in 2026. The final module is planned to be operational in 2027. Excavation of the far detector cavities began on July 21, 2017, and prototype detectors are being constructed and tested at CERN. The first of the two prototypes, the single-phase ProtoDUNE, recorded its first particle tracks in September 2018. CERN's participation in DUNE marked a new direction in CERN's neutrino research, and the experiments are referred to as part of the neutrino platform in the laboratory's research program.

A bit of history, the project was originally started as a US-only project called the Long Baseline Neutrino Experiment (LBNE); in around 2012–2014, a descope was considered with a near-surface detector to reduce cost. However, the Particle Physics Project Prioritization Panel (P5) concluded in its 2014 report that the research activity being pursued by LBNE "should be reformulated under the auspices of a new international collaboration, as an internationally coordinated and internationally funded program, with Fermilab as host," reverting to a deep underground detector. The LBNE collaboration was officially dissolved on January 30, 2015, shortly after the new collaboration recommended by P5 was formed on January 22, 2015. The new collaboration selected the name Deep Underground Neutrino Experiment (DUNE).

Just to excavate a mile underground to build the caverns, to house these detectors, construction workers will have to excavate eight hundred thousand tons or rock, which is about equivalent to the weight of eight aircraft detectors. Some have compared this construction to being like building a ship inside of a small bottle. The workers build the components aboveground that will fit down the shafts that are assembled underground. One might think that South Dakota is an obscure place for a billion-plus-dollar neutrino detector, but it actually has historical significance. In the 1960s, a chemist named Ray Davis constructed one of the first solar neutrino experiments in a gold mine, of all places, which at that time was not considered a successful operation. Ray Davis's experiment came up quite short, as if somehow the electron neutrinos were disappearing on their way from the sun to the home state detector in South Dakota. This caused some people to not believe in Ray Davis's experiment for some time. Eventually, Ray Davis was vindicated as physicists' understanding of neutrino physics evolved.

The world has now confirmed that electron neutrinos coming from the sun were oscillating to other flavors of neutrinos and therefore not showing up in Ray Davis's detector as electron neutrinos. Those oscillations are key, because not only do neutrinos pass through the matter with ease, but they also have split personalities or what physicists call flavors.

Neutrinos come in what many call three different flavors, which are electron neutrino, muon neutrino, and tau neutrino. This is really why neutrinos are so fascinating, because if neutrinos oscillate, they must have some mass, and that is the potential key to understanding why the universe has mass to begin with.

DUNE will carry on Davis's legacy, tracking the way a neutrino oscillates or changes flavors when it interacts with atoms, and they are going to use liquid argon time projection chambers to observe them. In physics, a time projection chamber (TPC) is a type of particle detector that uses a combination of electric field and magnetic field together with a sensitive-volume gas or liquid to perform a three-dimensional reconstruction of a particle trajectory or interaction.

Liquid argon time projection chamber is precision technology on a massive scale capable of producing photographic images of particles as they travel through the detector. For instance, you can tell the difference between the flavors from the trail they leave behind. While the electron bounces around and produces a shower like a

Ping-Pong ball, the muon is just like a bowling ball, and it just travels straight through the detector in a long line.

The construction for DUNE is a mammoth undertaking, and it will not be fully operational until the year 2027. The hope is that DUNE can provide a more comprehensive understanding of the universe that we all live in or unlock a whole new class of physics or, in a perfect world, both. Maybe we will find things we never even expect to find. Science is fun, exciting, and amazing. The original TPC was invented by David R. Nygren, an American physicist, at Lawrence Berkeley Laboratory in the late 1970s. Its first major application was in the PEP-4 detector, which studied 29 GeV electron-positron collisions at the PEP storage ring at SLAC.

A time projection chamber consists of a gas-filled detection volume in an electric field with a position-sensitive electron collection system. The original design (and the one most commonly used) is a cylindrical chamber with multiwire proportional chambers (MWPC) as endplates. Along its length, the chamber is divided into halves by means of a central high-voltage electrode disk, which establishes an electric field between the center and the end plates. Furthermore, a magnetic field is often applied along with the length of the cylinder, parallel to the electric field, in order to minimize the diffusion of the electrons coming from the ionization of the gas.

On passing through the detector gas, a particle will produce primary ionization along its tracks. The z coordinate (along the cylinder axis) is determined by measuring the drift time from the ionization event to the MWPC at the end. This is done using the usual technique of a drift chamber. The MWPC at the end is arranged with the anode wires in the azimuthal direction, which provides information on the radial coordinate. To obtain the azimuthal direction, each cathode plane is divided into strips along the radial direction.

In recent years, other means of position-sensitive electron amplification and detection have become more widely used, especially in conjunction with the increased application of time projection chambers in nuclear physics. These usually combine a segmented anode plate with either just a Frisch grid or an active electron-multiplication element like a gas electron multiplier. These newer TPCs also depart from the traditional geometry of a cylinder with an axial field in favor of a flat geometry or a cylinder with a radial field. Earlier researchers in particle physics also usually made use of a more simplified box-shaped geometry arranged directly above or below the beamline, such as in the CERN NA49 and NA35 experiments.

CHAPTER 14

So let's talk about CERN and dark matter, which is a form of matter that is thought to account for approximately 85 percent of the matter in the universe and about a quarter of its total energy density. The majority of dark matter is thought to be nonbaryonic in nature, possibly being composed of some as-yet undiscovered subatomic particles. Its presence is implied in a variety of astrophysical observations, including gravitational effects that cannot be explained by accepted theories of gravity unless more matter is present than can be seen. For this reason, most experts think dark matter to be abundant in the universe and to have had a strong influence on its structure and evolution.

Dark matter is called dark because it does not appear to interact with observable electromagnetic radiation, such as light, and is thus invisible to the entire electromagnetic spectrum, making it extremely difficult to detect using usual astronomical equipment. The primary evidence for dark matter is that calculations show that many galaxies would fly apart instead of rotating, or would not have formed or move as they do, if they did not contain a large amount of unseen matter. Other lines of evidence include observations in gravitational lensing, from the cosmic microwave background, from astronomical observable universe's current structure, from the formation and evolution of galaxies, from mass location during galactic collisions, and from the motion of galaxies within galaxy clusters. In the standard Lambda-CDM model of cosmology, the total mass-energy of the universe contains 5 percent ordinary matter and energy, 27 percent dark matter, and 68 percent of an unknown form of energy known as dark energy. Thus, dark matter constitutes 85 percent of total mass, while dark energy plus dark matter constitutes 95 percent of total mass-energy content.

Dark matter has not yet been observed directly; if it exists, it must barely interact with ordinary baryonic matter and radiation, except through gravity. The primary candidate for dark matter is some kind of elementary particle that has not yet been discovered, in particular, weakly interacting massive particles (WIMPs). Many experiments to directly detect and study dark matter particles are being actively undertaken, but none have yet succeeded. Dark matter is classified as cold, warm, or hot according to its velocity (more precisely, its free streaming length). Current models favor a cold, dark matter scenario, in which structures emerge by the gradual accumulation of particles.

Although the existence of dark matter is generally accepted by the scientific community, some astrophysicists, intrigued by certain observations that do not fit the dark matter theory, argue for various modifications of the standard laws of general relativity, such as modified Newtonian dynamics, tensor-vector-scalar gravity, or entropic gravity. These models attempt to account for all observations without invoking supplemental nonbaryonic matter.

When thinking about the early history of dark matter, many think of the hypothesis of dark matter as an elaborate history.

In a talk given in 1884, Lord Kelvin estimated the number of dark bodies in the Milky Way from the observed velocity dispersion of the stars orbiting around the center of the galaxy. By using these measurements, he estimated the mass of galaxy, which he determined is different from the mass of visible stars. Lord Kelvin thus included that "many of our star, perhaps a great majority of them, may be dark bodies." In 1906 Henri Poincaré, in the "The Milky Way and Theory of Gases," used "dark matter," or "matière obscure" in French, in discussing Kelvin's work. In 1933, Swiss astrophysicist Fritz Zwicky, who studied galaxy clusters while working at the California Institute of Technology, made a similar inference. Zwicky applied the virial theorem to the Coma Cluster and obtained evidence of the unseen mass that he called *dunkle materie* ("dark matter").

Zwicky estimated its mass based on the motions of galaxies near its edge and compared that to an estimate based on its brightness and number of galaxies. He estimated that the cluster has about four hundred times more mass than was visually observable. The gravity effect of the visible galaxies was far too small for such fast orbit; thus, mass must be hidden from view. Based on these conclusions, Zwicky inferred that some unseen matter provided the mass and associated gravitational attraction to hold the cluster together. Zwicky's estimates were off by more than an order of magnitude, mainly due to an obsolete value of the Hubble constant. The same calculation today shows a smaller fraction, using greater values from luminous mass.

Nonetheless, Zwicky did correctly conclude from his calculation that the bulk of the matter was dark. Further indications that the mass-to-light ratio was not in unity came from measurements of galaxy rotation curves. In 1939, Horace W. Babcock reported the rotation curve for the Andromeda nebula (known now as the Andromeda galaxy), which suggested that the mass-to-luminosity ratio increases radially. He attributed it to either light absorption within the galaxy or modified dynamics in the outer portions of the spiral and not to the missing matter that he has uncovered. Following Babcock's 1939 report of unexpectedly rapid rotation in the outskirts of the Andromeda galaxy and a mass-to-light ratio of 50, in 1940, Jan Oort discovered and wrote about the large nonvisible halo of NGC 3115.

Let's go back to the 1970s now. Vera Rubin, Kent Ford, and Ken Freeman's work in the 1960s and 1970s provided further strong evidence, also using galaxy rotation curves. Rubin and Ford worked with a new spectrograph to measure the velocity curve of edge on spiral galaxies with greater accuracy. This result was confirmed in 1978. An influential paper presented Rubin and Ford's results in 1980. They showed that most galaxies must contain about six times as much dark as visible mass; thus, by around 1980 the apparent need for dark matter was widely recognized as a major unsolved problem in astronomy.

At the same time that Rubin and Ford were exploring optical rotation curves, radio astronomers were making use of new radio telescopes to map the twenty-one-centimeter line of atomic hydrogen in nearby galaxies. The radical distribution of interstellar atomic hydrogen (HI) often extended the sampling of rotation curves, and thus of the total mass distribution, to a new dynamical regime. Early mapping of Andromeda with the 300-foot telescope at Green Bank and the 250-foot dish at Jodrell Bank already showed that the HI rotation curve did not trace the expected Keplerian decline. As more sensitive receivers became available, Morton Roberts and Robert

Whitehurst were able to trace the rotational velocity of Andromeda to 30 kpc, much beyond the optical measurements.

Illustrating the advantage of tracing the gas disk at large radii simply proves, or strengthens, the fact, and that paper combines that optical data (the cluster of points at radii of less than 15 kpc with a single point farther out) with the HI data between 20 and 30 kpc, exhibiting the flatness of the outer galaxy rotation curve; the solid curve peaking at the center is the optical surface density, while the other curve shows the cumulative mass, still rising linearly at the outermost measurement. In parallel, the use of interferometric arrays for extragalactic HI spectroscopy was being developed.

In 1972, David Rogstad and Seth Shostak published H-I rotation curves of five spirals mapped with the Owens Valley interferometer; the rotation curves of all five were very flat, suggesting very large values of mass-to-light ratio in the outer parts of their extended H-I disks. A stream of observations in the 1980s supported the presence of dark matter, including gravitational lensing of background objects by galaxy clusters, the temperature distribution of hot gas in galaxies and clusters, and the pattern of anisotropies in the cosmic microwave background.

CHAPTER 15

When people hear the name ATLAS, many may picture the image of a man cursed to forever hold the Earth on his shoulders. Let's get to know the real meaning of ATLAS, being one of seven particle detector experiments constructed at the Large Hadron Collider, the LHC, the "great particle accelerator" at CERN. ATLAS was really designed to take advantage of the energy available at the Large Hadron Collider and observe phenomena that may involve massive particles that were not able to be observed using earlier, lower-energy accelerators. The discovery of the Higgs boson was in July 2012, and ATLAS was one of the two Large Hadron Collider experiments involved in this amazing find. Of course, ATLAS was also designed to continue searching for proof and real evidence of particle physics beyond the standard model. The ATLAS detector is twenty-five meters in diameter, forty-six meters long. I know it contains about three thousand kilometers of cable and weighs approximately seven thousand tons. This experiment involved about three thousand physicists, and they are from well over 175 institutions in almost forty countries.

The design was really a combination of the two previous experiments, and it seems to have benefited from the detector R + D that had been done for the Superconducting Super Collider.

ATLAS is designed to be a general-purpose detector. When the proton beams produced at the LHC interact in the center of the detector, a variety of different particles with a broad range of energies is produced. ATLAS has a very important job, and that is to investigate many different types of physics that might become detectable in the energetic collisions of the LHC. It is well-known that some of these are only improved measurements of actual confirmations of the standard model, and many others are merely clues for new particle theories.

The new Higgs-like particle was detected by its decay into two photons and its decay for leptons. In March of year 2013, in light of the updated CMS and ATLAS results, an amazing announcement was made. CERN told the world that the new particle was in fact a Higgs boson. The experiments also provided proof that the properties of the particle as well as the ways it interacts with other particles were well matched with those of the Higgs boson. In 2013, two of the theoretical physicists who predicted the existence of the standard model Higgs boson, Peter Higgs and Francois Englert, were awarded the Nobel Prize in Physics. Analysis of more properties of the particles and data collected in 2015 and 2016 confirmed this further.

One theory at CERN is the research supersymmetry, which can potentially solve a lot of problems in theoretical physics, such as the hierarchy problems within gauge theory, and is present in almost all models of string theory. Models of supersymmetry involve new, highly massive particles. In many cases, these decay into quarks and stable heavy particles that are very unlikely to interact with ordinary matter. The stable particles would escape the detector, leaving as a signal one or more high-energy quark jets and a large amount of missing momentum. Other hypothetical massive particles, like those in the Kaluza-Klein theory, might leave a very similar signature, but their discovery would certainly indicate that there was some kind of physics beyond the standard model.

The ATLAS detector consists of a series of ever-larger concentric cylinders around the interaction point where the proton beams from the LHC collide. It can be divided into four major parts, such as the inner detector, the calorimeters, the muon spectrometer, and the magnet systems. Each of these is in turn made of multiple layers. ATLAS is designed to be a general-purpose detector. When the proton beams produced by the Large Hadron Collider (LHC) interact in the center of the detector, a variety of different particles with a broad range of energies is produced.

Rather than focusing on a particular physical process, ATLAS is designed to measure the very broadest possible range of signals. This is intended to ensure that whatever form a new physical processes or particles might take, ATLAS will be able to detect them and measure their properties. Experiments at earlier colliders, such as the Tevatron and Large Electron-Positron Collider, were designed based on a similar philosophy. However, the unique challenges of the Large Hadron Collider—its unprecedented energy and extremely high rate of collisions—require ATLAS to be significantly larger and more complex than previous experiments. At an incredible twenty-seven kilometers in circumference, the Large Hadron Collider collides two beams of protons together, with each proton carrying up to 6.5 TeV of energy, which is enough to produce particles with masses significantly greater than any particles that are currently known, if these particles even exist. ATLAS was to detect these particles, namely their masses, momentum, energies, lifetime, nuclear spin, and charges.

In order to identify all particles produced at the interaction point where the particle beams collide, the detector is designed in layers made up of detectors of different types, each of which is designed to observe specific types of particles. The different traces that particles leave in each layer of the detector allow for effective particle identification and accurate measurements of energy and momentum. As the energy of particles produced by the accelerator increases, the detector attached to it must grow to effectively measure and stop higher-energy particles.

As of the year 2017, ATLAS is the largest detector ever built, it is really one of a kind and its name is well deserved. One of the most important goal of ATLAS was to investigate a missing piece of the standard model, the Higgs boson. The Higgs mechanism, which includes the Higgs boson, gives mass to elementary particles, leading to differences between the weak force and electromagnetism by giving the W and Z bosons mass while leaving the photon massless. On the Fourth of July 2012 was when ATLAS, together with CMS, its sister experiment at the LHC, reported evidence for the existence of particle consistent with the Higgs boson at a confidence level of 5 sigma, with a mass around 125 GeV, or 133 times the proton mass.

The ATLAS detector consists of a series of ever-larger concentric cylinders around the interaction point where the proton beams from the Large Hadron Collider actually collide. It can be divided into four major parts: the inner detector, the calorimeters, the muon spectrometer, and the magnet systems. Each of these is in turn made of multiple layers. The detector is complementary: the inner detector tracks particles precisely, the calorimeters measure the energy of easily stopped particles, and the muon system makes additional measurements of highly penetrating muons. The two magnet systems bend charged particles in the inner detector and the muon spectrometer, allowing their momenta to be measured. The only established stable particles that cannot be detected directly are neutrinos; their presence is inferred by measuring a momentum imbalance among detected particles.

For this to work, the detector must be "hermetic"—meaning, it must detect all nonneutrinos produced, with no blind spots. Maintaining detector performance in the high-radiation areas immediately surrounding the proton beams is a significant engineering challenge. The inner detector begins a few centimeters from the proton beam axis, extends to a radius of 1.2 meters, and is 6.2 meters in length along the beam pipe. Its basic function is to track charged particles by detecting their interaction with material at discrete points, revealing detailed information about the types of particles and their momentum. The magnetic field surrounding the entire inner detector causes charged particles to curve; the direction of the curve reveals a particle's charge, and even the degree of curvature reveals its momentum.

The inner detector has three parts. The pixel detector is the innermost part of the detector. It contains three concentric layers and three disks on each endcap, with a total of 1,744 modules, each measuring two centimeters by six centimeters. The detecting material is a 250-centimeter-thick silicon. Each module contains sixteen readout chips and other electronic components. The smallest unit that can be read out is a pixel size designed for extremely precise tracking very close to the interaction point. In total, the pixel detector has over eight million readout channels, which is about 50 percent of the total readout channels of the whole experiment. Having such a large amount created a considerable design, and the engineering challenge was the radiation to which the pixel detector is exposed because of its proximity to the interaction point, requiring that all components be radiation hardened in order to continue operating after significant exposures.

The semiconductor tracker (SCT) is the middle component of the inner detector. It is very similar in concept and function to the pixel detector, but with long narrow strips rather than small pixels, making coverage of a larger area practical. Each strip measures eighty micrometers by twelve centimeters. The SCT is the most critical part of the inner detector for basic tracking in the plane perpendicular to the beam, since it measures particles over a much larger area than the pixel detector, with more sampled points and roughly equal accuracy. It is composed of four double layers of silicon strips, and it has 6.3 million readout channels and total area of sixty-one square meters.

A computer-generated cutaway view of the ATLAS detector would show its various components, such as muon detectors; magnet system: toroid magnets, solenoid magnets; inner detector: transition radiation tracker, semiconductor tracker, pixel detector; and calorimeters: liquid argon calorimeter, tile calorimeter.

The transition radiation tracker (TRT), the outermost component of the inner detector, is a combination of a straw tracker and a transition radiation detector. The detecting elements are drift tubes (straws), each four millimeters in diameter and up to 144 centimeters long. The uncertainly of track position measurements (position resolution) is about two hundred micrometers.

This is not as precise as those for the other two detectors, but it was necessary to reduce the cost of covering a larger volume and to have transition radiation detection capability. Each straw is filled with gas that becomes ionized when a charged particle passes through. The straws are held at about –1,500 V, driving the negative ions to a fine wire down the center of each straw, producing a current pulse (signal) in the wire. The wires with signals create a pattern of "hits" straws that allow the path of the particle to be determined. Between the straws, materials with widely varying indices of refraction cause ultrarelativistic charged particles to produce transition radiation and leave much stronger signals in some straws. Xenon and argon gas are used to increase the number of straws with strong signals.

Since the amount of transition radiation is greater for highly relativistic particles (those with a speed very near the speed of light), and because particles of a particular energy have a higher speed the lighter they are, particle paths with many very strong signals can be identified as belonging to the lightest charged particles: electrons and their antiparticles, positrons. The TRT has about 298,000 straws in total. The calorimeters are situated outside the solenoidal magnets that surround the inner detector. Their purpose is to measure the energy from particles by absorbing it. There are two basic calorimeter systems: an inner electromagnetic calorimeter and an outer hadronic calorimeter.

Both are sampling calorimeter; that is, they absorb energy in high-density metal and periodically sample the shape of the resulting particle shower, inferring the energy of the original particle from this measurement. The electromagnetic (EM) calorimeter absorbs energy from particles that interact electromagnetically, which include charged particles and photons. It has high precision, both in the amount of energy absorbed and in the precise location of the energy deposited. The angle between the particle's trajectory and the detector's beam axis (or more precisely, the pseudorapidity) and its angle within the perpendicular plane are both measured to within roughly 0.025 radians. The barrel EM calorimeter has accordion-shaped electrodes, and the energy-absorbing materials are lead and stainless steel, with liquid argon as the sampling material, and a cryostat is required around the EM calorimeter to keep it sufficiently cool. The hadronic calorimeter absorbs energy from particles that pass through the EM calorimeter but do interact via the strong force; these particles are primarily hadrons. It is less precise, both in energy magnitude and in the localization (within about 0.1 radians only).

The energy-absorbing material is steel, with scintillating tiles that sample the energy deposited. Many of the features of the calorimeter are chosen for their cost-effectiveness; the instrument is large and comprises a huge amount of construction material: the main part of the calorimeter, the tile calorimeter, is eight meters in diameter and covers twelve meters along the beam axis. The far-forward sections of the hadronic calorimeter are contained within the forward EM calorimeters cryostat and use liquid argon as well, while copper and tungsten are used as absorbers. The muon spectrometer is an extremely large tracking system consisting of three parts: (1) a magnetic field provided by three toroidal magnets, (2) a set of 1,200 chambers measuring with high spatial precision the tracks of the outgoing muons, and (3) a set of triggering chambers with accurate time resolution. The extent of this subdetector starts at a radius of 4.25 meters close to the calorimeters out to the full radius of the detector (11 meters).

Its tremendous size is required to accurately measure the momentum of muons, which first go through all the other elements of the detector before reaching the muons, which first go through all the other elements of the detector before reaching the muon spectrometer. It was designed to measure, stand-alone, the momentum of 100 GeV muons with 3 percent accuracy and 1 TeV muons with 10 percent accuracy.

It was vital to go to the lengths of putting together such a large piece of equipment because a number of interesting physical processes can only be observed if one or more muons are detected and because the total energy of particles in an event could not be measured if the muons were ignored. It functions similar to the inner detector, with muons curving so that their momentum can be measured, albeit with a different magnetic field configuration, lower spatial precision, and much larger volume. It also serves the function of simply identifying muons; very few particles of other types are expected to pass through the calorimeters and subsequently leave signals in the muon spectrometer. It has roughly one million readout channels, and its layers of detectors have a total area of twelve thousand square meters.

The ATLAS detector uses two large superconducting magnet systems to bend charged particles so that their momenta can be measured. This bending is due to the Lorentz force, which is proportional to velocity. Since all particles produced in the LHC's proton collisions are traveling at very close to the speed of light, the force on particles of different momenta is equal. In the theory of relativity, momentum is not linear or proportional to velocity at such speeds. Thus high-momentum particles curve very little, while low-momentum particles curve significantly; the amount of curvature can be quantified, and the particle momentum can be determined from this value.

The inner solenoid produces a two-tesla magnetic field surrounding the inner detector. This high magnetic field allows even very energetic particles to curve enough for their momentum to be determined, and its nearly uniform direction and strength allow measurements to be made very precisely. Particles with momenta below roughly 400 MeV will be curved so strongly that they will loop repeatedly in the field and most likely not be measured; however, this energy is very small compared to the several TeV of energy released in each proton collision.

The outer toroidal magnetic field is produced by eight very large air-core superconducting barrel loops and two endcaps air toroidal magnets, all situated outside the calorimeters and within the muon system. This magnet is situated outside the calorimeters and within the muon system. This magnetic field extends in an area twenty-six meters long and twenty meters in diameter, and it stores 1.6 gigajoules of energy. Its magnetic field is not uniform, because a solenoid magnet of sufficient size would be prohibitively expensive to build. It varies between 2 and 8 teslameters.

The ATLAS detector is complemented by a set of detectors in the very forward region. These detectors are located in the LHC tunnel, far away from the interaction point. The basic idea is to measure elastic scattering at very small angles in order to produce better measurements of the absolute luminosity at the ATLAS interaction point.

The detector generates unmanageably large amounts of raw data: about 25 megabytes per event (raw; aero suppression reduces this to 1.6 megabytes), multiplied by forty million beam crossings per second in the center of the detector. This produces a total of one petabyte of raw data per second. The trigger system uses simple information to identify, in real time, the most interesting events to retain for detailed analysis. There are three trigger levels. The first is based in electronics on the detector, while the other two run primarily on a large computer cluster near the detector. The first-level trigger selects about one hundred thousand events per second.

After the third-level trigger has been applied, a few hundred events remain to be stored for further analysis. This amount of data still requires over one hundred megabytes of disk space per second—at least a petabyte each year. Earlier particle detector readout and event detection systems were based on parallel shared buses such as VMEbus or FASTBUS. Since such a bus architecture cannot keep up with the data requirements of the LHC experiments, all data acquisition system proposals rely on high-speed point-to-point link and switching networks.

People designing the LHC experiments evaluated several such networks, including asynchronous transfer mode, ANT interface, fiber channel, ethernet, and IEEE 1355 (space wire).

Offline events reconstruction is performed on all permanently stored events, turning the pattern of signals from the detector into physics objects, such as jets, photons, and leptons. Grid computing is being extensively used for events reconstruction, allowing the parallel use of university and laboratory computer networks throughout the world for the CPU-intensive task of reducing large quantities of raw data into a form suitable for physics analysis. The software for these tasks has been under development for many years and will continue to be refined even now that the experiment is collecting data. Individuals and groups within the collaboration are writing their own code to perform further analysis of these objects, searching the patterns of detected particles for particular physical models or hypothetical particles.

CHAPTER 16

Perhaps one of the greatest fears among theoretical physicists concerning CERN and the Large Hadron Collider is that it might create miniature black holes that could descend to the core of the planet and literally devour it from within. It is important to note that black holes are only theoretical constructs and have never been proven to exist. Black holes were first discovered as purely mathematical solutions of Einstein's field questions and are not necessary in Tesla's electric universe model. To date, many believe black holes are science fiction. It is the past that tells us who we are; without it, we would lose our identity, said Stephen Hawking at an inauguration of Harvard's black hole initiative. He was talking about black holes in depth and went on to say that its very principle is if it could be recovered. Einstein communicated these fantastic cosmic ideas in a very simple, down-to-earth way. He always made physics interesting and fascinating, leaving one wanting to learn more.

So with the death and passing of Hawking, it does seem fitting to remember his words and also all his work as part of our identity. Stephen Hawking is probably best known for his realization that black holes do not grow forever like people once thought. They radiate off particles that make them slowly lose mass until eventually they die in a burst of light. This idea leads to the black hole information paradox, which we are still grappling with today.

It is difficult to overstate Stephen Hawking's impact on our understanding of the universe. In his PhD thesis, he showed us how the big bang theory worked kind of like a black hole in reverse. It exploded outward from infinitely dense singularity. This helps solidify the big bang theory as a scientific fact. Later, much of his work was aimed at finding a complete theory of the universe, a theory that unified all the fundamental forces of the universe. Stephen Hawking never won a Nobel Prize, but he was indeed ahead of his time.

Hawking loved science and was fascinated with black holes. He shone a light onto the darkest objects into the universe while he remained lighthearted. He concluded his talk at Harvard by saying black holes are not as black as they are painted; they are not the eternal prisons that they were once thought to be. Things can get out of a black hole, to the outside, and possibly to another universe, so if you feel you're in a black hole, don't give up; there is a way out and we

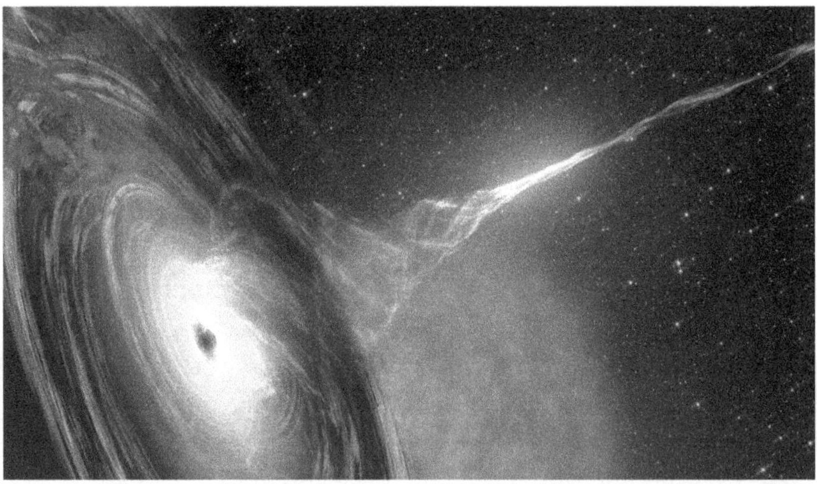

could still find those bursts of light from shrinking, radiating black holes created by the past or from new tiny black holes CERN creates in the Large Hadron Collider. As any theoretical physicist worth his salt will admit, particle physics and quantum mechanics are a world within fact and fantasy, and at times, they are indistinguishable. When it comes to CERN and the LHC, there is no storage of theoretical doomsday scenarios.

I would like to talk about several of the theoretical possibilities relating to the activities at CERN. Each one of my points represents either a scientific reality or a hypothetical possibility based on incredibly complex concepts and mathematical formulas that would be extremely difficult to explain. The first possibility is to do with time distortion and Stargates. It has been suggested that by colliding heavier atomic particles, such as lead ions, which CERN will soon be doing, space and time could be distorted, creating what Einstein called a Rosen bridge, or a Stargate, which is basically a wormhole between two different locations, dimensions, or periods of time. It has also been suggested that such distortions in the space-time continuum could lead to what has been referred to as the Groundhog Day effect, in which time folds back on itself, allowing manipulation of the past.

The next theoretical possibility are DNA sequencing and artificial synthesis. Since it is a fact that the synchrotron collider at Berkeley in Walnut Creek, California, was used to help sequence human DNA for the human genome project, it is certainly feasible that the Large Hadron Collider could also be employed in a similar way, but with much more precise results. There is evidence to suggest that artificial human or human-hybrid genomes have already been synthesized at collider facilities; it is certainly worth a Google.

The next doomsday scenario we have are strangelets, which are produced from a quark-gluon plasma soup sometimes generated after high-energy particle collision. Strangelets are the most explosive substance in the unknown universe, and according to theoretical physicists, they were responsible for the explosion at the so-called big bang. Contrary to popular belief, strangelets are not theoretical but have been confirmed to exist at the Brookhaven National Laboratory in Long Island, New York, where physicists working with relativistic heavy ion collider (also known as RHIC) are attempting not only to produce strangelets but also to contain them. The LHC is a much higher-energy collider than the RHIC. Strangelet production and containment is even more feasible at CERN.

In light of this information, it should give everyone pause when confronted with the fact that China is now preparing to construct a supercollider twice the size of the one at CERN. Also, Russia has a particle collider and has CERN physicists working with them. North Korea also works with Russia on their particle collider. Japan has big plans to build a massive hadron collider in the very near future. Unlike black hole, antimatter is not theoretical.

Not only can it be measured, but it is already being created and even contained in the Large Hadron Collider at CERN, though in very small amounts and for a short period of time. Antimatter has enormous explosive potential. A quarter gram of antimatter can produce an explosive yield equivalent to five kilotons of TNT. If CERN develops the capability to create and store significant amounts of antimatter (and some claim CERN already has), then highly destructive antimatter weapons will be developed.

Science has showed us that black holes have extremely strong gravitational pulls, so what are these tiny black holes pulling in? CERN is absolutely aware that the Large Hadron Collider has everything to do with the outside atmosphere, rhythm, and energy of the Earth and sun. This is why they have such a unique and astrologically coordinated schedule for firing up the LHC. There has been a petition online; people are saying they should stop the Large Hadron Collider because it could or will create black holes that could consume the whole universe and destroy the world. When confronted with this information, somewhat as a question to some CERN physicists, the response was, "Certainly not the universe. It is just our little planet that is at stake, and also the danger is a danger that can be assessed beforehand, and it would take about a week to assess the danger."

The big bang led to the birth of the universe about 13.7 billion years ago. When asking CERN if the black hole theory is acknowledged by the nuclear research organization, a physicist has admitted CERN started out with this theory as the main reason for doing the experiments, and when it turned out that there may be some real danger involved, it became second and third rank in the agenda. But that's not the main problem. The question is now whether experimenting with black holes is dangerous or not. One physicist with CERN has stated that there is a one in twelve probability of Earth being swallowed up by a black hole. Other physicists connected to the organization answered with this response: it wouldn't swallow the Earth within months or seconds; it would take at least five years, but still, such an outlook is something that should be discussed heavily before going ahead.

CHAPTER 17

The multiverse is a hypothetical group of multiple universes including the universe in which we live. Together, these universes comprise everything that exists: the entirety of space, time, matter, energy, the physical laws, and the constants that describe them. The different universes within the multiverse are called parallel universes, other universes, or alternative universes. Multiple universes have been hypothesized in cosmology, physics, astronomy, religion, philosophy, transpersonal psychology, and literature, particularly in science fiction and fantasy. In these contexts, parallel universes are also called alternate universes, quantum universe, interpenetrating dimensions, parallel dimensions, parallel worlds, parallel realities, quantum realities, alternate realities, alternate timelines, alternate dimensions, and dimensional planes.

The physics community has debated the various multiverse theories over time. Prominent physicists are divided about whether any other universes exist outside our own. Some physicists say the multiverse is not a legitimate topic of science inquiry. Concerns have been raised about whether attempts to exempt the multiverse from experimental verification could erode public confidence in science and ultimately damage the study of fundamental physics.

Some have argued that the multiverse is a philosophical rather than a scientific hypothesis because it cannot be empirically falsified. The ability to disprove a theory by means of scientific experiment has always been part of the accepted scientific method. Paul Hardt has famously argued that no experiment can rule out a theory if the theory provides for all possible outcomes. In 2007, Nobel laureate Steven Weinberg suggested that if the multiverse existed, "the hope of finding a rational explanation for the precise values of quarks, masses, and other constants of the standard model that we observe in our big bang is doomed, for their value would be accident of the particular part of the multiverse in which we live."

The multiverse is a theory in which our universe is not the only one, but states that many universes exist parallel to one another. These distinct universes within the multiverse theory are called parallel universe. A variety of different theories lend themselves to a multiverse viewpoint. Not all physicists really believe that these universes exist. Even fewer believe that it would ever be possible to contact these parallel universes. The idea of level 1 parallel universe basically says that space is so big that the rules of probability imply that surely, somewhere else out there, are other planets exactly like Earth.

In fact, an infinite universe would have infinitely many planets, and on some of them, the events that play out would be virtually identical to those on our own Earth.

We don't see these other universes because our cosmic vision is limited by the speed of light—the ultimate speed limit. Light started traveling at the moment of the big bang, about fourteen billion years ago, and so we can't see farther than about fourteen billion light-years (about farther, since space is expanding). This volume of space is called the Hubble volume and represents our observable universe.

The existence of level 1 parallel universes depends on two assumptions:

- The universe is infinite (or virtually so).
- Within an infinite universe, every single possible configuration of particles in a Hubble volume takes place multiple times.

If level 1 parallel universes do exist, reaching one is virtually (but not entirely) impossible. For one thing, we wouldn't know where to look for one because, by definition, a level 1 parallel universe is so far away that no message can ever get from us to them, or them to us. (Remember, we can only get messages from within our own Hubble volume.)

In a level 2 parallel universe, regions of space are continuing to undergo an inflation phase, and because of the continuing inflationary phases in these universes, space between us and the other universe is literally expanding faster than the speed of light and they are, therefore, completely unreachable. Two possible theories present reasons to believe that the level 2 parallel universe may exist: eternal inflation and ekpyrotic theory. In eternal inflation, recall that the quantum fluctuations in the early universes' vacuum energy caused a bubble universe to be created all over the place, expanding through their inflation stages at different rates.

The initial condition of these universes is assumed to be at a maximum energy level, although at least one variant, chaotic inflation, predicts that the initial condition can be chaotically chosen as any energy level, which may have no maximum, and the results will be the same. The findings of eternal inflation mean that when inflation starts, it produces not just one universe but an infinite number of universes. Right now, the only noninflationary model that carries any kind of weight is the ekpyrotic model, which is so new that it's still highly speculative.

In the ekpyrotic theory picture, if the universe is the region that results when two branes collide, then the branes could actually collide in multiple locations. Consider flapping a sheet up and down rapidly onto the surface of a bed. The sheet doesn't touch the bed only in one location but rather touches it in multiple locations. If the sheet were a brane, then each point of collision would create its own universe with its own initial conditions.

There is no reason to expect that branes collide in only one place, so the ekpyrotic theory makes it very probable that there are other universes in other locations, expanding even as you consider this possibility. Brilliant minds have said, "If you stay where you are, you'll run into yourself." I guess that's up for you to decide.

A level 3 parallel universe is a consequence of the many worlds interpretation (MWI) from quantum physics, in which every single quantum possibility inherent in the quantum wave function becomes a real possibility in some reality. When the average person (especially a science-fiction fan) thinks of a "parallel universe," he's probably thinking of level 3 parallel universes.

Level 3 parallel universes are different from the others posed because they take place in the same space and time as our own universe but you still have no way to access them.

You have never had and will never have contact with any level 1 or level 2 universe (we assume), but you're continually in contact with level 3 universes—every moment of your life, every decision you make, is causing a split of your "now" self into an infinite number of future selves, all of which are unaware of one another. Though we talk of the universe "splitting," this isn't precisely true. From a mathematical standpoint, there's only one wave function, and it evolves over time. The superpositions of different universes all coexist simultaneously in the same infinite dimensional Hilbert space.

These separate, coexisting universes interfere with one another, yielding the bizarre quantum behaviors of our four types of universes. Level 3 parallel universes have the least to do with string theory directly. A level 4 parallel universe is the strangest place (and most controversial prediction) of all, because it would follow fundamentally different mathematical laws of nature than our universe. In short, any universe that physicists can get to work out on paper would exist, based on the mathematical democracy principle: any universe that is mathematically possible has an equal possibility of actually existing.

CHAPTER 18

When people think about time travel, many think that it is just science fiction, is impossible, and could not happen. Other people believe in time travel or, at a minimum, that time travel is possible or has occurred. Most people wouldn't think of a nuclear research facility such as CERN as being associated with or involved with time travel. After reading the concepts of Stephen Hawking, Albert Einstein, Gilbert Newton Lewis, most of us tend to think of science, light speed, black holes, and wormholes. Those brilliant men were so close.

A wormhole, or Einstein-Rosen bridge, is a hypothetical topological feature that would fundamentally be a shortcut connecting two separate points in space-time. A wormhole, in theory, might be able to connect extremely far distances, such as a billion light-years, or more short distances, such as a few feet, different universes, and different points in time. Like black holes, wormholes arise as valid solutions to the equations of Albert Einstein's general theory of relativity, and like black holes, the phrase was coined in the year 1957 by Mr. John Wheeler, an American physicist. Also, like black holes, they have never been observed directly, but they crop up so readily in theory that some physicists are encouraged to think that real counterparts may eventually be found fabricated.

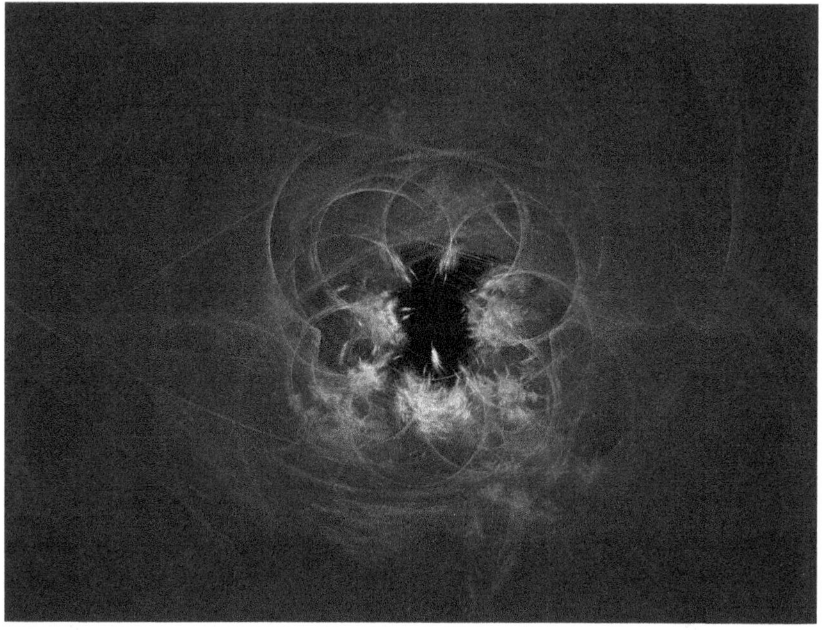

In 1916, the Austrian physicist Ludwig Hamm, while looking over Karl Schwarzschild's solution to Einstein's field questions, which describes a particular form of a black hole known as Schwarzschild's black hole, noticed that another solution was also possible, one that described a phenomenon that later came to be known as a white hole. A *white hole* is the theoretical time reversal of a black hole, and while a black hole acts as a vacuum, drawing in any matter that crosses the event horizon, a white hole acts as a source that ejects matter from its event horizon. Some have even speculated that there is a white hole on the other side of all black holes, where all the matter the black hole sucks up is blown out into some alternative universe, and even that what we think of as the big bang might in fact have been the result of such a phenomenon.

How to travel in time, to the past and to the future, has been a mystery for a very long time. Brilliant scientists have said that you need a machine to sustain a wormhole, and of course, the machines that they are talking about are located in Geneva, Switzerland, at the nuclear research facility known as CERN. It is there where new science continues to fascinate the human mind with wormholes. With a route metric computer, it only takes time and development before a new model can be born.

Time travel 101, the basics, is, first, to harness a wormhole, simply speed up one end and slow down the other end of the wormhole and step through, break on through to the other side, so to speak. Still, how does this all work? Has it been under our noses all this time? Being familiar with the concepts of wormholes, I know they are a consequence of the theory of Einstein's theory of general relativity. A wormhole, in theory, would act as a shortcut or a passageway through space and time. The wormhole creates a tunnel, effectively cutting through two locations in space and time, therefore eliminating the need for three-dimensional travel through space. Therefore, no more rocket ships needed. Similar to the movie *Stargate II.*

Many believe wormholes are everywhere and it's just a matter of seeing them and harnessing them. To achieve this, a machine or a gateway is necessary. Of course, a machine is needed to sustain a wormhole, just like the largest known machine in the world, the LCH, or Large Hadron Collider, located in Geneva. If a person did go through time and then went back, could the ripples be enough to change the future or even create an alternate future? Ripples would be best explained by this example: If you have a glass of water in front of you, think of the water in the glass as time. Time moves forward constantly untouched, as still as the water, but if you go back and try to change something (hand smacks table next to water glass), it creates a ripple effect.

Change has to catch up with time, and everything around it either changes or suffers. However, with Nikola Tesla's time-travel experience, he states, "I could see the past, present, and future simultaneously." The idea that humans can or could travel in time has captured the imagination of millions around the globe. When looking back at history, we find numerous texts that can be interpreted as evidence of time travel.

When Albert Einstein published his theory of relativity in the year 1905, it created a buzz in the scientific community, opening the page for many questions such as time travel to a possibility. There is also evidence of time travel in the Bible. In the Bible, the prophet Jeremiah was sitting together with a few of his friends, and there was a young boy, and Jeremiah told this young boy to go out of Jerusalem, to the hills nearby, and collect figs for everyone. Next, the boy went out and collected some fresh figs. As the story goes, the young boy heard some noise and sensed a strange wind in the air, then the boy became unconscious. He had what felt like a blackout or sorts. After a time, he woke up and he saw it was nearing evening. This boy ran back to the society area, and his city was full of strange soldiers. He yelled, "What's going on here? Where is Jeremiah and all the others?" An old man spoke up and said, "That was sixty years ago." It was a time-travel story from the Bible.

In the year 1895, Tesla made a shocking discovery suggesting that time and space could be influenced by magnetic fields. Tesla had been experimenting with radio frequencies along with power transmissions through the Earth's atmosphere, and this discovery would many years later lead to the Philadelphia Experiment, along with time-travel programs. The Philadelphia Experiment is an alleged military experiment supposed to have been carried out by the US Navy at the Philadelphia Naval Shipyard in Philadelphia, Pennsylvania, sometime around October 28, 1943. The US Navy destroyer escort USS *Eldridge* (DE-173) is claimed to have been rendered invisible (or "cloaked") to enemy devices.

The story first appeared in 1955, in letters of unknown origin sent to a writer and astronomer, Morris K. Jessup. It is widely understood to be a hoax; the US Navy maintains that no such experiment was ever conducted, that the details of the story contradict well-established facts about USS *Eldridge*, and that the alleged claims do not conform to known physical laws. In this experiment, Allende claimed the destroyer escort USS *Eldridge* (DE-183) was rendered invisible, teleported to New York, teleported to another dimension where it encountered aliens, and teleported through time, resulting in the death of several sailors, some of whom were fused with the ship's hull.

Jessup dismissed Allende as a "crackpot." In the early 1957, Jessup was contacted by the Office of Naval Research (ONR) in Washington, DC, and received a parcel containing a paperback copy of *The Case for the UFO* in a manila envelope marked "Happy Easter." The book had been extensively annotated in its margins, written with three different shades of pink ink, appearing to detail a correspondence among three individuals, only one of which is given a name: "Jemi." The ONR labeled the other two "Mr. A" and "Mr. B."

The annotators referred to one another as "Gypsies" and discussed two different types of "people" living in outer space. Their text contained nonstandard use of capitalization and punctuation and detailed a lengthy discussion of the merits of various elements of Jessup's assumptions in the book. There was an oblique reference to the Philadelphia Experiment. One example is that Mr. B reassures his fellow annotators who have highlighted a certain theory that Jessup advanced. Based on the handwriting style and subject matter, Jessup concluded a large part of the writing was Allende's. And others have the same conclusions, that the three styles of annotations are from the same person using three pens.

The ONR funded a small printing of one hundred copies of the volume by the Texas-based Varo Manufacturing Company, which later became known as the Varo edition, with the annotations therefore known as the Varo annotations. Jessup tried to publish more books on the subject of UFOs but was unsuccessful. Losing his publisher and experiencing a succession of downturns in his personal life led him to commit suicide in Florida on April 30, 1959. A long time before the top secret military programs were even thought about, Tesla has already made some discoveries that were fascinating in regards to a nature of time and the possibilities of being able to travel through time. The experiments of Tesla and high-voltage electricity, along with magnetic fields, led him to discovering that time and space may be deformed to essentially create a door that may lead to another time.

Nikola Tesla was born and raised in the Austrian Empire. Tesla received an advanced education in engineering and physics in the 1870s and gained practical experience in the early 1880s working in telephony and at Continental Edison in the new electric power industry. He immigrated to the United States in 1884, where he would become a naturalized citizen. He worked for a short time at the Edison Machine Works in New York City before he struck out on his own. With the help of partners to finance and market his ideas, Tesla set up laboratories and companies in New York to develop a range of electrical and mechanical devices.

His alternating current (AC) induction motor and related polyphase AC patents, licensed by Westinghouse Electric in 1888, earned him a considerable amount of money and became the cornerstone of the polyphase system, which that company would eventually market. Attempting to develop inventions he could patent and market, Tesla conducted a range of experiments with mechanical oscillators/generators, electrical discharge tubes, and early x-ray imaging. He also built a wireless-controlled boat, one of the first ever exhibited. Tesla became well-known as an inventor, as he would demonstrate his achievements to celebrities and wealthy patrons at his lab, and was noted for his showmanship at public lectures.

Throughout the 1890s, Tesla pursued his ideas for wireless lighting and worldwide wireless electric power distribution in his high-voltage, high-frequency power experiments in New York and Colorado Springs. In 1893, he made pronouncements on the possibility of wireless communication with his devices.

Tesla tried to put these ideas to practical use in his unfinished Wardenclyffe Tower project, an intercontinental wireless communication. After Wardenclyffe, Tesla experimented with a series of inventions in the 1910s and 1920s with varying degrees of success. Having spent most of his money, Tesla lived in a series of New York hotels, leaving behind unpaid bills. He died in New York City in January 1943.

Tesla went on to discover, through his own personal experiences, that traveling through time came with very real dangers. The very first experience Nikola Tesla had with traveling in time occurred in 1895. A *New York Herald* reporter wrote that he found the inventor Tesla in a café just after he had just been hit by 3.5 million volts of electricity. The reporter had also said that Mr. Tesla informed him that he would not make very good company to be around due to the fact that he almost died.

Tesla went on to say that a three-foot spark had jumped into the air and hit him on the shoulder. Next, Tesla went on to say that if it were not for his assistant turning the power off straight away, he would have been killed. The inventor went on to tell the reporter that when he was in contact with the residence from the electromagnet charge, he had found that he went out of his space-and-time window. He said that he had been able to see the past, the present, and the future, and all at the very same time. He did admit he had been paralyzed in the electromagnetic field, so he had been unable to help himself. Thankfully, his assistant had been beside him and was able to turn off the power before any severe and permanent damage had been done.

CHAPTER 19

Scientists have said there is a connection between CERN and Saturn that ties in the electric universe model and Thunderbolts Project. If their hypothesis is correct, it could not fail to alter many paths of scientific investigation. In part 1 of his presentation, physicist Eugene Bagashov began his analysis of ongoing mysteries surrounding the first ever so-called interstellar asteroid, 'Oumuamua. Eugene scrutinized the rather-surprising hypothesis that the object is not natural but rather a kind of extraterrestrial technology.

A new scientific paper provides stunning affirmation of one of the most striking predictions of the electric universe / catastrophic hypothesis. The paper, published in the journal *Icarus*, reports that the water on Saturn's moons and in its rings is remarkably similar to water on our own planet, a completely unexpected finding. Without resorting to black holes, dark matter, dark energy, neutron stars, or magnetic reconnections, I believe the greatest surprises of the space age are predictable patterns in an electric universe, to an age of planetary instability and earthshaking electrical events in ancient times. The Thunderbolts Project, the electric universe model, and the connection between CERN and Saturn are at the cutting edge of science, and much of this information might be new to a lot of people.

After looking at physics with CERN and looking at a number of things going on in the cosmos, looking at the ancient Sumerian writing, Babylonian art, and similar information, it becomes apparent that what CERN—that is, the people that are promoting the project at CERN, beyond the physicists and engineers, the people that are really behind all this—is clearly using occult practices. Looking at the occult connections between CERN and the planets, it becomes obvious that they are trying to reestablish some form of physical connection or, at least at minimum, a line of communication with Saturn.

There is an attempt to establish what are known as Birkeland currents. These are two electric-charged fields that arrange themselves in a twisted or helical fashion, comprised of an electric plasma, and it appears that they are trying to project Birkeland currents to the southern pole of Saturn, in the form of a twisted helix, like a plasma conduit between the southern pole of Saturn and CERN itself. When we talk about the Birkeland current, usually we are referring to the electric currents in a planet's ionosphere that follows magnetic field lines and sometimes used to describe any field-aligned electric current in a space plasma. They are caused by the movement of a plasma perpendicular to a magnetic field. Birkeland currents often show filamentary, or twisted, ropelike magnetic structure.

They are also known as filed-aligned currents, magnetic ropes, and magnetic cables. Originally, Birkeland currents referred to electric currents that contribute to aurora, caused by the interaction of the plasma in the solar wind with the Earth's magnetosphere. The current flows earthward down the morning side of the Earth's magnetosphere. It also flows earthward, down the morning side of the Earth's ionosphere, around the polar regions, and spaceward, up to the evening side of the ionosphere. These Birkeland currents are now sometimes called auroral electrojets. The currents were predicted in 1903 by Norwegian explorer and physicist Kristian Birkeland.

Is the purpose of the plasma conduit and CERN's real agenda being to free demonic entities from Saturn and bring them back to our plane of existence, our world? These entities reside in the gaseous body of Saturn. There are many different threads in the conspiracy realm, but according to the occult, according to ancient writing, there are demonic entities that reside within Saturn. Electricity is a much bigger part of our fundamental makeup of the universe than we are taught, and the reason why Saturn of all the other planets is that maybe, in our previous age, Saturn possibly played a huge role in creating our environment, in what was known as the golden age, which predates the Sumerian times and the Babylonian times, predates the flood and biblical times. The theory again, or the writings, of the occult practitioners that carry forward to this day in their existence and practices is that there was an alignment of three planets that were in very close proximity to Earth.

The first planet closest to Earth was Mars, the next was Venus, and behind that in a straight line, if you were to visualize this in a straight line coming up from Earth, was Saturn itself. Saturn was so close and so very large that it actually blotted out most of the sun; it obscured most of a it, except for the rim of the sun. We have ancient carvings that depict this alignment and close proximity of the three planets to Earth, thus establishing an electrical plasma connection between those three aligned planets and to the surface of the Earth itself and thereby creating a lot of the images that we see in stone carving and painting. What are really depicted, according to Thunderbolts Project, are not necessarily gods or entities that are alive but actually plasma configurations.

The radiation of plasma fields, the shapes, the morphologies of different plasma energies that are seen, in particular the plasma conduit—these are what's connecting those three planets with the Earth, including Saturn. It is difficult to imagine what the environment would have been. But looking at certain related material, it appears that there was some type of envelope or cocoon that almost encapsulated the whole planet; it was almost like it was an environment that was more stable around the whole globe. One reason Birkeland currents are particularly interesting is that in the plasma forced to carry them, they cause a number of plasma physical processes to occur (waves, instabilities, fine structure formation). These, in turn, lead to consequences such as acceleration of charged particles, both positive and negative, and element separation, such as preferential ejection of oxygen ions.

Both these classes of phenomena should have a general astrophysical interest far beyond that of understanding the space environment of our own Earth. Now, the relationship of Saturn to the Earth, which blocks most of the energy from the sun. The time of day is presented as crescent shapes of the sun as it peaks around at different quadrants of the clock, around Saturn, and therefore you have a change in seasons. Going way back in time, back to the golden age, when our atmosphere was much denser, higher in concentrations of oxygen, warmer, you would see the promoting of things that we would call giants, dinosaurs, and perhaps the Nephilim. We all know about the dinosaurs and the prehistoric history, but giant humanlike people?

The Nephilim were giants, the violent superhuman offspring produced when wicked angels mated with human women, way back in the days of Noah. The babies or hybrid born from this unnatural mating or relationship were no ordinary children. The Nephilim were giant bullies, tyrants who filled the Earth with violence. If you read the Bible, it describes them as the mighty ones of the old times, the men of fame. They left behind a legacy of violence and great fear.

It appears that CERN has handed out its real agenda in a new video: to open an abyss and "set free" the creatures who live there, the Nephilim. It is known by many people that CERN has a history of using art and film to convey their plans. One of these films is called *Symmetry*, which appears to depict the opening of a portal. Another of CERN's films was recently aired as a part of CERN's art exhibit, called C*o*llide. This is an annual exhibit of artists who bring together "art and science."

The occultists see Saturn as the "black sun." They originally saw our sun as a symbol of the light, and Saturn as a symbol of the dark sun. The worshippers of the black sun, being Saturn, the worshippers and adherents to what is known as the golden age of Cronus, *Cronus* being Saturn, they reach back into Sumerian, Babylonian, and Egyptian history. The electric universe people talk about is a being formally known as a brown dwarf but was thought to be the last of the planets. This is the reason Saturn was known as the dark star, the dark sun, or the black sun. The number of moons, the mysteries associated with these moons located both Jupiter and Saturn are phenomenal aspects of his whole story.

CHAPTER 20

Many scientists believe that CERN and its Large Hadron Collider experiments could be a cover for a much larger convert weapons operation. Could CERN be creating the ultimate weapon or even attempting to open a doorway to another reality? What are the people at CERN really up to? When we are dealing with the LHC, we must understand that this is a machine that could generate planetary residence effects, and very secretly, we would have a military possibility. If CERN could generate planetary effects in specific regions with the Large Hadron Collider, through residence or what have you, or in the sun, or on other planets, would this information dare be released to the general population? Most people believe this technology would be kept secret.

The speed at which the world is acquiring new technology *publicly* represents only what is a very small fraction of what is available on all the incredible advances that have been made in covert circles—if there are indeed the breakaway element inside the national security state, working with global corporations on technology that is so far above laptops and smartphones. I really believe that it is beyond absurd that on the few occasions where their operations must be run openly to a certain degree, we must be ready to seize the opportunity to not fall for the official story and dig a little bit deeper.

When it comes to CERN and its six-billion-dollar budget, there are some very unusual aspects surrounding its Large Hadron Collider (LHC) experiments, which are ultraexpensive, ultrasecret, and ultra-dangerous. There are other particle accelerators out there, but it all began during World War II. These machines have become bigger and bigger as scientists try to probe smaller and smaller aspects of particle physics; in other words, now you are not even dealing with protons, electrons, and neutrons. Now you are dealing with quarks that make them up.

A *quark* is basically a type of particle and fundamental constituent of matter. Quarks combine to form hadrons, which are composite particles. The most stable of the hadrons are neutrons and protons, which are the components of the nuclei. Because of a phenomenon, known as color confinement, quarks are never directly found or observed in isolation; they can only exist or be found within hadrons, which include mesons and baryons (such as neutrons and protons). When it comes to quarks, much of what is known about them comes from observations of hadrons at this time. Quarks have various properties, various intrinsic properties that include color charge, electric charge mass, and spin.

They are the only elementary particles in the standard model of particle physics to experience all four fundamental interaction, also known as fundamental forces, such as gravitation, electromagnetism, weak interaction, and strong interaction, as well as the only known particles whose electric charges are not integer multiples of the elementary charge. There is a total of six types of quarks that physicists also call flavors, which are as follows: up, down, strange, charm, top, and bottom. Up and down quarks have the lowest masses of all quarks.

The heavier quarks rapidly change into up and down quarks through a process called particle decay, which is simply the transformation from higher mass state to lower mass state. Because of this, up and down quarks are generally stale and the most common in the universe, whereas strange, charm, bottom, and top quarks can only be produced in high-energy collisions, like they are doing at CERN, involving cosmic rays and in particle accelerators. For every quark flavor there is a corresponding type of antiparticle, known as an antiquark, that differs from the quark only in that some of its properties, like the electric charge, have equal magnitude but opposite sign.

The quark model was independently proposed by two physicists, George Zweig and Murray Gell-Mann, in 1964. Quarks were introduced as parts of an ordering scheme for hadrons, and there was a very little evidence of their physical existence until elastic scattering experiments at the Stanford Linear Accelerator Center in 1968. Accelerator experiments have provided evidence for all six flavors. The top quark was first observed at Fermilab 1995 and was the last to be discovered.

The Collider Detector at Fermilab (CDF) experimental collaboration studies high-energy particle collisions from the Tevatron, the world's former highest-energy particle accelerator. The goal is to discover the identity and properties of the particles that make up the universe and to understand the forces and interactions between those particles. CDF is an international collaboration of about six hundred physicists (from about thirty American universities and national laboratories and about thirty groups from universities and national laboratories from Italy, Japan, UK, Canada, Germany, Spain, Russia, Finland, France, Taiwan, Korea, and Switzerland). The CDF detector itself weighs about five thousand tons and is about twelve meters in all three dimensions. The goal of the experiment is to measure exceptional events out of the billions of particle collisions in order to look for evidence for phenomena beyond the standard model of particle physics to measure and study the production and decay of heavy particles, such as the top and bottom quarks, and the W and Z bosons. Also to measure and study other phenomena such as diffraction.

The Tevatron collided protons and antiprotons at a center-of-mass energy of about 2 TeV. The very high energy available for these collisions made it possible to produce heavy particles, such as the top quark and the W and Z boson, which weigh much more than a proton (or antiproton). These heavier particles were identified through their characteristic decays.

The theory of physicist Murray Gell-Mann is that quarks are entirely mathematical. In order to understand the spin of different particles, finally scientists have come to a conclusion that particles are made up of other particles. Physicists have to make bigger colliders to probe smaller things at higher energies to reproduce the effects of earlier periods. Right after the big bang, this is what essentially what has been going on, somewhat like a "collider race." When scientists start building magnetic fields that powerful, you will start to get other effects that have nothing to do with particles.

Many may ask, What are some of the core aspects that will give us an opportunity to see the hidden side of how the Large Hadron Collider is doing these experiments in addition to what they tell us is the official reason? Are you curious?

You have the Large Hadron Collider, a circular collider that has counterrotating beams of protons, and above this you have the proton synchrotron, which is the last stage of acceleration of the proton stream that's injecting the protons into the Large Hadron Collider. The proton synchrotron is a smaller circular accelerator, and if you were to run an axis of rotation through the center of the Large Hadron Collider, then the proton synchrotron is sitting off that axis rotation, and in fact, if you were to bring the proton synchrotron down to the same plane as the LHC, the proton synchrotron is going to sit on the edge of the collider. In other words, you've got another rotating system canted off the LHC with its own strong magnetic fields, used to accelerate all this, and that's going to introduce a localized wobble.

The physics of the Large Hadron Collider, CERN will tell you, is all about particle acceleration, but the hidden aspect of this could be a torsion machine with very different sorts of physical effects than they are advertising. And there you have the possibility for a real secret project. The CERN facility has been embedded all in rock, in a nonlinear medium where immensely strong magnetic fields exist. So what happens to rock, particularly if it is crystal-bearing rock? The crystals under stress give off packets of sound called phonons.

In physics, a *phonon* is a collective excitation in a periodic, elastic arrangement of atoms or molecules in condensed matter, like solids and some liquids. Often designated a quasiparticle, it represents an excited state in the quantum mechanical quantization of modes of vibration of elastic structures of interacting particles. Phonons play a major role in many of the physical properties of condensed matter, like thermal conductivity and electrical conductivity. The study of phonons is an important part of condensed matter physics. The concept of phonons was introduced in 1932 by Soviet physicist Igor Tamm.

The name *phonon* comes from the Greek word *phone*, which translates to "sound" or "voice," because long-wavelength phonons give rise to sound. The name is based on the word *phonon*. Shorter-wavelength, higher-frequency phonons are responsible for the majority of the thermal capacity of solids. If you were to look at CERN's actual camera, the CMS detector, the ATLAS detector, you will see that these things have large crystals, lead quartz crystals, and other extremely exotic things that have been put into these detectors to detect and to photograph particle collisions as they are moving through these crystals. The CERN scientists have deliberately designed nonlinear mediate crystals that are reacting to all this.

When looking at CERN, you've got the public story, which is all about particle physics, but when you stop and look at the machine itself, you've basically got a torsion machine, you've got a hyperdimensional machine, and yes, CERN is looking for higher dimensions, and every now and then, CERN has been known to admit that they may have found evidence of that.

CHAPTER 21

Along with science and very advanced physics, supernatural things are happening at CERN, and this time they are happening in the clouds above the mysterious nuclear research facility. Most of us know that clouds are just big clumps of water droplets, of course after becoming water vapor and floating into the air. And that's basically how clouds are made. Clouds can be big and fluffy like a castle made out of cotton candy, such as the cumulus clouds, or they can be thin or even wispy, like thin white lines drawn in the sky, as in the cirrus clouds. Then there are the stratus clouds; they form something that looks kind of like a blanket that has been laid across a very big area of the sky. Have you ever looked up in the sky and seen, for example, a dinosaur or maybe a sheep figure in the clouds?

Over CERN, bizarre and scary cloud formations have been seen, documented, and photographed. High above CERN, a picture was taken, or shall we say captured, of a breathtaking cloud formation. This photograph shows an amazing cloud or whatever it is that took form right over CERN, the European organization that operates the biggest machine in the world, the LHC, the Large Hadron Collider, located a mere three hundred feet below Earth's surface, smashing particles together.

It seems CERN could be playing with fire, creating all sorts of weirdness and possible black holes. When the largest machine in the world is smashing particles together at almost the speed of light and they are experimenting or messing with things, especially things that many scientists have already stated could directly cause the creation of a mini black hole here on Earth, that would then grow and grow, with the potential to actually "swallow our entire planet," and this would all take place in a very short period.

As they, the CERN's scientists, are doing these dangerous experiments, we've seen a lot of over-the-top weather conditions, activities, and things in the sky over Switzerland. There are bizarre clouds over CERN, and its Large Hadron Collider could possibly prove that portals are opening. There are new images of strange cloud formations seen above CERN, and the LHC could be the shocking truth that it is the world's biggest experiment, with the latest conspiracy theories surrounding the monster machine, the largest machine in the whole world, the LHC.

People have raised major concerns over what the LHC is being used for at CERN. Should we all be concerned about what CERN is doing and how it is affecting our Earth? I leave this for you to decide. Several brilliant minds, many intelligent scientists, and even the late Stephen Hawking believe we should be.

With the very high energy testing and many experiments being performed at CERN, and with how much energy the LHC has been pulling into itself, could this open a black hole right here on Earth? Could the supermachine, and all the others similar to it and, in many ways, just like it, be what is causing the wild weather across our planet lately? A small group of engineers and I recently watched a short film about one of the many experiments being performed at CERN. The video showed CERN's schedule for the Large Hadron Collider, in which we are able to view the film showing the new experiment at the facility, which has been called AWAKE, due to begin promptly on June 24, 2016.

Many of the popular conspiracy theories about CERN have included that it has been used as a portal to literally allow Saturn to return to Earth. This massive machine, this LHC, is the world's largest and most powerful machine and is actually being used to crash and collide particles at close to the speed of light, to discover much more about physics and the possibility of there being parallel universes, other dimensions, stargates, and of course, portals. The curious machine developed across a seventeen-mile ring of pure conducting magnets has had critic after critic make claims that CERN could inadvertently create a black hole that may swallow up the whole world, but some of these wild conspiracies are among the strangest to date yet seem spot-on to the masses.

Now CERN, of course, denies trying to change our weather, but it has carried out experiments to create an artificial cloud to better understand global warming, which does fuel the conspiracies. The official line on what the AWAKE experiments are about is to develop a new type of accelerator to cut the size of the huge particle physics experiments down by a factor of a hundred or more so they can be carried out on tabletops. This AWAKE experiment, also known as the Advanced Proton-Driven Plasma Wakefield Acceleration Experiment, will use a whole new method that will get particles going much faster in a shorter amount of time. Results are expected in the year 2018.

CHAPTER 22

Across the world, many people worry about our air, water, and environment; others worry about our sweet Mother Earth. I wonder if CERN and its Large Hadron Collider could be having an effect on our planet, weather conditions, and even causing earthquakes. CERN uses giant magnets, which are superconducting magnets, and they are actually one hundred thousand times more powerful than the magnetic shields around the planet of our own magnetosphere, which is created by a planet with an active dynamo.

Science studies teach us that a *magnetosphere* is basically a region of space surrounding an astronomical object in which charged particles are affected or manipulated by that object's magnetic field. I have learned that planets having active magnetospheres, just like Earth, are capable of actually blocking the effects of solar radiation or cosmic radiation. This is studied under the specialized scientific subjects or plasma physics, space physics, and aeronomies. CERN has many people concerned with what it is doing to our environment and the only world we have. When the machines at CERN are running and confining particles to a circular pathway, they generate at ninety-degree angles, magnetic lines of force radiate outward, right through our planet, and then out into the magnetosphere, and they change the shape of the force fields that protect us from the gamma rays, x-rays, and accelerated particles coming to Earth from the sun and the greater cosmos.

This is affecting the magnetosphere and the magnetopause out in the outer reaches of the planet, specifically to our own atmosphere. In the space environment close to a planetary body, the magnetic field resembles a magnetic dipole. Farther out, field lines can be significantly distorted by the flow of electrically conducting plasma as emitted from the sun or nearby star, and possibly solar wind could play a role. Along with HAARP, the atmosphere is being heated up and the weather is changing because of the magnetic influence of the magnets. HAARP stands for the High-Frequency Active Auroral Research Program.

It was initiated as an ionosphere research program funded by the US Air Force, the US Navy, the University of Alaska Fairbanks, and the Defense Advanced Research Projects Agency, also known as DARPA. It was built and designed by British Aerospace Engineering, also known as BAE Advanced Technologies (BAEAT). HAARP's original purpose was to simply analyze the ionosphere and investigate the potential for developing ionospheric enhancement technology for radio communications and surveillance. As a university-owned facility, HAARP is a high-power, high-frequency transmitter used for study of the ionosphere. Work on HAARP and its facility began in 1993. The current working IRI was completed in 2007; its prime contractor was BAE Technologies. As of 2008, HAARP has incurred around $250 millions in tax-funded construction and operating costs.

In May 2014, it was announced that the HAARP program would be permanently shut down later in the year. After discussions between the parties, ownership of the facility and its special equipment was transferred to the University of Alaska Fairbanks in August 2015. HAARP is a target of conspiracy theorists, who claim that it is capable of weaponizing weather. Scientists and commentators say that the advocates of this theory are uninformed, as claims made fall well outside the abilities of the facility, if not the scope of natural science. The most prominent tool at HAARP is the Ionospheric Research Instrument (IRI), a high-power frequency transmitter facility operating in the high-frequency band. The IRI is used to temporarily excite a limited area of the ionosphere. Other instruments, such as VHF and an induction magnetometer, are used to study the physical processes that occur in the excited region.

CERN is causing magnet lines of force to propagate, to spread through the crust and the mantle of the planet. In the weak spots of the mantle, this is triggering earthquakes. In conjunction with HAARP, HAARP is specifically targeting weak spots and targeting specific locations to trigger earthquake. HAARP is pure Tesla technology, as is virtually everything that's going on at CERN. The planet right now is being Tara formed. There is another aspect to it; the scientists at CERN are producing the most powerful explosive in the known universe.

This explosive material occurred if you believe in the big bang scenario. They are described as occurring prior to the God particle, the Higgs boson, which they claimed to have discovered, and in this timeline from the explosion of the singularity, strangelets were produced.

Strangelets are the most explosive substance in the known universe, composed of quarks and gluons. *Gluons* are actually a force that binds quarks together. The issue with these is they are being produced by the Large Hadron Collider (LHC) and they cannot be contained. They move to the center, to the core of the Earth, where the magnetic lines of force are stabilized, and this how a neutron star is formed. It is the electromagnetic collapsing of the planet. It is not a black hole scenario. It is not gravity. It is the attractive forces, nuclear attractive forces of the strangelets at the core that are also going to be causing massive earthquakes in the near future.

Many people from across the Earth have claimed to have heard very loud booms, and nobody can figure out where these loud noises are actually coming from.

Others have heard trumpets, what sounds like enormous trumpets from the sky. People of all faiths and nationalities have heard these sounds from all across the globe. What is really going on with all this, and are we in the end-times? Scientists believe the loud booms and even louder sky trumpets being heard all over the world are created by CERN in origin. There are, in addition to the magnetic lines of force that are being generated by the superconducting magnets, naturally occurring currents of electrical waves that are called telluric currents. These currents are phenomena observed in Earth's crust and mantle in September of 1862. An experiment to specifically address Earth's currents was carried out in the Munich Alps (Lamont 1862). Including minor processes, there are at least thirty-two different mechanisms that cause telluric currents.

Both telluric and magnetotelluric methods are used for exploring the structure beneath the Earth's surface. For mineral exploration, the targets are any subsurface structure with a distinguishable resistance in comparison to its surroundings. These currents are being generated by Earth, and I can explain. Our beautiful planet Earth is basically a very low-voltage battery, and these currents are broadcast by the Earth up into our ionosphere and then reflected back down to the Earth's surface. And this happens all the time. So what happens when you are colliding particles is that you are generating much more powerful telluric currents that do reflect off the ionosphere and then come back and strike the Earth's surface.

They do not cause the earthquakes, but they are causing these sounds the world has been hearing. These happen in coincidence with activities that are occurring with CERN. In William Hope Hodgson's novel *The Night Land*, the Earth Current, a powerful telluric current, is the source of power for the Last Redoubt, the arcology home of man after the sun has died. Hodgson's Earth Current is a spiritual force as well as an electrical one, warding off the monsters of *The Night Land*.

A thirteen-year-old prodigy has offered proof that CERN recently destroyed our universe, shifting us into a parallel universe. Max Laughlin is possibly the smartest kid in the world, and he thinks that CERN destroyed our universe. The truth is, we are all living inside a universe that is so complex that if we can grasp what's happening for a moment, we'll fall down on our knees and cry in surrender to its marvelous beauty. Science just barely starts to scratch the surface to the nature of reality, and still, its discoveries are more shocking than we are able to imagine. It proves quantum entanglement, unified field of consciousness, free energy, superhuman abilities, singularity, parallel universes, and even alternate realities.

All this is mind-boggling that you would never think a kid can understand something so complex. But maybe we need a kid, someone who is brave enough to think about brave new ideas and theories, because most of the world we live in today was built upon such.

Max Laughlin, a brilliant thirteen-year-old young man, has proof that we have been shifted into a parallel universe. Max is a child genius and is considered one of the smartest people in the world. At the age of only thirteen, he came up with his own free-energy device. According to Max Laughlin, the nuclear research facility known as CERN has actually destroyed our universe and we now and have been living in a parallel universe that was closest to our old universe. To understand the complexity of the universe can make you feel like your head is going to blow up. What we do know about the universe, as from books and school, barely begins to scratch the surface of its complexity. All this information and complicated science can be mind-scrambling, as it is interesting and even more fascinating. The universe really is the biggest teacher of all, and we are merely trying to learn its lessons one day at a time and, basically, one book at a time.

Earth's magnetic field is defiantly changing; anyone watching a compass needle pointed steadily north might suppose that Earth's magnetic field is a constant, but it's not. Researchers have long known that changes are afoot. The north magnetic pole is known to routinely move, as much as forty kilometers a year, causing compass needles to drift over time. Moreover, the global magnetic field has weakened 10 percent since the nineteenth century.

A new study provided by the European Space Agency Constellation of Swarm Satellites reveals that changes may be happening even faster than we thought. Data from Swarm, combined with observations from other sources, shows clearly that the field has weakened by about 3.5 percent at high latitudes over North America, while it has strengthened about 2 percent over Asia. These changes have occurred over the relatively brief period between 1999 and the middle of the year 2016. Earth's magnetic field protects us from solar storms and cosmic rays. Less magnetism means more radiation can penetrate our planet's atmosphere.

CHAPTER 23

The largest, most sophisticated, and most expensive machine in the entire world is the Large Hadron Collider, and it's located in Geneva, Switzerland. The LHC lies down low beneath the ground, three hundred feet. The real construction of CERN, when they broke ground, began in the year 1954. CERN is home of the LHC, the largest particle accelerator on the planet. Inside the tunnels built at the nuclear facility and inside what is called the main ring, the temperatures are colder than outer space. The main ring is the particle accelerator, which gets all the notoriety in the media and press usually. It is twenty-seven kilometers in diameter and, again, has been constructed three hundred feet below the surface of the Earth. It spans across two borders, one being Switzerland, and the other is France.

The area that is the coldest is within the ring itself. Try to picture it as a hollow tube. CERN refers to it as the pipe, and within that area, there are magnets that are superconducting. In order for them to be superconducting, they need to be cold, cryogenically cold, with helium, down to almost absolute zero, and in fact, it is really colder than outer space, with the tubes of the main ring itself. The tunnels are very cold themselves simply by their association with the pipe itself, which is really the main ring, which is cryogenically cold.

Another very big part of what is CERN is doing is trying to understand the Higgs field.

To make it simple, the Higgs field is a theoretical model of what is typically referred to as dark matter and dark energy, so if you picture everything in the universe that we can touch, see, and measure as being dark matter, that would be about 4 percent of the unknown universe. The remainder is comprised of what they typically call dark energy and dark matter. If we go along the lines of this theory, the Higgs field is really much like a matrix. The matrix is really like a fabric, a weaving or matrix of what is known as weakly interacting massive particles, or WIMPs. WIMPs are connected to strangelets in the sense that their particles are smaller than atoms. These are weakly interacting massive particles at the nuclear level of the quantum level. Their interaction as far as nuclear force, their bonding force, is very weak, and therefore the Higgs field is theoretically capable of being opened or torn apart like a fabric is torn if the veil is parted.

WIMPs are connected to strangelets in the sense that their particles are smaller than atoms; they are actually the building blocks that make up an atom. When you are talking about colliding particle and shattering them and particles spinning off, you're talking about quantum particles that are spinning off from the larger atoms or protons specifically that are being collided. Strangelets are a combination of two quantum particles; one is a quark, and one is a gluon. And these bind together to form what is known as strangelets.

Strangelets are somewhat concerning to people, especially to folks in the conspiracy circles, as they can be very dangerous. According to a few scientific journals, one characteristic of strangelets is that they are considered to be the most powerful explosive force in the known universe; the other characteristic is, they are the cousin of the black hole. This is because they exhibit much of the same types of characteristics of the black hole. Most people believe that black holes suck in all living matter, including light. The quark-gluon strangelet also attracts matter, but it does not attract light. But it does attract matter and other atoms to it. The third characteristic is, it's kin to the black hole, because it is so heavy and so dense that it will penetrate out of the ALICE detector at the LHC.

Some scientists and many people do worry about possible dangers that could occur at the CERN facility. The Large Hadron

Collider machine is very powerful, one of a kind, and could it be dangerous to the world? If folks listen to the scientists at the nuclear facility, they say, "We have it all under control," and yet at the same time, out the other side of their mouth they claim to have two goals, two things that they are trying very hard to accomplish. The first thing is to create microscopic black holes, and the other thing is to create interdimensional portals. When we discuss CERN, I would like to talk about the fact that things are occurring below the Earth, at the quantum level, and the microscopic level. There are also many things happening aboveground and outside the Earth itself.

The magnets being used at the nuclear research facility do have a gravimetric effect upon the Earth itself, especially to the Earth's mantle, the Earth's crust, and even the Earth's magnetic sphere, which has also been called the Earth's shield, which protects us all from gamma rays and x-rays coming in from the cosmos. There is a distortion that is readily visible on the satellites that monitor our magnetosphere and our magnetopause, and those shields are being affected. They are being changed; the shape, the morphology of those shields are being changed every time we see the powering up of the superconducting, cryogenically cold magnets that are located three hundred feet below the Earth's surface. What CERN is doing could really be having an effect on the Earth, even bigger than global warming.

CHAPTER 24

If someone asks you how in the world or universe you measure antimatter, simply tell them they need access to an Alpha Magnetic Spectrometer. The Alpha Magnetic Spectrometer, also designated AMS-02, is a particle physics experiment module that is mounted on the International Space Station (ISS). The module is a detector that measures antimatter in cosmic rays. This information is needed to understand the formation of the universe and search for evidence of dark matter.

The principal investigator is Nobel laureate particle physicist Samuel Ting. The launch of space shuttle *Endeavour* flight STS-134, carrying AMS-02, took place on May 16, 2011, and the spectrometer was installed on May 19, 2011. By April 15, 2015, AMS-02 had recorded over sixty billion cosmic ray events and ninety billion after five years of operation since its installation in May 2011. In March 2013, Professor Ting reported initial results, saying that AMS had observed over four hundred thousand positrons, with the positron-to-electron fraction increasing from 10 GeV to 250 GeV. (Later results have shown a decrease in positron fraction at energies over about 275 GeV.) There was "no significant variation over time, or any preferred incoming direction. These results are consistent with the positrons origination from the annihilation of dark matter particles in space, but not yet sufficiently conclusive to rule out other explanation." The results have been published in *Physical Review Letters*. Additional data are still being collected.

Just a little background or history, if you will, on the AMS. The Alpha Magnetic Spectrometer was proposed in 1995 by the Antimatter Study Group, led by MIT particle physicist Samuel Ting, not long after the cancellation of the Superconducting Super Collider. The original name for the instrument was Antimatter Spectrometer, with the stated objective to search for primordial antimatter, with a target resolution of antimatter/matter. The proposal was accepted, and Ting became the principal investigator.

An AMS prototype designated AMS-01, a simplified version of the detector, was built by the International Consortium under Ting's direction and flown into space aboard the space shuttle *Discovery* on STS-91 in June 1998. By not detecting any antihelium, the AMS-01 established an upper limit of 1.1×10^{-6} for the antihelium/helium flux ratio and proved that the detector concept worked in space. This shuttle mission was the last shuttle flight to the Mir space station. After the flight of the prototype, the group, now labeled the AMS Collaboration, began the development of a full research system designated AMS-02. This development effort involved the work of five hundred scientists from fifty-six institutions and sixteen countries organized under the United States Department of Energy (DOE) sponsorship. The instrument that eventually resulted from a long evolution process has been called "the most sophisticated particle detector ever sent into space."

Rivaling very large detectors used at major particle accelerators, it has cost four times as much as any of its ground-based counterparts. Its goals have also evolved and been refined over time. As built, it is a more comprehensive detector that has a better chance of discovering evidence of dark matter along other goals. The power requirements for AMS-02 were thought to be too great for a practical independent spacecraft. So AMS-02 was designed to be installed as an external module on the International Space Station and use power from the ISS. The post-space shuttle *Columbia* plan was delivering AMS-02 to the ISS by space shuttle in 2005 on station assembly mission UF4.1, but technical difficulties and shuttle scheduling issues added more delays.

AMS-02 successfully completed final integration and operational testing at CERN in Geneva, Switzerland, which included exposure to energetic proton beams generated by the CERN SPS particle detector. AMS-02 was then shipped by the specialist hauler to ESA's European Space Research and Technology Centre (ESTEC) facility in the Netherlands, where it arrived on February 16, 2010. Here it underwent thermal vacuum, electromagnetic compatibility, and electromagnetic interference testing. AMS-02 was scheduled for delivery to the Kennedy Space Station in Florida, United States, in late May 2010. This was, however, postponed to August 26, as AMS-02 underwent final alignment beam testing at CERN. A cryogenic, superconducting magnet system was developed for the AMS-02.

With Obama's plans to extend International Space Station operation beyond 2015, the decision was made by AMS management to exchange the AMS-02 superconducting magnet for the nonsuperconducting magnet previously flown on AMS-01. Although the nonsuperconducting magnet has a weaker field strength, its on-orbit operational time at ISS is expected to be ten to eighteen years versus only three years for the superconducting version. In January 2014, it was announced that funding for the ISS has been extended until 2024.

In 1999, after the successful flight of AMS-01, the total cost of the AMS program was estimated to be $33 million, with AMS-02 planned for flight to the ISS in 2003. After the space shuttle *Columbia* disaster in 2003, and after a number of technical difficulties with the construction of AMS-02, the cost of the program ballooned to an estimated $2 billion. For several years, it was uncertain if AMS-02 would ever be launched because it was not manifested to fly on any of the remaining flights. After the 2003 *Columbia* disaster, NASA decided to reduce shuttle flights and retire the remaining shuttles by 2010. A number of flights were removed from the remaining manifest, including the flight for AMS-02. In 2006, NASA studied alternative ways of delivering AMS-02 to the space station, but they all proved to be expensive.

In May 2008, a bill was proposed to launch AMS-02 to ISS on additional shuttle flight in 2010 or 2011. The bill was passed by the full House of Representatives on June 11, 2008. The bill then went before the Senate Commerce, Science, and Transportation Committee, where it also passed. It was then amended and passed by the full Senate on September 25, 2008, and was passed again by the House on September 27, 2008. It was signed by President George W. Bush on October 15, 2008. The bill authorized NASA to add another space shuttle flight to the schedule before the Space Shuttle program was discontinued. In January 2009, NASA restored AMS-02 to the shuttle manifest. On August 2010, AMS-02 was delivered from CERN to the Kennedy Space Station by a Lockheed C-5 Galaxy.

It was delivered to the International Space Station on May 19, 2011, as part of the station assembly flight ULF6 on shuttle flight STS-134, commanded by Mark Kelly. It was removed from the shuttle cargo bay using the shuttle's robotic arm and handed off to the station's robotic arm for installation. AMS-02 is mounted on top of the Integrated Truss Structure, on USS-02, the zenith side of the S3-element of the truss. AMS-02 was installed on the ISS.

The design of the Alpha Magnetic Spectrometer is amazing. The detector module consists of a series of detectors that are used to determine various characteristics of the radiation and particles as they pass through. Characteristics are determined only for particles that pass through from top to bottom. Particles that enter the detector at any other angles are rejected. From top to bottom, the subsystems are identified as follows:

- Transition radiation detector measures the velocities of the highest energy particles.
- Upper time of flight counter, along with the lower time of flight counter, measures the velocities of lower energy particles.
- Star tracker determines the orientation of the module in space.
- Silicon tracker measures the coordinates of charged particles in the magnetic field.

- Permanent magnet bends the path of charged particles so they can be identified.
- Anticoincidence counter rejects stray particles that enter through the side.
- Ring imaging Cherenkov detector measures the velocity of fast particles with extreme accuracy.
- Electromagnetic calorimeter measures the total energy of the particles.

Some may ask, What are the scientific plans or goals for the AMS?

The AMS-02 will use the unique environment of space to advance knowledge of the universe and lead to the understanding of its origin by searching for antimatter and dark matter and measuring cosmic rays. Antimatter and all the science around it leave more questions than answer in many cases. Experimental evidence indicates that our galaxy is made of matter; however, scientists believe there are about one hundred to two hundred billion galaxies in the universe, and some versions of the big bang theory of the origin of the universe require equal amounts of matter and antimatter.

Theories that explain this apparent asymmetry violate other measurements. Whether or not there is significant antimatter is one of the fundamental questions of the origin and nature of the universe. Any observations of an antihelium nuclear would provide evidence for the existence of antimatter in space. In 1999, AMS-01 established a new upper limit of 10^{-6} for the antihelium/helium flux ratio in the universe. AMS-02 was designed to search with a sensitivity of 10^{-9}, an improvement of three orders of magnitude over AMS-01, sufficient to reach the edge of the expanding universe and resolve the issue definitively.

What is *dark matter* exactly? The visible matter in the universe, such as stars, adds up to less than 5 percent of the total mass that is known to exist from many other observations. The other 95 percent is dark matter, which is estimated at 20 percent of the universe by weight, or dark energy, which makes up the balance. The exact nature of both still is unknown.

One of the leading candidates for dark matter is the neutralino. If neutralinos exist, they should be colliding with one another and giving off an excess of charged particles that can be detected by AMS-02. Any peaks in the background positron, antiproton, or gamma ray flux could signal the presence of neutralinos or other dark matter candidates but would need to be distinguished from poorly known confounding astrophysical signals.

Cosmic radiation during transit is a significant obstacle to sending humans to Mars. Accurate measurements of the cosmic ray environment are needed to plan appropriate countermeasures. Most cosmic rays studied are done by balloon-borne instruments with flight times that are measured in days; these studies have shown significant variations.

AMS-02 is operative in the ISS, gathering a large amount of accurate data and allowing measurements of the long-term variation of the cosmic ray flux over a wide energy range, for nuclei from protons to iron. In addition to understanding the radiation protection required for astronauts during interplanetary flight, this data will allow the interstellar propagation and origins of cosmic rays to be identified.

What kind of results? In July 2012, it was reported that AMS-02 had observed over eighteen billion cosmic rays. In February 2013, Samuel Ting reported that in its first eighteen months of operation, AMS had recorded twenty-five billion particle events, including nearly eight billion fast electrons and positrons.

The AMS paper reported the positron-electron ratio in the mass range of 0.5 to 350 GeV, providing evidence about the weakly interacting massive particle (WIMP) model of dark matter. On March 30, 2013, the first results from the AMS experiment were announced by the CERN press office. The first physics results were published in *Physical Review Letters* on April 3, 2013.

A total of $6.8x10^6$ positron fraction (of the total electron plus positron events) steadily increased from energies of 10 to 250 GeV, but the slope decreased by an order of magnitude above 20 GeV, even though the fraction of positrons still increased. There was no fine structure in the positron-fraction spectrum, and no anisotropies were observed. The accompanying physics viewpoint said that "the first results from the space-borne Alpha Magnetic Spectrometer confirm an unexplained excess of high-energy positrons in Erath-bound cosmic rays." These results are consistent with the positrons originating from the annihilation of dark matter particles in space but not yet sufficiently conclusive to rule out other explanations.

Ting said, "Over the coming months, AMS will be able to tell us conclusively whether these positrons are a signal for dark matter, or whether they have some other origin." On September 18, 2014, new results with almost twice as much data were presented in a talk at CERN and published in *Physical Review Letters*. A new measurement of positron fractions up to 500 GeV was reported, showing that positron fraction peaks at maximum of about 16 percent of total electron + positron events, around an energy of 275 +/- 32 GeV. At higher energies, up to 500 GeV, the ratio of positrons to electrons begins to fall again.

CHAPTER 25

Near CERN, there was a plane crash, of Germanwings Flight 9525. This horrific tragedy occurred on March 24, 2015, and has been called the Alps Disaster of Flight 9525. Some have claimed the pilot deliberately crashed the Airbus A320 over Europe, and other people believe that large magnets at CERN might have had an effect on the plane's control system and instruments, causing this crash. Germanwings Flight 9525 was a scheduled international passenger flight between Barcelona, Spain, and Dusseldorf, German. The pilot in command was Captain Patrick S., aged thirty-four, and the copilot was Andreas L., aged twenty-seven. There were 144 passengers and six crew members on board at the time Flight 9525 crashed. It is known that there were many other aircraft in the area on the same day, at the same time, and none of them were affected by gravimetric wave that passed through the Alps. As another note, any and all other aircraft did not have any other issues or any problems with their control systems that day.

Flight 9525 took off from runaway 07R at Barcelona-El Prat Airport at 10:01 a.m. The aircraft was due to arrive at Dusseldorf Airport by 11:30 a.m. By 10:27 a.m. the airplane was flying at its cruising altitude of thirty-eight thousand feet in the sky. At 10:30 a.m., the flight was cleared by the air traffic control direct to the IRMAR waypoint, and this was actually confirmed by the flight crew.

Captain: "Direct IRMAR, MERCI 18G."

The plane now left Spanish airspace and entered French territory.

First Officer: "If you need to go to the bathroom, now is your chance."

Next, Captain: "Good idea. I think I will go."

At 10:30 a.m., the captain told the copilot that he was leaving the cockpit and asked him to take over any communications.

Some people believe that when the captain was leaving for the restroom, the first officer set the autopilot's altitude selector to one hundred feet. The next thing to happen was that the airplane started to descend, started to go down, and both engines' speeds decreased. At the specific time of exactly 10:33:47, the controller asked the flight crew what cruise level they were cleared for.

Marseille Center: "Germanwings, Marseille. Confirm, what cruising altitude are you cleared for?"

There was no answer from the copilot.

Marseille Center: "Germanwings, this is Marseille. Do you read me?"

Over the following thirty seconds, the controller tried to contact the flight crew again on two occasions, without any answer. At 10:34 a.m., it is believed that the captain tried to re-enter the flight deck. At this time, Marseille control and the controller from French air defense system called the flight at various frequencies, without any success. Other aircraft in the immediate area attempted to contact the flight and any of the crew on the flight of 9525. The aircraft was descending at 10:39:30.

The electronics seemed to have no control. Heard through communications next was repeated.

GPWS: "Pull up, pull up. Terrain, pull up!"

Germanwings Flight 9525 crashed into the Massif des Trois-Évêchés, a region of the French Alps. The French Bureau of Enquiry and Analysis for Civil Aviation and Safety (BEA) opened an investigation into the crash. According to the French and German prosecutors, the crash was caused by the copilot.

Many researchers are looking at this crash and looking at the remains of the aircraft and thinking that the wreckage is much more consistent with something that is scattered about, that came apart in the air, littered the area, rather than wreckage from an impact. The conspiracy people interested have mentioned the crash could have been caused by what is known as directed energy weapons. There is a theory out there that a direct energy weapon in the form of what is more specifically defined "kinetic energy" weapon may have been used to disintegrate the aircraft; this is because the wreckage is in such small particles. The bodies have been basically pulverized beyond what would normally be seen in airplane impacts and similar crashes, and it does appear that there was an outside source being used to bring this aircraft down.

When people talk about direct energy weapons, really what they are talking about, or referring to, is light amplification by stimulated emissions of radiations, also known as lasers. Other scientists refer to accelerated particles, perhaps protons, perhaps other subatomic particles that are accelerated in a particle accelerator and then used to direct those particles toward a target, in which the target is destroyed, simply based on the mass and the speed of the particles themselves, without any explosives being used. This is well-known, and this is no longer a science-fiction thing.

One March 24, 2015, witnesses did see the actual aircraft explosions, each explosion taking approximately eight seconds each, which may back up the idea that it was some new age weapons not seen or heard about by regular civilians. There is a theory out there, something that gravimetric waves could have had an effect upon the avionics, the control systems and instruments of Germanwings Flight 9525. I believe there is that effect being spawned upon the Earth by magnets at CERN. Several conspiracy theorists believe CERN could have been responsible for the Airbus A320 crashing in the Alps in March of 2015. The locations of the crash site was Prads-Haute-Bléone, France.

To be more specific, the Airbus A320-211 crashed one hundred kilometers (sixty-two miles) northwest of Nice in the French Alps. All 144 passengers and six crew members were killed. The French Bureau of Enquiry and Analysis for Civil Aviation Safety (BEA) opened an investigation into the crash; it was joined by its German counterpart, the Federal Bureau of Aircraft Accident Investigation (BFU), and was assisted by the US's very own FBI. Hours after the crash, the BEA sent seven investigators to the crash site; these were accompanied by representative from Airbus and CFM International. The CVR (cockpit voice recorder), which was damaged but still usable, was recovered by rescue workers and was examined by the investigation team. The following week, Marseille prosecutor Brice Robin announced that the flight data recorder, which was blackened by fire but still usable, had also been found. Investigators isolated 150 sets of DNAs for "comparisons."

CHAPTER 26

Stop and think about what the LHC is doing. It is counterrotating. This is torsion. It's got another machine on top of it, canted off the axis of rotation, for professional wobble. This is a machine that can mimic planetary effects and therefore possibly be in resinous with them or create them, which makes me and many others begin to wonder if there is a hidden esoteric occult project. And CERN has hinted at this in their logo, which has three twisted 666 numbers. Three seems to be a kind of theme or practice that goes back to some of the work of the Nazi generals, their staff, and their secret work on the "bell." It was the idea of developing supersecret projects right in public view.

CERN certainly seems to follow this pattern with all the secret experiments being conducted. Some people do not realize that in building this machine, scientist had to literally invent new technologies that they did not have in order to make this machine work, even for the particle physics story. CERN uses little square crystal, lead quartz crystals, and other very exotic things that are very expensive to engineer. This project ran into the billions of dollars, and on top of this, they had to invent a computer technology that was able to handle the massive amounts of data that this thing was generating and separate the signal from the noise. The computers are making the selection of the data for the scientists to look at, so it becomes possible, particularly if you grant the fact that you are dealing with a hyperdimensional machine.

No physicist in my thinking worth their salt would be able to look at that and say, "We better plan for the possibility that this thing might have effects that none of us had anticipated." Just look at it—strong magnetic fields, counterrotation, cotorsion, and so on and forth. We need to design and have "data selection filters" in the computer program to pull anything like that. We need to pay attention to. The kind of data CERN has and uses is so far out of the mainstream public consumption physics, so to speak. By the nature of the case, that data is going to be kept secret and withheld from the public and be only released sparely, and another thing is, we are working with a machine that could cause planetary resinous effects, then immediately you've got a military possibility.

If it is possible to generate "planetary effects" in specific regions with this machine through resinous, on other planets or in the sun, it is very unlikely they would share this information. Any of the details about this wouldn't be given to the public, most likely. On one hand, CERN is studying these unusual effects that are taking place, and on the other hand, they have this public face of finding the magical moment right after the big bang. And CERN set all this up publicly in order to find the God particle, which they claim that they do have. There has been much research done on the Nazi-Bell, but many ask, How did it disappear? And many other people may well ask, What is the Nazi-Bell?

The Bell was a purported top secret Nazi scientific technological device, secret weapon, or Wunderwaffe. It was described by multiple Polish journalists and even an author by the name of Igor Witkowski in *Prawda o Wunderwaffe* (2000). It was later popularized by military journalists and even an author by the name of Nick Cook, as well as writers such as Joseph P. Farrell and others who associate it with Nazi occultism and even antigravity or free-energy research.

Die Glocke has risen up and become a very popular subject of speculation, and a following similar to science-fiction fandom exists around it and other alleged Nazi miracle weapons or Wunderwaffe. The truth is, the mainstream scientists and reviewers, such as former aerospace scientist David Myhra, express skepticism that such a device existed. Scientists that worked on the Nazi-Bell Project are known to have been killed, and there are some similarities between CERN and what we know about the Bell. With all these Nazi ties, with this trail, do you think CERN's Hadron Collider could be a stage of the Nazi-Bell Project or could be related to it? I believe that a connection to the thinking of the German scientists and the Bell exists, because again you've got counterrotation; you've got something that clearly, when turned on, the cause and effect of which may not be what they have expected, namely levitation.

Now, going back to CERN, when they first turned on the machines, few know what actually happened—they had to shut down testing immediately, and they said, "One of the coolant tanks for these giant magnets was pierced and began to heat up, so we had to shut it down." I wonder why one of the coolant tanks would rupture, and I suspect that what happened was when they turned it on, CERN got some sort of effect. Possibly, CERN was getting a gigantic torsion effect that they were not anticipating. The testing was shut down, and the scientists had to go back and do a lot of reconfiguring before they could turn on the LHC again.

CERN physicists provided, possibly invented, the explanation that there was rupture inside the coolant tank. If this is true, this this is a fact: Why and how did the tank actually rupture? Could the machine begin to have been levitated when first turned on? Some have speculated the machine was pulled out of its moorings or caused some other localized effect that they had not anticipated. Because of the excessive secrecy surrounded by this nuclear research facility, folks are not given the exact details of what really happened. CERN is able to "stonewall" forever their secret experiments because there is no process legally or even diplomatically to get any information about the tests and experiments, so it makes it very difficult to call them out about their activities.

Let's suppose a nearby country started experiencing earthquakes out of the blue and this happened to be a result of experiments CERN has been doing. There is still no way for them to address it because CERN is a sovereign entity unto itself. It is a kind of like the physics equivalent of the Bank of International Settlements. CERN has authority, on its own, to take out loans and things like that; it is in the charter that it has a quasisovereign status. So when they brought lawsuits in Germany and the United States, to prevent CERN from being shut down, the lawsuits were dismissed because the people bringing the lawsuits had no standing, and the courts acknowledged that they had no jurisdiction over CERN. So what does that tell you? Is this nuclear research facility above the law?

This makes it clear that CERN is a sovereign entity and a lawsuit can be brought against it, and it has so many countries involved. It is a cosmological equivalent of the International Bank of Settlements, and that should really give people pause. Why CERN would need sovereign status should tell you that there is a secretiveness to this whole project that it is not entirely about what they are telling us it's all about. Would they dare lie to us or not tell us the whole truth? The particle physics thing is for public consumption; you've got a planet-size torsion machine that I think is the real project here.

Let's not forget that one of the movers and shakers on helping establish it was this Nazi lawyer by the name of Walter Hallstein, who was an adviser to people that helped write the charter that set up CERN, that you have this kind of influence behind it. This is not coincidental; the fact that you've got this sovereign status and got this kind of physics conception involved and embodied in the machine itself tells me that this is about much more than particle physics and that this is a very secret project.

CHAPTER 27

CERN is well-known for its amazing scientific achievements, one of its biggest being finding the great Higgs boson (the God particle). Many people from all around the world have heard of the LHC (the Large Hadron Collider), and others have heard of the dark conspiracies around CERN. Sure, CERN has a huge Lord Shiva statue at their facility there in Geneva, and some believe that CERN and the Vatican have ties, dark secrets and connections that few know about or speak of. So you have to admit, CERN is interesting, so interesting that even Hollywood has taken a great interest in the nuclear facility, its science, its conspiracies, and its ties to the Vatican in Rome.

Hollywood has had their eye on CERN and its activities and have decided to create a film, make a movie about CERN, its collider and its dealings with the Vatican. There was a movie produced about all this. Its title is *Angels and Demons,* starring the very famous Tom Hanks (*Forrest Gump*) and many more talented Hollywood stars. The movie has many twists and turns and keeps one guessing. The movie starts off with a theme about a papal conclave, which is simply a meeting of the College of Cardinals, convened to elect a bishop of Rome, also known as the pope. The pope is considered by Roman Catholics to be the apostolic successor of Saint Peter and earthy head of the Catholic Church. So about CERN, the pope, and this movie is fascinating.

The Hollywood stars and the plot are interesting. For starters, Gunther Glick and Chinita Macri are, respectively, an investigative reporter and a camerawoman who, in the world of Dan Brown's *Angels and Demons*, work for the British Broadcasting Corporation and are assigned to cover the papal election presented in the novel. Glick is described as looking rather odd, with a thin face and slim build. Chinita is of African American descent (implying that she is originally from the United States), slightly overweight, with a jovial manner. So wrap your mind around that, if you choose to have a mind visual. Macri is depicted as more conscious and less of a risk-taker than Glick, but also very protective of him. They are considered nuisances by the protagonists for much of the novel because they come along to relate for the television audience the events of the night.

Glick has been fired away from a fictional British gossip magazine to work on "less important" (in Macri's estimation) stories for the BBC. Glick is called by an unknown individual (revealed as the assassin) who scoops him on the murder/torture of four members of the College of Cardinals and planned bombing of Vatican City. The plot is creative. CERN director Maximilian Kohler discovers one of the facility's top physicists, Leonardo Vetra, murdered, his chest branded with an ambigram of the word *Illuminati*.

Kohler contacts Robert Langdon, an expert on the Illuminati, who determines that the ambigram is authentic. Kohler calls Vetra's adopted daughter, Vittoria, home, and it is ascertained that the Illuminati, an ancient antireligious organization thought extinct, have stolen a canister containing antimatter, a substance with destructive potential comparable to a nuclear weapon. When at CERN, the canister is stored on a unique electrical charger that ensures the antimatter's stability, but when removed, its backup battery provides power for twenty-four hours, after which the antimatter would fall out of suspension and, on coming into contact with the physical matter of the container, explode. The canister is located somewhere in Vatican City, with a security camera in front of it, as its digital clock counts down to an explosion due to occur at midnight, which will wipe out the Vatican.

Langdon is initially convinced that the Illuminati cannot be responsible, for two reasons:

1. The Illuminati went extinct centuries ago, and their remnants were absorbed into the Freemasons.
2. The Illuminati, as men of scientific truth, would never sanction the murder of a fellow scientist.

Kohler explains that Vetra might be an exception, as he was also an ordained Catholic priest. Langdon and Vittoria make their way to Vatican City, where the pope has recently died.

They are told that the four preferiti, the cardinals who are most likely to be elected pope, are missing. Langdon and Vittoria search for the preferiti in hopes that they will also find the antimatter canister. Their search is assisted by Camerlengo Carlo Ventresca (the late pope's closest aide), the Vatican Swiss Guard, and Commander Olivetti. Langdon tells Vittoria how the illuminati created a citywide map known as the Path of Illumination, a trail once used by the Illuminati where one was required to follow a series of subtle clues left in various churches in and around Rome. The clues indicate the secret meeting place of the Illuminati.

Langdon's theory is that the Path was marked by sculptures created by a mysterious Illuminati artist: an illuminati member placed as a mole within the Vatican itself. Langdon is granted access to the Vatican Archives by the camerlengo, where he believes a document containing the clues to the Path of Illumination is located. The clues to the Illuminati markers are placed inside Galileo's famous book called *Diagramma*. Langdon then sets off on the Path of Illumination on hopes of saving the preferiti and recovering the antimatter canister. The plot is amazing. The Path leads Langdon and Vittoria to four churches in Rome, each one containing works of art by Baroque artist Gian Lorenzo Bernini (who Langdon realizes is the illuminati artist) depicting angels and associated with one of the primordial elements: earth, air, fire, water.

Langdon realized the hour preferiti will be murdered in a way thematically related to each location-related elements. The first cardinal is branded with an earth ambigram and had soil forced down his throat, suffocating him; the second is branded with an air ambigram and has lungs punctured; the third is branded with a water ambigram and is wrapped in chains and left to drown at the bottom of a fountain. During their search for the Illuminati lair, Langdon and Vittoria are seen getting closer. After finding the bodies of the first two preferiti, Langdon hurries to the Santa Maria de la Vittoria Basilica and finds the preferiti abductor in the act of setting the third cardinal on fire. The kidnapper is an unnamed assassin who is working under the orders of the Illuminati master Janus, whose true identity is unknown.

Commander Olivetti is killed, and the assassin kidnaps Vittoria. Langdon escapes and accosts the assassin at the final element's marker (later) but is unable to save the cardinal. As a movie critic, so to speak, I'd say my favorite part of the movie is when Langdon must complete the Path of Illumination in order to find the assassin and rescue Vittoria. His search leads him to Castel Sant'Angelo, which he realizes is the Church of Illumination, the Illuminati's secret lair. Under the papal fortress is a tunnel that leads directly into the pope's private library in the Vatican. Langdon frees Vittoria, and together they send the assassin falling several hundred feet to his death.

The two hurry back to Saint Peter's Basilica, where they find that Kohler is Janus and that he has come to murder the camerlengo in private. Hearing the camerlengo scream in agony from being branded with the Illuminati diamond (a symbol combining all four illuminati ambigrams,) the Swiss Guards burst into the room and open fire on Kohler while he was confronting the camerlengo and telling him to give it to the media. With time running out, the Swiss Guard evacuates the basilica. The camerlengo rushes back in, claiming that he has received a vision from God, who revealed the location of the antimatter canister to him.

With Langdon in pursuit, the camerlengo ventures into the catacombs and finds the canister sitting atop the tomb of Saint Peter. Langdon and the camerlengo retrieve the antimatter and get in a helicopter with only minutes to spare. The camerlengo manages to parachute safely onto the roof of Saint Peter's just as the canister explodes harmlessly in the sky. The crowd in Saint Peter's Square look in awe as the camerlengo stands triumphantly before them. Because of this "miracle," the cardinal debates whether to elect the camerlengo as the new pope. Langdon manages to survive the explosion, using a window cover from the helicopter as a parachute, a trick he learned while touring CERN with Maximilian Kohler, and lands in the Tiber River.

As Langdon regains consciousness, he finds himself in a hospital located on an island. He is given the video camera that he placed in the pocket of his tweed jacket. The video shows the camerlengo branding himself with the illuminati diamond and confessing that he himself is Janus and who set in motion the night's chain of events in order to sabotage the Vatican. He also confesses that he killed the pope with an overdose of heparin, a powerful anticoagulant, because the pope revealed he had fathered a child.

After viewing Kohler's tape, Langdon, Vittoria, and the cardinals confront the camerlengo. Shortly before the novel began, the pope met with Leonardo Vetra, who believed that antimatter was capable of establishing a link between science and God. Vetra's beliefs caused great discomfort to the camerlengo. While discussing with Vetra, the pope revealed that his support was caused by science having given him a son. Without waiting to hear the explanation (that the child was the result of artificial insemination), and horrified that the pope appeared to have broken his vow of chastity, the camerlengo plotted to rectify the situation. He poisoned the pope and, under the guise of an Illuminati master (Janus), recruited the assassin to kill Vetra, steal the antimatter, and kidnap and murder the preferiti. The camerlengo planted the antimatter in Saint Peter's Basilica, feigned his last-minute vision from God, and retrieved the canister just in time to save the Vatican from the ensuing explosion, hoping to unite the struggling Catholic Church.

The Illuminati involvement was merely a plot engineered by the camerlengo. Upon the discovery and the camerlengo's attempts to justify his murder of the pope, Cardinal Saverio Mortati, dean of the College of Cardinals, reveals that the camerlengo is, in fact, the late pope's biological son, conceived with a nun through artificial insemination. Overcome with guilt, Ventresca soaks himself in oil and sets himself on fire before a crowd of onlookers in Saint Peter's Square. His ashes are recovered by Mortati, who places them in an urn placed inside his father's sarcophagus. It is revealed that the cardinal's endorsing of him would have made him the pope by acclamation. Mortati is unanimously elected pope by the cardinals, and Langdon and Vittoria reunite at Hotel Bernini. The last brand, the Illuminati diamond, is given to Langdon on indefinite loan, providing that he returns it to the Vatican in his will to cover his own involvement.

CHAPTER 28

The Gotthard Base Tunnel (GBT; German: Gotthard-Basistunnel; Italian: Galeria di base del San Gottaardo; Romansh: Tunnel da basa dal Son Gottard) is a railway tunnel through the Alps in Switzerland. It opened on June 1, 2016, and full service began on December 11, 2016. With a route length of 57.09 kilometers (35.5 miles), it is the world's longest railway and deepest traffic tunnel and the first flat, low-level route through the Alps. It lies at the heart of the Gotthard axis and constitutes the third tunnel connecting the cantons of Uri and Ticino, after the Gotthard Tunnel and the Gotthard Road Tunnel.

The link consists of two single-track tunnels connecting Erstfeld (Uri) with Bodio (Ticino) and passing below Sedrun (Graubünden). It is part of the New Railways Link through the Alps (NRLA) project, which also includes the Ceneri Base Tunnel farther south (scheduled to open late 2020) and the Lotscheberg Base Tunnel on the other main north-south axis. It is referred to as a base tunnel since it bypasses most of the existing Gotthard railway line, a winding mountain route opened in 1882 across the Saint-Gotthard Massif, which was operating at its capacity before the opening of the GBT. The new base tunnel establishes a direct route usable by high-speed rail and heavy freight trains.

The main purpose of the Gotthard Base Tunnel is to increase local transport capacity through the Alpine barrier, especially for freight, notably on the Rotterdam-Basel-Genoa corridor, and more specially to shift freight volumes from trucks and reduces the environmental damage caused by heavy trucks. The tunnel provides a faster connection between the canton of Ticino and the rest of Switzerland, as well as between northern and southern Europe, cutting the Basel/Zürich-Lugano-Milan journey time for passenger trains by one hour (and from Lucerne to Bellinzona by forty-five minutes).

After 63 percent of Swiss voters accepted the NRLA project in a 1992 referendum, first preparatory exploratory work began in 1996. The official start of construction began on November 4, 1999, at Amsteg. Drilling operations in the earthen tunnel were completed on October 15, 2012, in a breakthrough ceremony broadcast live on Swiss TV, and in the western tunnel on March 23, 2011. The tunnels constructor, AlpTransit Gotthard AG, originally planned to hand over the tunnel of Swiss Federal Railways (SBB CFF FFS) un operating condition in December 2016, but on February 4, 2014, the handover date was changed to June 5, 2016, with the start of an 850-day opening countdown calendar on the AlpTransit homepage. As of 1998, the total project cost of the project was CHF 6.323 billion; as of December 2015, the final cost is projected as CHF 9.560 billion. Nine people died during construction.

The Gotthard Base Tunnel, with a length of 57.09 kilometers (35.47 miles) and a total of 151.84 kilometers (94.3 miles) of tunnels, shafts, and passages, is the longest railway tunnel in the world, with a geodetic distance of 55.782 kilometers (34.661 miles) between the two portals. It is also the first flat route through the Alps or any other major mountain range, with a maximum height of 549 meters (1,801 feet) above sea level, corresponding to that of Berne. It is the deepest railway tunnel in the world, with a maximum depth of 2,450 meters (8,040 feet) comparable to that of the deepest mines on Earth. Without ventilation, the temperature inside the mountain reaches forty-six degrees Celsius (115 degrees Fahrenheit).

Like the two tunnels passing below the Gotthard, the Gotthard Base Tunnel connects two Alpine valleys across the Saint-Gotthard Massif: the Urner Reusstal in the canton of Uri, in which flows the river Reuss, and the Valle Leventina, the largest valley in the canton of Ticino, in which the river Ticino flows. Unlike most other tunnels, the Gotthard Base Tunnel passes under serval distinct mountain massif, two of them being major subranges of the Alps, the Glarus Alps and the Saint-Gotthard Massif, with the valley of the Anterior Rhine, the Surselva in the canton of Graubünden, between them. The tunnel passes under these two ranges more than two kilometers (6,600 feet) below the Chrüzlistock (2,709 meters; 8,888 feet) and the Piz Vatgira (2,983 meters; 9,787 feet), near the Lukmanier Pass.

While the cantons of Uri and Ticino are part of the German- and Italian-speaking areas of Switzerland respectively, the Surselva is mainly Romansh-speaking. The Alps strongly influence the European climate—and that of Switzerland in particular—and there can be substantially different weather conditions at each end of the GBT, described by the Ticinese architect Mario Botta as thus: "The light changes at the Gotthard: that of the Mediterranean Sea is not the same as that of the continent, that of the central lands, that of Europe far away from the sea." On average, the temperatures is two to three degrees Celsius (4 to 5 degrees Fahrenheit) higher on the south side than the north side, but on some day, temperature difference is well over ten degrees Celsius (eighteen degrees Fahrenheit).

The north portal lies in the north of the municipality of Erstfeld at an elevation of 460 meters (1,510 feet) east of Reuss. There, the tunnel penetrates the western slopes of the Bälmeten and Chli Windgällen (although only marginally) before passing below the valley of the Chärstelenbach, a creek in the Maderanertal. From there, the tunnel runs parallel to the small valley of Etzli, below the Witenalpstock. The main crest of the Glarus Alps, which is the watershed between the Reuss and the Anterior Rhine, is crossed below the Chrüzlistock, the crest having an elevation of about 2,700 meters (8,900 feet) at this point. From the crest and border, the tunnel runs parallel to the small valley of the river stream (Val Strem) before passing below Sedrun and the Anterior Rhine.

From the bottom of the valley, the tunnel proceeds toward the valley of the of the Rein da Nalps (Val Nalps) and passes east of Lai da Nalps, before crossing the Gannaretsch range below the western summit of Piz Vatgira (2,981 meters; 9,780 feet). This is the deepest point of the tunnel, with a rock layer of 2,450 meters (8,040 feet) above it. The tunnel then passes below the valley of the Rein da Medel (val Medel) and west Lai da Saontga Maria. After a few kilometers, the tunnel crosses the watershed between Anterior Rhine and the Ticino, just north of Pizzo dell'Uomo, which is 8,284 feet. This point corresponds to the main chain of the Alps and is the main drainage divide between the Rhine and the Po. For a few kilometers, the tunnel passes below two western tributaries of the Brenno in the Valle Santa Maria before crossing the last range, west of the Passo Predèlp (about 2,5000 meters; 8,200 feet) and east of Faido.

It then follows the eastern slopes of the large Valle Leventina, the valley of the Ticino, for about eighteen kilometers (11 miles) to the south portal at Bodio, at an elevation of 312 meters (1,024 feet), just three kilometers (1.9 miles) before Biasca, where the Brenno converges with the Ticino. The closest railway stations to the portals are Altdorf and Biasca. The first regularly served railway stations on the base line (as of 2016/2017) are those of Arth-Goldau (Schwyz), a railway node with links to Lucerne and Zurich, and Bellinzona (the "Gate of Ticino"), with links to Locarno, Luino, and Lugano (via the Monte Ceneri Rail Tunnel).

The journey from Arth-Goldau to Bellinzona takes not more than an hour. The station of Altdorf is planned to be served by 2021. There also have been talks of using that of Biasca. The travel between Altdorf and Biasca would last less than twenty-five minutes.

CERN, home of the Large Hadron Collider, was the host of a very strange tunnel opening ceremony recently at the world's largest rail tunnel near CERN. There were many interesting observations and more at Gotthard Base Tunnel. It is the longest tunnel in the whole wide world, near Piz Vatgira. It is fifty-seven kilometers, or 35.4 miles, long and is the deepest railway tunnel in the world. It is 1.4 miles deep. The tunnel cuts right through the Alps and the Swiss through a party to celebrate its completion. The tunnel was blessed on opening day, and many important people and leaders from Germany, France, and Italy attended this ceremony.

This tunnel opening ceremony, or show, consisted of strange perversions. As it slowly coasted through the dark tunnel with many onlookers on the sidelines, watching, attractive, mindless men and women on the train, in their underwear, began to touch and caress one another. They seemed to be in a trance of some kind, and in the background, horror music of the creepiest kind was being played throughout the tunnel. Next to come, walking through the center of evil creatures in costumes, was a topless angel, a mindless woman, with no facial expression, holing a lamb high in the air as sacrifice. So there was horror music, a topless angel, and a lamb to be sacrificed.

Could it be their false declaration that Lucifer has not been defeated by Jesus? This tunnel opening seemed to be a lot about religion and demonic creatures. Next, coming through the tunnel was a Baphomet parade, with the sound of bell ringing, cohesive to the wicked creatures, people, walking. Next, another railcar slowly came through the tunnel. This time, the train car was full of evil creatures and Satan was in the midst. One this car, the creatures on board moved around as the Satan character on board bobbed up and down and screamed aloud and appeared to be controlling the insignificant creatures on the ride or journey with him. Next, the creature's types began to roll off either side of the train car, and after they were all off, the devil guy, Apollyon, Abaddon, jumped off the train car. He seemed to be in a trance, almost humping the air, or with short dancing-like spurts. The audience, the funders, looked at this spectacle in complete amazement.

Next, the lights were totally blue in the tunnel; it was almost like an evil circus. Characters were now climbing up high into the air on ropes and round hoops. The creepy music became even more bizarre, and horned, demon-like figures strutted about as this went on. The sounds of Satan himself could be heard over and over as these demon-like characters danced about. The feeling in the air would best be described as unsettling. Creatures in shiny, faceless black costumes rolled about as the devil figure growled, screamed, and laughed. The audience watched on from the shadows, seated comfortably and in knowledge of all and what was to come.

Next, mindless people dressed in total black slowly walked through, all holding sticks, branches, high into the air, as bells rang to an evil-like music that was very unsettling. The devil character was close behind with his horns. Then, coming through the tunnel were a mix of people in miscellaneous costumes. The music became even spookier than before, with wicked drumbeats and bells that shattered the comfort of one's soul. These figures ranged in colored outfits, clothes, but many held high the head or skull of a dead animal. These people walked slowly through as the devil character seemed to be directing them, almost disciplining them as they moved through.

When a person is addicted to food, drugs, gambling, sex, or anything that can steal energy away from them, they can all become corrupted and are essentially invoking the devil. This is indeed a microcosm of what is happening on a global scale as humanity gradually gives away all its energy to "dark entities," like the global elite who are ushering in a brand-new world order under false pretenses.

On the video screen, we next see workers falling to their death, down a bottomless pit. Another way to think about a bottomless pit is a wormhole to another dimension, a tunnel to the underworld. Now, three ghosts rose from the pit, a giant eyeball on the big screen, which appeared to be the Illuminati's all-seeing eye, watching over the ceremony, as the workers now returned as ghosts, draped in veils.

As if this creepy parade weren't enough, it got even more interesting, as this ceremony was also held outside the tunnel. In the next spectacle, many workers in orange uniforms were on a stage, in a trancelike state. In the back of this stage was a huge, massive screen, similar to a drive-in movie screen. It projected the video of mountains, and high above were several CERN workers in their orange outfits, appearing to climb this video mountain screen. These workers seemed to be fitted with cables and were hoisted up a rocky wall, a mountain wall illusion, only to fall to their demise, driving home the idea that their lives were expendable.

The rock wall finally collapsed completely as the tunnel-boring machine used to carve out the tunnel finally broke through. Once the rocks fell and the portal had been opened, the workers were seen jerking their bodies as if they were possessed. The demonic power, or power that had been sealed behind the mountains, had been released, like the evils from inside Pandora's box, and had infiltrated the souls of CERN workers, who actually began to strip off their clothes and began to spar with one another before descending into an orgiastic dance. The ritual orgy is very important in satanism. Demonic entities feed like vampires on energy.

In another scene at this ceremony, there were many ghostlike figures or people in ghost attire slowly walking forward in a large group. They were like unclean spirits leading the way with Satan behind them, on the large screen. At this gathering, the audio and the sound were something that one might expect to experience in the depths of hell, or a horror movie, and not at a top-rated nuclear facility on the Franco-Swiss border. If you had seen this ceremony, you would have seen their version of the tree of life, an upside-down tree. Now, according to Pagans, their tree of life encompasses all realms of existence; it is eternal in nature, having no beginning or ending.

The tree of life is a symbol of immortality and healing of the soul. Its fruit is said to keep the gods youthful. Their tree of life has many meanings. The balance of harmony in nature, wisdom, strength, and rebirth, just as a tree would shed its leaves in the fall, hibernate in the winter, and be reborn with new leaves in the spring. The upside-down tree does not have any leaves. It is also said that the tree unites the upper and lower worlds. Its roots reach deeper into the lower worlds, while its branches grow into the upper world. The trunk of the tree of life connects the two worlds to Earth's planes; it is through this connection that gods can communicate through the tree of life.

The tree is upside down. If something is right side up and spills, that's a big difference. Think about a glass of wine or water. If it is standing straight up and some is spilled out, the force is not as fast in comparison to if the glass is flipped over and all the liquid spills out. CERN is really telling you, all of us, in an occult fashion what is really going to happen. However, CERN's tree of life is not a tree for all; their tree is Satan and telling you that the Antichrist is about to come and many in this world truly want him.

Since the thirteenth century, the 2,106-meter-high (6,909 feet) Gotthard Pass has been an important trade route from northern to southern Europe. Control of its access route led to a birth of the Swiss Confederacy. The Gotthard Pass is located halfway between Lake Lucerne and Lake Maggiore. It is the shortest link between the navigable Rhine and the Po. The traverse of the pass took days. Quite late, compared to other pass routes through the Alps on a north-south axis, Simlon, Sanbernardino, Brenner. Namely, in 1822, the first Saint-Gotthard Pass road was established after centuries-long usage of a bridle path. From 1842 onward, a daily course by the Gotthard Post, a stagecoach drawn by five horses with ten seats, still took about twenty-three hours from Como to Fluelen.

In 1882, with the inauguration of the Gotthard Railway Tunnel, the travel time between Altdorf and Biasca was reduced dramatically to only hours, though often accompanied with overnight stays in huge Fin de siècle-hotels, for example in Biasca. In those days, it was still an adventure and it was only affordable to the very rich. In the autumn of 1921, the final stagecoach traversed the pass. Electrification of the railway line in 1922 significantly reduced travel time even more. Refilling water boilers of a steam locomotive was no longer necessary.

There were also the technical advantages of electrical engines and future technical improvements. It is said that the first car traversed the pass in 1901, which still took more than a day. From 1924, car transport on trains through the railways tunnel began. The sections between Göschenen and Andermatt, the Schöllenen ravine, and especially the Tremola, had countless hairpin turns and serpentine curves from the peak of the pass to Airolo on the southern side of the pass, dropping one thousand meters (3,300 feet) in altitude, posing a huge challenge for automobiles. From 1953 onward, the pass road was sequentially improved and expanded at several sections along the Gotthard route, finally ending in 1977 with an opening of an expressway fully circumventing the Tremola.

Transit time was further dramatically reduced with the opening of the Gotthard Road Tunnel and the finalization of the northern part of A2 motorway through the Urner Reusstal, with many additional tunnels (then leading from Basel to the Gotthard Road Tunnel), in 1980. With the completion in 1986 of the A2 motorway in the Valle Leventina, the huge valley leading from Airolo down to Bellinzona, and the surmounting of the Monte Cereri between Bellinzona and Lugano in 1983, finally a continuous motorway was established from the northern border of Switzerland in Basel to the southern border in Chiasso, or the shortest motorway route from North-German Hamburg as far as Southern-Italian Sicily, bringing down the competitiveness of the railway line.

Today, both the rail and the road routes are among the most important passages through the Alps on the north-south axis. After the opening of the auto tunnel, in 1980, traffic increased more than tenfold. The existing tunnel was at its capacity by 2013. A second tunnel will be built next to the first, following a national referendum. Construction is to start in 2020 and will be finished in 2027.

As early as 1947, Engineer Eduard Gruner imagined a two-story base tunnel from Amsteg to Biasca, both rail and road, with a stop at Sedrun, to provide a faster and flatter passage through the Swiss Alps. Similarly to Gruner's ideas, the GBT cuts through the Gotthard Massif some 600 meters (2,000 feet) below the older tunnel. On the historic track, the Gotthard railway only trains up to 1,300 tons (1,400 short tons; 1,300 long tons) when using two locomotives, or up to 1,500 tons (1,700 short tons; 1,500 long tons), with an addition bank engine at the end of the train, able to pass through the narrow mountain valleys and through spiral tunnels climbing up to the portals of the old tunnel at a height of 1,151 meters (3,776 feet) above sea level. Since the GBT is in full service, standard freight trains of up to 3,600 tons (4,000 short tons; 3,500 long tons) are able to pass this natural barrier.

Because of ever-increasing international truck traffic, Swiss voters chose a shift in transportation policy in September 1992 by accepting the NRLA proposal. A second law, the Alpine Protection Act of February 1994, requires a shift of as much tonnage as possible from truck transport to train transport. The goal of both the laws is to transport trucks, trailers, and freight containers through Switzerland from Basel to Chiasso, and beyond by rail, to relieve the overused roads, and that of the Gotthard in particular, by using intermodal freight transport and rolling highways (where the entire truck is transported).

The GBT substantially contributes to the requirements of both laws and enables a direct flat route from the ports of the North

Sea (notably Rotterdam) to those of the Mediterranean Sea (notably Genoa), via the Rhine corridor. Passenger trains can travel up to 250 kilometers per hour (155 miles per hour) through the GBT, currently reducing travel times for trans-Alpine train journeys about forty minutes, and by one hour once the adjacent Zimmerberg and Ceneri Base Tunnels are completed. This is viewed as a revolution, especially in the isolated region of Ticino, which is separated from the rest of the country by the Alps and the Gotthard. The two stations of Bellinzona and Lugano (respectively named "Gate of Ticino" and "Terrace of Ticino") were entirely renovated for the opening of the GBT, among other improvements.

As of 2016, the Gotthard Base Tunnel is the longest railway tunnel in the world. It is the third Swiss tunnel to bear this title, after the Gotthard Tunnel (15 kilometers or 9.3 miles, 1882) and the Simplon Tunnel (19.8 kilometers or 12.3 miles, 1905). It is the third tunnel built under the Gotthard, after the Gotthard Tunnel and the Gotthard Road Tunnel.

CHAPTER 29

CERN is all about science and physics. You would imagine that the nuclear research facility thinks of everything, and it is no different when it comes to where they decided to build the largest machine in the entire world, the Large Hadron Collider, the amazing LHC. A large portion of CERN, the laboratory for particle physics, is located within the territory of Saint-Genis-Pouilly. The ALICE experiment is located on the periphery of the town, and the main entrance to the primary CERN campus (Meyrin) and the ATLAS experiment are located only three kilometers from the center of Saint Genis.

CERN is the world's largest fundamental physics research laboratory, and its presence has largely been responsible for the development of the community of Saint Genis since the middle of the 1960s. It was in the year 1887 that the current name, Saint-Genis-Pouilly, first appeared on the state civil register. Previously, Saint-Genis-Pouilly was called Pouilly-Saint-Genis, and before that, the two towns were separately identified. Historically, the spelling *Saint-Genix* had been widely used. CERN calls a great area of Saint-Genis-Pouilly home. In Roman times, it was called Apolliacum. The entire town and the temple were dedicated to Apollyon the Destroyer, also known as Shiva, Lord Shiva, Horus, Abaddon, and some have called him Satan or the devil.

The very city that CERN is sitting on is the ancient temple of the god Apollyon, which is called today in the Hindu temples as Shiva or Lord Shiva, the god of destruction and recreation. I ask myself, Destruction of what? It is the only god, the only deity, that claims they want to destroy the universe for the purpose of recreating it. Would it be shocking to find out that CERN would like to release Apollyon from the bottomless pit, from hell, using science, physics, and witchcraft?

The Hebrew term *Abaddon*, means Avaddon, which means "doom," and its Greek equivalent, *Apollyon*, appears in the Bible as both a place of destruction and an angel of the abyss. In the Hebrew Bible, *Abaddon* is used with reference to a bottomless pit, often alongside the place Sheol, which means the "realm of the dead." In the New Testament book of Revelation, an angel called Abaddon is described as the king of an army of locusts. His name is first transcribed in Greek. In Revelation 9:11, his name in Hebrew is Abaddon, also known as the angel of death, and then translated in the Greek language to mean "the destroyer." Abaddon has also been called a king, the angel of the bottomless pit.

In the Revelation 9:11, Abaddon is described as destroyer, the angel of the abyss, and as king of a plague of locusts resembling horses with crowded human faces, women's hair, lion's teeth, wings, iron breastplates, and a tail with a scorpion's stinger, who torments for five months anyone who does not have the seal of God on their foreheads, and it is said to him was given they key to the bottomless pit and he opened the bottomless pit, whose name in Hebrew tongue is Abaddon, but in the Greek tongue hath his name Apollyon.

Revelation 9:1–2, 11 in the Bible says the bottomless pit is connected to the god Apollyon and his temple of Apollyon, which is right now sitting dead center in CERN, which is the largest scientific consortium in the world, involving thousands of top physicists in the world, from twenty-one member-states, all working in tandem to discover the fundamentals that hold the universe together. CERN is well-known for discovering the God particle, but has anyone noticed how the Large Hadron Collider's name is very similar to the name Had or Hades? In Greek mythology those names mean "god of the underworld." The underworld is believed to be heaven or hell, where the dead are believed to be going for eternity. Another interesting fact is the choice of geological location of CERN's facility and how the Large Hadron Collider is built over the burial ground of Apollyon the Destroyer.

It is particularly located in the French town of Saint-Genis-Pouilly. The name *Pouilly* comes from the Latin name of the city of Apolliacum, because in the Roman times, a temple existed in honor of Apollyon and the people who lived there believed it was a gateway to some kind of underworld. To this day, the ancestors speak of Apollyon and his burial grounds. The truth is, CERN built their nuclear research facility on the exact same spot as the temple of Apollyon, which in the Greek language is Abaddon. In the Hebrew Bible, Abaddon is mentioned as the god of the bottomless pit, often appearing alongside the place of Sheol, a realm of the dead people. Also, it appears in the Bible as an angel of destruction and abyss. Abaddon, the spiritual being, is also a destroyer in the Christian apocalyptic theology. In Revelation, the destroyer is released. Many may ask, Does CERN have or hold the key to free the devil from hell?

The good Bible says in Revelation 9:11, they have a king over them, the angels of the abyss, and the king's name is Abaddon. And again, in the Greek language, his name is Apollyon. The fact that CERN was even built on a place where stood an ancient temple to the God of destruction, and that the people of the day believe even way back then that it was a gateway to hell or the bottomless pit, is just a little more proof that CERN can be used to unlock the bottomless pit and free the devil, as described in Revelation 9:11, literally opening a doorway to hell.

Some people know that CERN began their real work on September 29, 1954. However, this is the year of the Rosh Hashanah, the beginning of the Hebrew calendar, and do not think that this is a coincidence. Some religious people have said this is the time of the trumpets. This is the time that CERN started their quest and began using the Large Hadron Collider (LHC) to tear open time, space, and the veil.

In CERN's tunnel opening ceremony, the main character was wearing horns, exactly like the horned god appears. This god goes by several names, such as Dianus, Faunus, Actaeon, and one of his names is Cern. I am not kidding! One of the horned god's names is Cern. Is this just a coincidence? I don't think so. This nuclear research facility is in full control and knows exactly what it is doing, even when they used 666 for their logo, three twisted 6s.

The horned god is a Wiccan deity, a god with horns or antlers on his head. The horned god is one of the two primary deities found in Wicca and some related forms of neopaganism. The term *horned god* itself predates Wicca and is an early twentieth-century syncretic term for a horned or antlered anthropomorphic god with partly pseudohistorical origins, partly based on historical horned deities. The horned god represents the male part of religion's duotheistic theological system, the consort of the female triple goddess of the moon or another mother goddess. In common Wiccan belief, he is associated with nature, wilderness, sexuality, hunting, and the life cycle. Whilst depictions of the deity vary, he is always shown with either horns or antlers upon his head, often depicted as being theriocephalic (having a beast's head), in this way emphasizing "the union of the divine and the animal," the latter of which includes humanity. The horned god has been explored within several psychological theories and has become a recurrent theme in fantasy literature.

In traditional and mainstream Wicca, the horned god is viewed as the divine male principality, being both equal and opposite to the goddess. The Wiccan god himself can be represented in many forms, including as the sun god, the sacrificed god, and the vegetation god, although the horned god is the most popular representation.

The pioneers of the various Wiccan or witchcraft traditions, such as Gerald Gardner, Doreen Valiente, and Robert Cochrane, all have claimed that their religion was a continuation of the pagan religion of the witch cult following historians who had purported the witch cult's existence, such as Jules Michelet and Margaret Murray.

For Wiccans, the horned god is "the personification of the life force energy in animals and the wild" and is associated with the wilderness, virility, and the hunt. Doreen Valiente writes that the horned god also carries the souls of the dead to the underworld.

Wiccans generally, as well as some other neopagans, tend to conceive of the universe as polarized into gender opposites of male and female energies. In traditional Wicca, the horned god and the goddess are seen as equal and opposite in gender polarity. However, in some of the newer traditions of Wicca, and especially those influenced by feminist ideology, there is much more emphasis on the goddess, and consequently, the symbolism of the horned god is somewhat less developed than that of the goddess.

In Wicca, the cycle of the seasons is celebrated during eight Sabbats, called the Wheel of the Year. The seasonal cycle is imagined to follow the relationship between the horned god and the goddess. The horned god is born in winter, impregnates the goddess (just like what was seen and shown in the Gothard tunnel ceremony, where world leaders were present), and then dies during the autumn and winter months and is then reborn by the goddess at Yule. The different relationships throughout the year are sometimes distinguished by splitting the god into aspects, the oak king and the holly king. The relationships between the goddess and the horned god are mirrored by Wiccans in seasonal rituals. There is some variation between Wiccan groups as to which Sabbat corresponds to which part of the cycle.

Some Wiccans regard the horned god as dying at Lammas, August 1, also known as Lughnasadh, which is the very first harvest Sabbat. Others may see him dying at Mabon, the autumn equinox, or the second harvest festival. Still other Wiccans conceive of the horned god dying on October 31, which Wiccans call Samhain, the ritual of which is focused on death or Halloween in many parts around the world. He is then reborn on winter solstice, which is December 21. Other important dates for the horned god include Imbolc, when, according to Valiente, he leads a wild hunt. In Gardnerian Wicca, the Dryghten prayer recited at the end of every ritual meeting contains the lines referring to the horned god:

> In the name of the lady moon and the horned
> lord of death and resurrection.

CHAPTER 30

Many people are familiar with the pope, the Vatican, rumors, and stories of inappropriate behavior from someone we should be able to trust. Is this just the tip of the iceberg with the Catholic Church and the Vatican? Could it be possible that CERN and the Vatican have a very special connection, a very important secret, a plan to welcome aliens from another place, another universe, or another dimension into our world? Wrap your mind around that. A nuclear research facility and the largest religious organization in the entire world joining together, in cahoots, if you will.

I believe that the Vatican has many slithering secrets and that many of them are hidden right in plain sight. One of many clear examples is the "statues of the Vatican." The Vatican is actually layered out like a serpent and an upside-down cross. If you were to fly over and above Saint Peter's Basilica, you would be able to look down and see the whole body of a serpent.

It is true that a whole lot of people have a few concerns about the Vatican and CERN's connections and their real motivation behind this strange alliance. Could these two organizations be hiding something from the believers? I think, whether you are religious or not, a whole lot of people feel religion holds a very important part in preparing or helping the superlarge masses of the world for terrestrial contact.

It is key in the government's alien disclosure project; without it, it may not happen, so they are getting on board with the Vatican. In the year 2019, parts of the United States military were given orders to report any alien activity, sightings, or encounters of any kind. Even though no real disclosure has been yet given by the pope after many rumors flying around, there is definitely something going on. I believe some kind of "buildup" is occurring, and if one is to go as far as to add in the Large Hadron Collider (LHC) machine at CERN, then all the pieces of this jigsaw would really start coming together.

One rumor floating around out there is that Pope Francis has been prepared and ready to talk, spill the beans, and acknowledge the real existence of extraterrestrial life to the whole wide world. I begin to wonder if there could be much more truth about this than was originally thought. With all the UFO sightings, all the footage and information coming in from all around the world being presented, it can start to become overwhelming. It does seem like Pope Francis was very keen to introduce the aliens to all of us. This was said by more than one outsider associated with the Vatican. Whether or not these claims are true, two things are for sure: we are supposed to now believe that ETs are real and do exist and that this pope is committed to transforming the way that all of us live in this world of ours.

A well-known researcher and writer, Tom Horn, has said that he has some astronomers at the Vatican observatory at the top of Mount Gram and they talked to him openly that they are searching for extra-terrestrial intelligence and planets that are inside our solar system. It does seem that the Vatican clearly takes the whole life beyond our planet Earth very seriously. Mr. Tom Horn has also said that he was in contact with a NASA scientist and that she told him that there is absolutely no question that there are ETs, extraterrestrial beings, and that they are out there, and if we really want, we can indeed contact them.

It is true that the Vatican has been pushing themselves to the very forefront in the observing and observation of what is out there. I think the Vatican is looking for these beings and they also know that these alien beings are on their way to our world and that many are here already; it is just a matter of time before the big announcement is made. The Vatican believes, probably knows that something is up there, out there, and is coming here, as they have been searching for aliens a very long time.

All around the world and in the United States of America, many of the Democrats all talk about going green, and others in the party, who may be a little more extreme, are really into the Green New Deal, which is embraced by the more radical in the party.

It seems the world may be in the middle of what has been called the green revolution, because it is revolving right now. The year 2020 and the green revolution, in my personal opinion, are just part, a small piece, of the New World Order or a one-world government and is an attempt to bring you, me, and every one of us under the umbrella of these coming aliens.

Perhaps a New World Order and its master plan will be sold to all of us as an amazing, new, and great idea, such as, "Let's have just one united world and with aliens." The aliens are observing us, many believe abducting us, and even do experiments on our bodies while we lie in a dreamlike state, unable to remember much or nothing at all in these cases. Yes, the aliens are watching us intensely, our nature and even our behavior. Maybe it is because we are destroying Mother Earth, or do they have a more sinister plan in store for us, the occupants of this big blue ball known as Earth? One or two of the biggest questions here has to be how the Vatican can be so sure that something from way up there could be coming to our world, way down here. And also, what does CERN have to do with all this? The Vatican's many astronomers, with their huge telescopes—some of them are even positioned inside the United States—are watching the skies continuously, and apparently, they can see what is coming toward Earth. And that the Catholic Church is calling it or what it is they see the alien saviors.

This green revolution is real, it is happening, and the Vatican is connected to this green revolution and is even connected to CERN and its Large Hadron Collider (LHC) in Geneva. The Vatican is in the very forefront of introducing themselves to these so-called alien saviors, and all this is true, real, and in our faces anymore. It makes sense why Pope Francis recently declared to the world that he would baptize any alien visitors, which is an acceptance of the truth in itself.

From my research, basic knowledge, and associated information, I have learned that in this green revolution, they will want the nonbelievers and the nonthinkers to believe that the aliens are coming, and this is in order to prepare us for the inevitable alien contact. The truth is, in many ways, the world has been prepared for contact with these beings through the media, science, and television, so it is really not much of a surprise that religion will play a very big role in all this. Isn't the future exciting, or is it becoming scary? There was a rumor going around in Rome. It was said that several priests at the Vatican had died under very unusual circumstances. The first was a man named Martin. He was an Irish Catholic priest and a writer on the Catholic Church. He was originally ordained as a Jesuit priest, and he tried to reveal secrets to the world just before he died of a cerebral hemorrhage.

His death was due to a fall in his Manhattan apartment in the year 1999, just four days after his seventy-eighth birthday, and coincidentally, the Large Hadron Collider was finally constructed about the same time of his death. Another strange incident occurred during an interview on an Italian TV news channel, where the topic was all about "another Jesuit Priest who was trying to tell the world the truth about what was really going on with the Vatican and was later found dead and with a rope around his neck." Next, a third Jesuit priest, in an attempt to tell the people details about exactly what is really going on at the Vatican, also died, and of very suspicious circumstances. The three priests knew exactly what the Vatican is up to, and their sudden deaths are potentially a sign that the Vatican could be involved in a very dubious plan to join a one-world government and religion.

It is true that many races and religions believe that aliens are demons from the sky, or, more likely, another dimension, which, if you were to ask me, would suggest why the well-informed people also believe that some kind of evil form or entity could be coming through CERN. A *stargate* is a wormhole or portal between two different dimensions. If CERN opens a portal to another dimension, who really knows what could come out? The year 2019 seems to have portals in many commercials, movies, and TV shows. CERN could potentially tear a hole in the veil of our reality. The pope is ready to welcome whatever comes from the other side, while the Bible warns us of things to come and, in Revelation 9:11, also a of darkness to come.

Theories, rumors, and conspiracies are all very interesting, but it has been said that the Vatican is in possession of artifacts from the past that would and could explain alien secrets and what is going on with that. It is also said that the Vatican knows all the secrets, such as preflood ruins, underground worlds, forbidden history, forgotten technology, occult conspiracy, ancient gods, and yes, even alien saviors.

Could the Vatican be preparing for the arrival of these extraterrestrials? They seem to be intentionally creating dogma that is going to position the Roman Catholic Church to be at the forefront of an official disclosure moment. The Vatican is obviously involved in ways that we cannot even imagine, and they have a gigantic telescope located at Mount Gram. It is called the LUCIFER Telescope. The Vatican is constantly monitoring things with the LUCIFER device, and sometimes they have to wait for all the UFOs to get out of the way. The Large Binocular Telescope (LBT) is an optical telescope for astronomy located on the 10,700-foot (3,300-meter) Mount Graham, in the Pinaleño Mountains of southeastern Arizona, United States. It is just a part of the Mount Graham International Observatory.

The LBT is currently one of the world's most advanced optical telescopes; using two 8.4-meter-wide (330 inches) mirrors, with centers 14.4 meters apart, it has the same light-gathering ability as an 11.8 meter-wide (464 inches) single circular telescope and detail of a 22.8 meter-wide one. Its mirrors individually are the joint second-largest optical telescope in continental North America, behind the Hobby-Eberly Telescope located in West Texas; it is also the largest monolithic, nonsegmented mirror, in an optical telescope. Strehl ratios of 60 to 90 percent in the infrared H band and 95 percent in the infrared M band have been achieved by the LBT, which was originally named the Columbus Project.

It is a joint project of these members: the Italian astronomical community, represented by the Istituto Naziondale di Astrofisica; the University of Arizona; the University of Minnesota; the University of Notre Dame; the University of Virginia; the LBT Beteiligungsgesellschaft located in Germany; and the Max Planck Institute for Extraterrestrial Physics in Munich, to name just a few. The telescope design has two 8.4-meter mirrors mounted on a common base, hence the name binocular. LBT takes advantage of active or adaptive optics, provided by Arcetri Observatory. The collecting area is two 8.4-meter aperture mirrors, which works out to about 111 meter squared) combined.

This area is equivalent to an 11.8-meter circular aperture, which would be greater than any other single telescope, but it is not comparable in many respects since the light is collected at a lower diffraction limit and is not combined in the same way. Also, an interferometric mode will be available, with a maximum baseline of 22.8 meters for aperture synthesis imaging observations, and a baseline of 15 meters for nulling interferometry. This feature is along one axis, with the LBTI instrument at wavelengths of 2.9 to 13 micrometers, which is the near infrared. The telescope was originally designed by a group of Italian firms and assembled by Ansaldo in its Milanese plant.

The choice of location sparked considerable local controversy, both from the San Carlos Apache Tribe, who view the mountain as sacred, and from environmentalists, who contended that the observatory would cause the demise of an endangered subspecies of the American red squirrel, the Mount Graham red squirrel.

Environmentalists and members of the tribe filed some forty lawsuits, eight of which have ended up before a federal appeals court, but the project ultimately prevailed after an act of the United States Congress. The telescope and mountain observatory survived two major forest fires in thirteen years, the more recent in the summer of 2017. Likewise, the squirrels continue to survive. Some experts now believe their numbers fluctuate, depending upon nut harvest without regard to the observatory.

The telescope was dedicated in October 2004 and saw first light with a single primary mirror on October 12, 2005, which viewed NGC 891. The second primary mirror was installed in January 2006 and became fully operational in January 2008. The first light with the secondary mirror was on September 18, 2006, and for the first and second, together it was on January 11–January 12, 2008. The first binocular light images show three false-color reignition of the spiral galaxy NGC 2770. The galaxy is eighty-eight million light-years from our Milky Way, a relatively close neighbor. The galaxy has a flat disk of stars and glowing gas tipped slightly toward our line of sight.

The first image taken combined ultraviolet and green light and emphasizes the clumpy regions of newly formed hot stars in the spiral arms. The second image combined two deep-red colors to highlight the smoother distribution of older, cooler stars. The third image was a composite of ultraviolet, green, and deep-red lights and shows the detailed structure of hot, moderate, and cool stars in the galaxy. The cameras and images were produced by the Large Binocular camera team, led by Emanuele Giallongo at the Rome Astrophysical Observatory. In binocular aperture synthesis mode, LBT has a light-collecting area 111 meters, equivalent to a singular 11.8-meter (39-foot) surface, and will combine light to produce the image sharpness equivalent to a single 22.8-meter (75-foot) telescope. However, this requires a beam combiner that was tested in 2008 but has not been a part of regular operation.

It takes images with one side at 8.4-meter aperture or takes two images of the same object using different instruments on each side of the telescope. In the summer of 2010, the first light-adaptive optics (FLAO), an adaptive optics system with a deformable secondary mirror rather than correcting atmospheric distortion farther downstream in the optics, was inaugurated. Using one 8.4-meter slide, it surpassed Hubble sharpness (at certain light wavelengths), achieving a Strehl ratio of 60 percent to 80 percent rather than the 20 percent to 30 percent of older adaptive optic systems, or the 1 percent typically achieved without adaptive optics for telescope of this size. Adaptive optics at a telescope secondary (M2) was previously tested at MMT observatory by the Arcetri Observatory and University of Arizona team.

The telescope has also made appearances on an episode of the Discovery channel TV show *Really Big Things*, National Geographic Channel's *Big, Bigger, and Biggest*, and the BBC program *The Sky at Night*. The BBC radio documentary *The New Galileo* covered the LBT and the JWST. LBT, with the XMM-Newton, was used to discover the galaxy cluster 2XMM J083026 + 524133 in 2008, over seven billion light-years away from Earth. In 2007, the LBT detected a twenty-sixth-magnitude afterglow from the gamma ray burst GRB 070125. In 2012, LBT observed the OSIRIS-REx spacecraft, an unmanned asteroid sample return spacecraft in space while it was en route.

LUCIFER, or the Large Binocular Telescope Near-Infrared Spectroscopic Utility with Camera and Integral Field for Extragalactic Research, is the near-infrared instrument for the LBT. The name of the instrument was changed to LUCI in 2012. LUCI operates in the 0.9-2.5 micrometer spectral range using a 2,048x2,049 element Hawaii-2RG detector array from Teledyne and provides imaging and spectroscopic capabilities in seeing- and diffraction-limited modes. In its focal plane area, long-slit and multislit masks can be installed for single-object and multiobject spectroscopy. A fixed collimator produces an image of the entrance aperture in which either a mirror (for imaging or a grating) can be positioned.

Three-camera optics with numerical apertures of 1.8, 3.75, and 30 provide image scales of 0.25, 0.12, and 0.015 arcsec/detector element for wide-field, seeing-limited, and diffraction-limited observable. LUCI is operated at cryogenic temperatures and is therefore enclosed in a cryostat of 1.6-meter height and cooled down to about negative two hundred degrees Celsius two closed cycles coolers.

CHAPTER 31

Often, rituals are associated with religion, but their roots lie in human nature itself. Brushing teeth every morning is a common ritual. Texting your kids at a specific or certain time every day is a ritual. A professor in college once told me that a ritual is anything our day is mocked with, and it keeps order in our lives. Why do we do all this? Hard to say, but it is probably because we cannot do all this. Human beings are conscious creatures simply reacting to their surrounding in very imaginative ways; it is one of the defining characteristics of human beings.

This is just the beginning in my research and my story about rituals. Burning incense, bowing, processions, prayers, baptisms, dancing—what do all these actions have in common? They are what we call rituals, and like the word *religion*, the word *ritual* is a simple word that attempts to describe an extremely complex idea. Everything from folding your hands when you pray to human sacrifice. The word *ritual* basically covers it all, but when we have a word that tries to capture so much complexity in just one word, it is truly difficult to define. Some scholars have tried to offer objective definitions of what a ritual is. In the 1960s, the anthropologist Victor Turner (cultural anthropologist) defined a *ritual* as prescribed formal behavior that has reference to beliefs in mystical beings or power. The 1987 edition of the *Encyclopedia of Religion* defines *rituals* as "those conscious and voluntary, repetitive, and stylized symbolic bodily actions that are centered on cosmic structures and/or sacred presence."

In August of the year 2016, a video was released of a Satanic ritual performed at CERN. The video appears to have been taken secretly from a man looking through a window in one of the buildings. During the ritual in the said video, several people in cloaks walk up to a large statue, and the statue these people walk toward is the Hindu god Shiva, Lord Shiva. After this, a woman takes off her cloak and lies on the ground. This is followed by her being stabbed by one of the other people wearing a cloak. The person recording the video of all this becomes very frightened by what he has witnessed, panics, and runs off in fear. It is not every day that one of us stumbles upon a human sacrifice taking place in front of a bronze dancing Shiva statue.

The video of a woman being sacrificed on the property of CERN, a nuclear research facility, is now being viewed by the masses and has gained a whole lot of attention, especially from the conspiracy theorists. Next comes a video by the folks at Stranger Than Fiction News, which provides some more insight into the video very shortly after its release. They were able to confirm that this human sacrifice ritual video did take place within the restricted boundaries of the CERN facility, so it is very likely that the people in this video were CERN employees or associates of CERN in some way. It is also believed that the man that recorded this video could have been in on this sacrifice ritual. The reason being, after carefully watching the ritual video over and over, you look at the reflection of the glass; the cameraman can be seen, clearly wearing a cloak, just like the others he was filming outside of the window, next to Lord Shiva.

Eventually, CERN did react to these claims. On their frequently asked questions page, they finally addressed the sacrifice video of a young woman by saying, "It's a hoax, perpetrated by some of the employees there." One of the questions sent to CERN was this: "I saw a video of a strange ritual at CERN. Is it real?" CERN responded with the following: "No, this video is from the summer of 2016 and is a work fiction." CERN does not condone this kind of action, which breaches CERN's professional guidelines, and states that those employees that were involved were identified and appropriate measures were taken.

The nuclear research facility also states, "Any behavior that can have a detrimental impact on how our organization is perceived, by our neighbors, our member-states, and the wider international community, hence could impact eventually CERN's reputation, and fate shall not be tolerated." CERN even mentions this video on their guidelines page, saying that they were continuing an investigation of this matter that could lead to disciplinary actions for those involved in this ritual, although on the frequently asked questions page, CERN says they've already identified the people responsible and have taken the necessary actions for those involved in this ritual. This CERN ritual is a video that depicts an occult ritual occurring in the grounds of CERN, a European particle physics research organization.

The video shows several people dressed in black cloaks surrounding a statue of the Hindu deity Shiva (Lord Shiva) and apparently stabbing a woman in a human sacrifice. The video ended with the person filming crying out and running away. The video became viral in August 2016. There are many conspiracy theories concerning CERN. CERN later stated in its FAQ that the video was "fiction" and the actions violated its professional guidelines, as would indeed a real ritual sacrifice. After all this, these conspiracies and such, there was reaction. A CERN spokesperson stated that the video was a hoax and that no one was actually harmed. The enactment was performed without any official's permission.

CERN stated that it "doesn't tolerate this kind of spoof" and that it can "give rise to misunderstandings about the scientific nature of [their] work." The video caused controversy both by creating a mockery of existing theories and fueling existing conspiracy theories about CERN activities. Given that the ritual was performed in front of a statue of a deity, some believed the ritual was Satanic in nature. These further fueled theories that CERN's goal was to use their Large Hadron Collider (LHC) to create a portal to hell, summon the Antichrist, or resurrect the ancient gods. And we thought global warming was a threat? CERN is all about science and potentially Satan, according to many people, both scientists and regular people in the world.

This is not the first time CERN has been accused of doing things like this. For a while now, many people have led their suspicions that CERN was up to something fishy or even sinister, because of their statue of Shiva, Lord Shiva. Some have tried to use this as evidence of them trying to resurrect ancient gods. This statue was a gift from India to celebrate its association with CERN in the 1960s. This statue was chosen because in the Hindu religion, this god does a cosmic dance, which CERN correlates with cosmic dance of subatomic particles.

Nataraja (Sanskrit) is a depiction of the Hindu god Shiva, also known as Lord Shiva, as the cosmic ecstatic dancer. His dance is called Thandavam, or Nadanta, depending on the context, such as the Anshumadbhed agama and Uttarakamika agama, the dance relief or idol featured in all major Hindu temples or Shaivism. The classical form of the depiction appears in stone reliefs, as at the Ellora Caves and the Badami Caves, by around the sixth century. Around the tenth century, it emerged in Tamil Nadu in its mature and best-known expression in Chola bronzes, of various heights, typically less than four feet, some over. The Nataraja reliefs have been identified in historic artwork from any parts of South Asia, in Southeast Asia, such as in Bali, Cambodia, and in Central Asia.

The sculpture is symbolic of Shiva as the lord of dance and dramatic arts, with style and proportions made according to Hindu texts on art. It typically shows Shiva dancing in one of the Natya Shastra poses, holding Agni (fire) in his left back hand, the front hand in gajahasta (elephant hand) or danadahasta (stick hand) mudra, the front right hand with a wrapped snake that is in abhaya (fear not) mudra, while pointing to a Sutra text, and the back hand holding a musical instrument, usually a damaru. His body, fingers, ankles, neck, face, head, earlobes, and dress are shown decorated with symbolic items, which vary with historic period and region.

He is surrounded by a ring of flames, standing on a lotus pedestal, lifting his left leg (or in rare cases, the right leg), and balancing over a demon shown as a dwarf (Apasmara or Mulakaya) who symbolizes ignorance. The dynamism for the energetic dance is depicted with the whirling hair, which spreads out in thin strands as a fan behind his head. The details on the Nataraja artwork have been variously interpreted by Indian scholars since the twelfth century for its symbol in India and popular used as a symbol of Indian culture, in particular as one of the finest illustrations of Hindu art.

CHAPTER 32

The nuclear research facility known as CERN built the Large Hadron Collider machine on the LHC complex, which is situated at Saint-Genis-Pouilly. In Roman times, it was called the Apolloacum, a town dedicated to Apollyon, where a temple was built to worship the demonic deity. Apollyon, the Greek name, like Shiva, also means the destroyer. It is given in Revelation 9:11 as the angel of the bottomless pit. In a nutshell, Satan is utilizing CERN as a mechanism to release his fallen angels from the bottomless pit onto the Earth, so they can eventually destroy mankind. Fiction or fact?

CERN is releasing a frequency of 4096 hertz. Some people that have a strong understanding of both science and religion believe that the key to the bottomless pit is the break in an encrypted dimensional code, one specific to Saturn cue, requiring 4096 Cubin. In one video produced by CERN, we can see Shiva's dance of destruction. To me, this is validation that CERN is definitely on some kind of spiritual conquest to open up new dimensions. This is a very dark and evil dance with many references to Lucifer, who can be seen in this CERN video dressed in all black. This dance represents humanity doing an incantation dance within a circle as a ritual to invoke a portal opening through the guidance of who they know as Lucifer standing outside of the circle.

Enchanters believe the circle and pentagram protect them from the evil spirits they are summoning from magical favors or knowledge. The ritual of channeling fallen angels or demons for scientific knowledge is called alchemy. The perfection of the human body and soul was thought to permit or result from the alchemical magnum opus and, in the Hellenistic and Western mystery tradition, the achievement of gnosis. In Europe, the creation of a philosopher's stone was variously connected with all these projects. In English, the term is often limited to descriptions of European's alchemy, but similar practices existed in the Far East, the Indian subcontinent, and the Muslim world.

In Europe, following the twelfth century Renaissance produced by the translation of medieval Islamic works on science and the rediscovery of Aristotelian philosophy, alchemists played a significant role in early modern science (particularly chemistry and medicine). Some of the very first alchemists attempted to purify, mature, and perfect certain materials. Common aims were chrysopoeia, the transmutation of "base metal" (e.g., lead) into "noble metal" (particularly gold); the creation of an elixir of immortality; the creation of panaceas able to cure any disease; and the development of an alkahest, a universal solvent.

Islamic and European alchemists developed a structure of basic laboratory experiments theory, terminology, and experimental methods, some of which are still in use today. However, they continued antiquity's belief in four elements and guarded their work in secrecy, including cyphers and cryptic symbolism. Their work was guided by Hermetic principles related to magic, mythology, and religion. Alchemy was an ancient branch of natural philosophy, a philosophical and protoscientific tradition practiced throughout Europe, Africa, and Asia, originating in Greco-Roman Egypt in the first few centuries AD. It is very interesting that Benjamin Franklin, Thomas Edison, Nikola Tesla, and even Apple cofounder Steve Jobs were all alchemists.

The secret society of the Rosicrucianism is based on alchemy. Rosicrucianism is a spiritual and cultural movement that arose in Europe in the early seventeenth century after the publication of several texts that purported to announce the existence of a hitherto-unknown esoteric order to the world and made seeking its knowledge attractive to many. The mysterious doctrine of the order is "built on esoteric truths of the ancient past" that, "concealed from the average man, provide insight into nature, the physical universe, and spiritual realm." The manifestos do not elaborate extensively on the matter but clearly combine references to Kabbalah, Hermeticism, alchemy, and mystical Christianity.

The Rosicrucian manifestos heralded a "universal reformation of mankind" through a science allegedly kept secret for decades until the intellectual climate might receive it. Controversies arose on whether they were a hoax, whether the Order of the Rosy Cross existed as described in the manifestos, and whether the whole thing was a metaphor disguising a movement that really existed, but in a different form. The truth is, the people that are involved in all this in today's age are a denomination of scientists, physicians, physicists, and engineers under the Masonic craft. There is a spiritual law that you must present the spell, incantation, curse and in the open before it will be effective on the intended target.

The witch, wizard, shaman, warlock, enchanter, according to this law, is allowed to utilize symbols, backward-masked messages, coded language, etc., as long as it is presented "in the open"; even though the intended target, victim, or victims can be comprehending it, it still qualifies under the spiritual law. This is the reason many entertainers, professional athletes, wealthy businesspeople of pagan secret societies use secret hand symbols, backward-masking music, witch language, because they are under the contract they make with Satan to obtain the riches, fortune, and fame.

There are sacrifices, rituals, and curses that must be practiced and implemented, always at a higher price than the enchanter can afford, which will eventually cost them their life and eternal soul in the lake of fire. *Paganism* was originally a pejorative and derogatory term for polytheism, implying its inferiority. Paganism has broadly connoted the "religion of the peasantry," and after the Middle Ages, the term *paganism* was applied to any unfamiliar religion, and the term presumed a belief in false gods. Most modern pagan religions existing today—modern paganism, or neopaganism—express a worldview that is pantheistic, polytheistic, or animistic, but some are monotheistic.

The origin of the application of the term *pagan* to polytheism is debated. In the nineteenth century, paganism was adopted as a self-descriptor by members of various artistic groups inspired by the ancient world. In the twentieth century, it came to be applied as a self-descriptor by practitioners on modern paganism, neopagan movements, and polytheistic reconstructionist. Modern pagan traditions often incorporate beliefs or practices, such as nature worship, that are different from those in the largest world religions and has even found its way into CERN, science, physics, and the New World Order. The nuclear research facility CERN says they simply seek answers on questions, such as these: What is the universe made of? How did the universe start? Some people just want to know what CERN's endgame is.

I believe it is to bring Satan's high-ranking officers out of the bottomless pit, and this in order to expedite the New World Order agenda. As these demonic spirts come forth, out of the bottomless pit and elsewhere, and through the portals being created for them by CERN, it thins the veil of the spirit realm that God put in place to protect humanity. The spirit realm, or spirit world, according to spiritualism, is the world or realm inhabited by spirits, both good and evil, of various spiritual manifestations. Whereas religion regards an inner life, the spirit world is regarded as an external environment for spirits.

Although it is independent from the natural world, both the spirit world and the natural world are in constant interaction. Through mediumships, these worlds can consciously communicate with each other. The spirit world is sometimes described by mediums from the natural world in trance. As these spirts come forth, bringing dark matter, which is a substance that real dark magicians use to create things, and the dark energy associated with it, through these portals CERN is creating, or wormholes, as they call it, it creates and manifests a powerful atmosphere, or climate, if you will, of very dark energy.

The dark matter will make it much easier for Satanists, witches, secret society members, and enchanters to perform and manifest their witchcraft and spellbound the masses with political race and gender wars, which will create chaos and confusion to entice humanity to embrace sinful cultures and values in order to prepare them to take the mark of the beast, which is 666, without any resistance when the time comes. The New World Order agenda includes creating and laying down a firm foundation for the core purpose of why secret societies of the Freemasons and Greek letter organizations, among others, were created. They are all part of the network that makes up what is called the Illuminati.

Their job is to be the secret foot soldiers and construction workers of the New World Order. The New World Order, or NOW, is claimed to be an emerging clandestine totalitarian world government by various conspiracy theories. The common theme in conspiracy theories about a New World Order is that a secretive power elite with a globalist agenda is conspiring to eventually rule the worlds through an authoritarian world government—which will replace sovereign nation-states—and an all-encompassing propaganda whose ideology hails the establishment of the New World Order as the culmination of history's progress. Many influential historical and contemporary figures have therefore been purported to be part of a cabal that operates through many front organizations to orchestrate significant and financial events, ranging from causing systemic crises to pushing through controversial policies, at both national and international levels, as steps in an ongoing plot to achieve world domination.

The majority of leadership within major corporations, law enforcement, government, entertainment, politics, including the presidency, are members of Masonic and Greek letter secret societies. It is important to know that these secret societies of today are a modern-day extensions of the pagan mystery schools of Egypt and Babylon, which practiced all types of sinful abominations according to God's Word, such as baal worship, witchcraft, black magic, rituals of sexual perversion, and human sacrifices, which included children.

How can such a huge and massive project such as the CERN project fly under the radar from the majority of mainstream society? The answer is, with simple and very effective technique, which was utilized by the ancient Roman emperors, called bread and circus. The way this technique worked was, when the people began questioning and inquiring about the corruption in the Roman government, the emperor learned that they could simply use a distraction technique, which was coined "bread and circus," which is to have a circus and give out free bread. The emperors would build and fill massive coliseums and make a sport of the Christians by feeding them to the lions for the public's entertainment.

In today's world, the same ancient bread-and-circus concept holds true. The shadow government behind the public face of our government, which is run by the network of pagan secret societies, also known as the Illuminati, is still building coliseums, along with a wide variety of entertainment platforms, to distract the people from knowing the diabolical plans of the Illuminati in their ongoing construction of the Antichrist's New World Order. Before the early 1990s, New World Order conspiracists were limited to two American countercultures, primarily the militantly antigovernment right and, secondarily, that part of fundamentalist Christianity concerned with the end-time emergence of the Antichrist.

The New World Order globalists have great power and control the six major media outlets. This is in order to distort and limit knowledge of governmental activities, such as with the nuclear research facility known as CERN. Globalism refers to various systems with scope beyond the mere international. It is used by political scientists to describe "attempts to understand all the interconnections of the modern world and to highlight patterns that underlie (and explain) them." While primarily associated with world systems, it can be used to describe other global trends.

It is true that the globalist also uses their deceptive control of the media to influence and implement dark and deceptive programming of the public's mainstream values, fashions, and political views, which they own and control, and this is regardless of which side an individual selects. In higher levels of government, it's known as political theater, to distract the mainstream with a staged blue-and-red civil war, while the shadow government moves the goal closer and closer to a completed New World Order for the Antichrist, Satan's servant. In Christian eschatology, the Antichrist, or anti-Christ, is someone recognized as fulfilling the biblical prophecies about one who will oppose Christ and substitute himself in Christ's place.

The term (including one plural form) is found five times in the New Testament, solely in the First and Second Epistle of John. The Antichrist is announced as the one "who denies the Father and the Son." The similar term *pseudochristos*, or "false Christ," is found in the gospels. In Matthew (chapter 24) and Mark (chapter 13), Jesus alerts his disciples not to be deceived by the false prophets, which will claim themselves as being Christ, performing "great signs and wonders." Two other images often associated with the Antichrist are the "little horn" in Daniels final vision and the "man of sin" in Paul the apostle.

Antichrist is translated from the combination of two ancient Greek words. In Greek, *xplotoc* means "anointed one," and the word *Christ* is derived from it. *Avti* means not only *anti* in the sense of "against" and "opposite of" but also "in place of." Therefore, an Antichrist opposes Christ by substituting himself for Christ. The five uses of the term *Antichrist* in the Johannine epistles do not clearly present a single latter-day individual Antichrist. The articles "the deceiver" or "the Antichrist" are usually seen as marking out a certain category of persons rather than an individual.

You have been warned; it is the last hour, and as you have heard, the Antichrist cometh.

CHAPTER 33

The CERN project is the largest and most epic project since the attempt to build the ancient Tower of Babel. Some model scholars have associated the Tower of Babel with known structures, notably the Etemenanki, a ziggurat dedicated to the Mesopotamian god Markduk in Babylon. According to stories, a united humanity in the generations following the great flood, speaking a single language and migrating westward, comes to the land of Shinar. It is there that they agree to build a city and a tower that is tall enough to reach heaven. God, observing their city and tower, confounds their speech so that they can no longer understand one another and scatters them around the world.

CERN, the nuclear research facility, is now the modern-day Tower of Babel. The goal of the Tower of Babel in Babylon was to open up new dimensions or portals to allow Satan's fallen angels to come through, in order to give humanity the forbidden knowledge and the magical secrets that they deceptively believed would elevate them to a god or goddess. There are about ten thousand engineers and physicists from eighty-five countries who have come together and built a seventeen-mile-long machine on the Franco border called the Large Hadron Collider. What is very interesting is that Cernunnos was the horned god of the underworld. Is it just a coincidence that the name Cern is short for the name of this pagan underworld god, Cernunnos?

Cernunnos is the conventional name given in Celtic studies to depictions of the horned god of Celtic polytheism. Cernunnos was a Celtic god of fertility, life, animals, wealth, and the underworld. The name itself is only attested once, on the first-century Pillar of the Boatmen, but he appears all over Gaul and among the Celtiberians. Cernunnos is depicted with the antlers of a stag, seated cross-legged, associated with animals, and holding or wearing torcs. This deity is known from over fifty examples in the Gallo-Roman period, mostly in northeastern Gaul. Not much is really known about the god from literary sources, and details about his name, his followers, or his significance in Celtic religion are unknown.

Speculative interpretations identify him as a god of nature, life, or fertility. The Cernunnos-type antlered figure, or horned god, on the Gundestrup cauldron is on display at the National Museum of Denmark in Copenhagen. The Theonym Cernunnos appears on the Pillar of the Boatmen, a Gallo-Roman monument dating back to the early first century CE, to label a god depicted with stag's antlers in their early stage of annual growth. Both antlers have torcs hanging from them. The name has been compared to divine epithet Carnonos in a Celtic inscription written in Greek characters at Montagnac.

The name Cernunnos occurs only once in the Pillar of the Boatmen, now being displayed din the Musée National Du Moyen Age in Paris. Constructed by Gaulish sailors probably in 14 CE, it was discovered in 1710 within the foundations of the cathedral of Notre Dame de Paris, site of ancient Lutetia, the Civitas capital of the Celtic Parisii. In Wicca and other forms of neopaganism a horned god is revered; this divinity syncretizes a number of horned or antler gods from various cultures, including Cernunnos. The horned god reflects the seasons of the year in an annual cycle of life, death, and rebirth. In the tradition of Kernunno, the horned god is sometimes specifically referred to as Cernunnos, or sometimes also as Kernunno.

Gardnerian Wicca, or Gardnerian witchcraft, is a tradition in the neopagan religion of Wicca, whose members can trace initiatory decent from Gerald Gardner. The tradition is itself named after Gardner, who was born in 1884 and died in the year 1964. He was a British civil servant and amateur scholar of magic. The term *Gardnerian* was probably coined by the founder of Cochranian witchcraft, Robert Cochrane, in the 1950s or 1960s, who himself left that tradition to found his own, and he even has his own book out around that time period, titled *Book of Shadows*. The book covers witchcraft, physics, and even nuclear science.

Basically, the goal of CERN is to recreate the big bang. The research facility says that they desire to understand the particles that make up matter. One physicist explained it like this: If you study a complex object and discover what was holding the object together was glue, and you wanted to replicate the object, however there was no glue like that anywhere in the whole wide world, no matter where you looked or how hard you looked, you found out that all the ingredients for the glue was lost, then you would have to find out what the glue was made of so you could recreate it. However, you would not be able to really study the glue in its solid form; you would have to break it apart into separate particles to the ground foundation to see what it was made of in its liquid form, then make your own glue so you could then recreate the object. This is what CERN is doing. They have built the LHC (the Large Hadron Collider) to smash particles into smaller particles because they want to understand how to build their own creations at will.

CERN, on the cover, would have you believe they exist because they want to discover what the universe is made of and how it all started almost fourteen billion years ago. The physicists at CERN will tell the public that they are simply seeking answers, using some of the most powerful machines in the world, on our planet and in the known universe. You must understand that this entire CERN project is sponsored by New World Order globalists, who are Luciferians—they want to be just like God!

CERN believes that smashing these particles at the speed of light can open up black holes or wormholes to other dimensions. Their goal is to connect with other dimensions, which we know as the spirit realm. Connecting to the spirit realm outside the connection with God, however, is called sorcery; this is very high-level witchcraft. This is exactly what the goal was with the Tower of Babel in Babylon. Babylon means "a gate of the gods." The Tower of Babel was constructed for the purpose of the people in that day to worship Lucifer or Satan and his fallen angels. It was going to be utilized as a device to open up a giant portal to the spirit world. CERN's Large Hadron Collider (LHC) is Satan's second attempt at this; it is to connect to other dimensions, also known as creating a Stargate.

CERN is planning to connect to other dimensions. The titanic machine may possibly create or discover previously unimagined scientific phenomena or even unknowns, for instance, and extra dimensions. Out of this door CERN will open may come something, or we may send something through it. If CERN can collide particles, they can open up black holes in the universe in order to communicate with other dimensions through the black holes. This, in essence, is the spirit realm. The black holes are a Stargates or doorways to the spirit realm. When these black holes are opened during particle collisions, black matter and energy go out of the portals along with evil spirits. Witches, sorcerers, and magicians utilize the matter, the dark matter, which is spiritual material, to create replicas of earthly creations. Basically, a counterfeit of God's creations, because their doctrine is for themselves to become a god or goddess.

This entire CERN project was constructed on occult doctrine. In front of CERN stands a huge statue of Shiva, a Hindu god, also known as Apollyon the Destroyer. In the mystery religions of the secret societies, this is taught: order out of chaos, symbolic of the phoenix, a bird of Greek mythology that, after a long life, dies in a fire of its own making, only to rise again from the ashes, from religious and naturalistic symbolism in ancient Egypt to a secular symbol for armies, communities, and even societies. The phoenix is a very prominent symbol in many secret societies. It is the occult's belief that Shiva destroys in order to rebuild. We see a constant thing with order out of chaos. CERN did build the Large Hadron Collider on the LHC complex, which is in the territory of Saint-Genis-Pouilly, and in Roman times, it was called Apolliacum, which was an entire town that was truly bound to Apollyon the Destroyer.

CHAPTER 34

John Jay McCloy (born John Snader McCloy; March 31, 1895–March 11, 1989) was an American lawyer and banker who served as assistant secretary of war during World War II. This man also had a strong hand in getting CERN off the ground; he was made high commissioner of Germany after World War II, and a little later, he was on the Warren Commission, which whitewashed the Kennedy assassination findings. He was one of CERN's founding fathers.

Many people feel like they have reason to be suspicious when it comes to CERN, especially with the strange connections associated to this research facility. One question to be asked is, Why did scientists tried to stop CERN from doing their Large Hadron Collider (LHC) experiments, even going to court to sue some cases? Research and information led many to believe these scientists were highly concerned with CERN's activities, dark science, and even with the standard model of quantum mechanics, a strangelet, or otherwise known as quark-gluon plasma. Many people have never heard of a strangelet.

Strangelets—what are they? One description would be a quark-gluon plasma (QGP) or quark soup, a state of matter in quantum chromodynamics (QCD) that exists at extremely high temperatures and/or density. This QGP is a state of matter that existed a few billionths of a second after the big bang, when matter was, so to speak, sort of beginning to congeal but was not in any recognizable state. When it comes to a quark-gluon plasma (QUP), CERN has admitted that it might be capable of producing that state of matter in some of the collisions that they generate. The problem that the people bringing the lawsuits saw in that is that if you were to look into a quark-gluon plasma, it acts like a mini black hole, or more accurately, it acts like the gray goo in the nanotechnology's fantasies.

Gray goo (also spelled grey goo) is a hypothetical end-of-the-world scenario involving molecular nanotechnology in which out-of-control self-replicating robots consume all biomass on Earth while building more of themselves, a scenario that has been called ecophagy (eating the environment, more literally eating the habitation). The original idea assumed machines were designed to have this capability, while populations have assumed that machines might somehow gain this capability by accident. Self-replicating machines of the macroscopic variety were originally described by mathematician John Von Neumann and are sometimes referred to as Von Neumann machines or clanking replicators.

The term *gray goo* was coined by nanotechnology pioneer Eric Drexler in his 1986 book *Engines of Creation.* In 2004, he stated, "I wish I had never used the term *gray goo.*" *Engines of Creation* mentions "gray goo" in two paragraphs and a note, while the popularized idea of gray goo was publicized in a mass-circulation magazine, *Omni,* in November of the year 1986.

When Eric Drexler first wrote his book on nanotechnology, he proposed the gray goo hypothesis, that you could create a nanomachine that would convert all matter into a gray goo and that everything would end up as a gray goo—well, a quark-gluon plasma acts kind of like this, because what it does is, any matter that comes into contact with it is converted into this quark-gluon glue, so to speak. The scientists that were bringing the lawsuits against CERN began to fear that if it was successful in creating a sustained quark-gluon plasma, it would start acting like a mini black hole and begin to draw all matter that it comes into contact with and create an even bigger quark-gluon plasma (QUP) until the entire planet is converted into that. So the people began bringing lawsuits against this possibility to shut it down. CERN responded, and their response was very interesting. CERN responded by saying the following: "There is only a few billionths of a chance that that would happen." They also provided this example: if we drop a pencil on our desk, quantum mechanics will tell you that there is a remote possibility that the pencil will fall all the way through the desk and onto the floor, but the chances of that happening are vanishing small statistically. And that was the example CERN gave to reassure everybody that even if CERN does create a quark-gluon plasma, the chances of it doing anything like that are vanishing small; the chances are zero, CERN explains.

The people bringing lawsuits against CERN were actually successful, but the courts dismissed them because the courts had no jurisdiction over CERN. This was true of the German courts and even a suit in the United States (USA). CERN is a sovereign entity, giving no one jurisdiction in any court proceedings. In international law, a sovereign state, a sovereign country, or simply a state, is a non-physical judicial entity that is represented by one centralized government that has sovereignty over a geographical area. International law defines *sovereign states* as having a permanent population, defined territory, one government, and even the capacity to enter into regulations with other sovereign states. It is also normally understood that a sovereign state is neither dependent on nor subjected to any other power or state.

While according to the declarative theory of statehood, a sovereign state can exist without being recognized by other sovereign states, unrecognized states will often find it hard to exercise full treaty-making powers and engage in diplomatic relations with other sovereign states.

CHAPTER 35

Science has certainly come a long way since the days of Einstein, Tesla, and Westinghouse. We have put a man on the moon, created the internet, created artificial intelligence, and these are just a few major achievements the world has accomplished. The nuclear research facility CERN has mastered particle collision and has particle physicists working together from all over the world, and they have discovered the great Higgs boson, also known as the God particle. CERN knows everything about particles and can confirm that everything in the entire universe is made up of just three little particles. The truth is, all of matter, every atom in the universe, and everything is made of just three different elementary particles. Everything is made up of just one electron, one up quark, and one down quark.

The electron is an interesting particle and plays a very important role in the universe as it is one-third of everything. The electron is a subatomic particle whose electric charge is negative on elementary charge. Electrons belong to the first generation of the lepton particle family and are generally thought to be elementary particles because they have no known components or substructure. The electron has a mass that is approximately 1/1836 that of the proton. Quantum mechanical properties of the electron include an intrinsic angular momentum (spin) of a half-integer value, expressed in units of the reduced Planck constant.

Being fermions, no two electrons can occupy the same quantum state, in accordance with the Pauli exclusion principle. Like all elementary particles, electrons exhibit properties of both particle and waves: they can collide with other particles and can be diffracted like light. The wave properties of electrons are easier to observe with experiments than those of other particles like neutrons and protons because electrons have a lower mass and hence a longer de Broglie wavelength for a given energy. Electrons play an essential role in numerous physical phenomena, such as electricity, magnetism, chemistry, and thermal conductivity, and they also participate in gravitational, electromagnetic, and weak interactions.

Since an electron has charge, it has a surrounding electric field, and if that electron is moving relative to an observer, said observer will observe it to generate a magnetic field. Electromagnetic fields produced from other sources will affect the motion of an electron according to the Lorentz force law. Electron radiates or absorbs energy in the form of photons when they are accelerated. Laboratory instruments are capable of trapping individual electrons as well as electron plasma in outer space. Electrons are involved in many applications, such as electronics, welding, cathode ray tubes, electron microscopes, radiation therapy, laser, gaseous ionization detectors, and particle accelerators, just like the detectors being used in Geneva, Switzerland, at CERN.

The next particle we will talk about is a very special particle. It is one-third of what the whole universe is made of. This particle is the up quark. The up quark, or u quark (symbol: u), is the lightest of all quarks, a type of elementary particle, and a major constituent of matter. It, along with the down quark, forms the neutron (one up quark, two down quarks) and protons (two up quarks, one down quark) of atomic nuclei. It is part of the first generation of matter and has an electric charge of +2/3 e and a bare mass of 2.2+0.5 -0.4 MeV/ c2. Like all quarks, the up quark is an elementary fermion with spin 1/2 and experiences all four fundamental interactions: gravitation, electromagnetism, weak interaction, and strong interaction.

The antiparticle of the up quark is the up antiquark (sometimes called antiup quark or simply antiup), which differs from it only in that some of its properties, such as a charge, have equal magnitude but opposite sign. Its existence (along with that of the down and strange quarks) was postulated in 1964 by Murray Gell-Menn and George Zweig to explain the Eightfold Way classification scheme of hadrons. The up quark was first observed by experiments at the Stanford Linear accelerator. Center in 1968.

In the beginnings of particle physics (first half of the twentieth century), hadrons such as protons, neutrons, and pions were thought to be elementary particle. However, as new hadrons were discovered, the "particle zoo" grew from a few particles in the early 1930s and 1940s to several dozens of them in the 1950s. The relationships between each of them were unclear until 1961, when Murray Gell-Mann and Yuval Ne'eman (independently of each other) proposed a hadron classification scheme called the Eightfold Way, or, in more technical terms, SU(3) flavor symmetry. The classification scheme organized the hadrons into isospin multiplets, but the physical basis behind it was still unclear.

In 1964, Gell-Mann and George Zweig (independently of each other) proposed the quark model, then consisting only of up, down, and strange quarks. However, while the quark model explained the Eightfold Way, no direct evidence of the existence of quarks was found until 1968 at the Stanford Linear Accelerator Center. Deep inelastic scattering experiments indicated that protons had substructure and that protons made of three more-fundamental particles explained the data (thus confirming the quark model). At first people were reluctant to describe the three bodies as quarks, instead preferring Richard Feynman's parton description, but over time, the quark theory became accepted. Despite being extremely common, the bare mass of the up quark is not well determined but probably lies between 1.8 and 3.0 MeV/c2. Lattice QCD calculations give a more precise value: 2.01+\- 0.14 MeV/c2.

When found in mesons (particles made of one quark and one antiquark) or baryons (particles made of three quarks), the effective mass (or "dressed mass") of quarks becomes greater because of the binding energy caused by the gluon field between each quark (see mass-energy equivalence). The base mass of up quarks is so light it cannot be straightforwardly calculated because relativistic effects have to be taken into account. Due to strong force mediated by gluons in the gluon field, the quarks move at roughly 99.995 percent of the speed of light, leading to Lorentz factor of roughly 100. As a result, the combined rest mass of quarks is barely 1 percent of proton or neutron mass.

CHAPTER 36

The universe and everything in it, the Earth, we humans, all the life around us, and all the objects like television, phones, and computers, are all made from elementary particle of matter. The universe and all matter were created approximately fourteen billion years ago in a giant burst of energy, the big bang. At a research complex near the west end of Lake Geneva, straddling the border between France and Switzerland, sits CERN, the European organization of particle physics research. Thousands of scientists and researchers from all over the world have come to CERN, the focus of whose attention is the Large Hadron Collider, the LHC, which has just inaugurated its seventh experiment MoEDAL.

The LHC ring is twenty-seven kilometers in circumference and houses thousands of magnets that guide counterrotating beams of protons into collisions that generate the unprecedented energy of fourteen million electron volts per collision. The LHC ring lies one hundred meters underground. The protons traveling opposing directions then accelerate to collision energy, which is close to the speed of light. The MoEDAL collaboration has built and detected a search for the electronic monopole, a hypothetical particle, with a magnetic charge, the discovery of which would be a fundamental importance.

MoEDAL (Monopole and Exotic Detector at the LHC) is a particle physics experiment at the Large Hadron Collider. The Monopole Detector is an array of four hundred modules, each consisting of a stack of ten sheets of plastic, the total area of which is 250 square meters.

The MoEDAL detector is essentially a giant camera waiting to photograph the telltale signs of new physics, and the plastic detectors are film. The proton beams collide, recreating quite literally a tiny big bang. If magnetic monopoles exist, they will be created in this fireball, rushing away from its hot fire center just like scrap metal from a bomb, and the trajectory is to be recorded by the detector. The magnetic monopoles will rip through the plastic sheets of the detector, breaking through its long chain molecules, creating a minute trail of damage through all ten sheets of plastic. The path of damage in the plastic sheets is revealed by the process of etching in a caustic solution of sodium hydroxide monopoles path. Eventually the two cones meet, to form a whole.

The clear indication of the path of monopole is an aligned set of holes with the trajectory pointing back to the collision point. Just one event like this could herald the existence of the magnetic monopole and revolutionize our understanding of the physical universe. MoEDAL shares the cavern at point 8 with LHCb, and its prime goal is to directly search for the magnetic monopole (MM) or dyon and other highly ionizing stable massive particles (SMPs) and pseudostable massive particle. To detect these particles, the project uses nuclear track detectors (NTDs), which suffer characteristic damage due to highly ionizing particles. As MMs and SMPs are highly ionizing, NTDSs are perfectly suited for the purpose of detection.

It is an international research collaboration whose spokesperson is the University of Alberta's James Pinfold. It is the seventh experiment at the LHC, was approved and sanctioned by the CERN research board on May 2010, and started its first test deployment in January 2011. In 2012, MoEDAL accuracy surpassed accuracy of similar experiments. A new detector was installed in 2015, but as of 2017, it also did not find any magnetic monopoles, setting new limits on their production cross-section. A solid-state nuclear track detector, or SSNTD (also known as an etched track detector or a dielectric track detector, DTD), is a sample of a solid material (photographic emulsion, crystal, glass, or plastic) exposed to nuclear radiation (neutrons or charged particles, occasionally also gamma rays), etched, and examined microscopically.

The tracks of nuclear particle are etched faster than the bulk material, and the size and shape of these yield information about the mass, charge, energy, and direction of motion of the particles. The main advantages over other radiation detectors are the detailed information available on individual particles, the persistence of the tracks allowing measurements to be made over long periods of time, and the simple, cheap, and robust construction of the detector.

The basis of SSNTDs is that charged particles damage the detector within nanometers along the rack in such a way that the track can be etched many times faster than the undamaged material. Etching, typically for several hours, enlarges the damage to conical pits of micrometer dimensions, which can be observed with a microscope. For a given type of particle, the length of the track gives the energy of the particle. The charge can be determined from the etch rate of the track compared to that of the bulk. If the particles enter the surface at normal incidence, the pits are circular; otherwise, the ellipticity and orientation of the elliptical pit mouth indicate the direction of incidence. SSNTDs are commonly used to study cosmic rays, long-lived radioactive elements, radon concentration in houses, and the age of geological samples.

A material commonly used in SSNTDs is polyallyl diglycol carbonate (PADC), also known as Tastrak, CR-39, and CR39. It is a clear, colorless rigid plastic with the chemical formula $C_{12}H_{18}O_7$. Etching to expose radiation damage is typically performed using solutions of caustic alkalis, such as sodium hydroxide, often at elevated temperatures, for several hours.

CHAPTER 37

The NA62 experiment (known as P-326 at the stage of proposal) is a particle physics experiment in the north area of the SPS accelerator at CERN. The experiment was approved in February 2007. Data taking began in 2015, and the experiment is expected to become the first in the world to probe the decays of the charge kaon with probabilities down to10^{-12}. The experiment's spokesperson is Cristina Lazzeroni (since January 2019). The collaboration involves 333 individuals from at least thirty institutions and thirteen countries from all around the world.

The experiment is designed to conduct precision tests of the standard model by studying the rare decays of charged kaons. The principal goal, for which the design has been optimized, is the measurement of the rate of the ultrarare decay $K^+ \rightarrow \pi^+ + \nu + \nu$ with a precision of 10 percent by detecting about one hundred decay candidates with a low background in two years of data taking. This will lead to the determination of the CKM matrix element $|V_{td}|$ with a precision better than 10 percent. This element relates very accurately the likelihood that top quarks decay to down quarks.

In order to achieve the desired precision, the NA62 experiment requires a certain level or background rejection with respect to signal strength. Namely, high-resolution timing (to support a high-rate environment), kinematic rejection (involving the cutting on the square of the missing mass of observed particles in the decay with respect to the incident kaon vector), particle identification, hermetic vetoing of photons out to large angles and of muons within the acceptance, and redundancy of information. Due to these necessities, the NA62 experiment has constructed a detector that is approximately 270 meters in length. The foundation of the NA62 experiment is observing the decays of kaons. In order to do this, the experiment receives two beams from the SPS.

The primary beam, called P42, is used for the production of the K^+ beam. The 400 GeV/c proton beam is split into three branches and strikes three targets (T2, T4, and T6). This produces beams of secondary particles that are directed through the underground target tunnel (TCC2). At the exit of T4, the beam of transmitted protons passes through apertures in two vertically motorized beam-dump / collector modules, TAX 1 and TAX 2 for P42, in which holes of different apertures define the angular acceptance of the beam and hence allow the flux of protons to be selected over a wide range. In order to protect the components of the apparatus, a computer surveillance program allows the currents in the principal magnets along the P42 beamline to be monitored and close TAX 2 in case of error.

A secondary beamline, K12HIKA+, is a kaon beamline. The beam is designed to come from a high flux of 400GeV/c protons in the North Area High Intensity Facility. The target/beam tunnel, TCC8, and the cavern, ECN3, where the detectors of experiment NA48 have been installed, have a combined length of 270 meters. It is planned to reuse the existing target station, T10 (located 15 meters from the beginning of TCC8), and to install the secondary beam along the existing (straight) K12 beamline, of length 102 meters to the exit of the final collimator, which marks the beginning of the decay fiducial region and points to the NA48 detectors (notably the liquid krypton electromagnetic calorimeter, LKR). These beams lead to 4.5 MHz of kaon decays in the fiducial region, with a ratio of ~6% for K^+ decays per hadron flux.

Placed immediately before the decay region of the kaons, the GTK is designed to measure the time, direction, and momentum of all the beam tracks. The GTK is a spectrometer and can provide the measurement from the incoming 75 GeV/c kaon beam. The measurements of the GTK are used for decay selections and for background reduction. The GTK is composed of three different stations labeled GTK1, GTK2, and GTK3 based on the order in which they are found relative to the beam path. They are mounted around four achromat magnets (which are used to deflect the beam). The entire system is placed along the beamline and is inside the vacuum tank. Once the kaon's beam has gone through the decay region, the straw tracker will track the decay elements. The system measures the direction and the momentum of the secondary charged particles that come from the decay region. The spectrometer is made with four chambers intersected with a high-aperture dipole magnet. Each of the chambers consists of multiple straw tubes positioned to offer four coordinates. Out of 7,168 straws in the whole system, only one was flawed. The leaking straw was sealed and the detector operated normally during the 2015 run. The experiment has run multiple tests to ensure that the new detector components were working properly. The first physics run with a nearly complete detector took place in 2015. NA62 collected data in 2016, 2017, and in the year 2018 before the CERN Long Shutdown 2. Data analysis is ongoing, and several results are in preparation. As part of the experiment, several papers have been and are in the process of being created.

CHAPTER 38

CERN is known for its science, for its discoveries, and for being the home of the Large Hadron Collider. Another amazing machine located there in Geneva at the nuclear research facility is the Synchro-Cyclotron, or Synchrocyclotron (SC), which was originally built in 1957. It was CERN's first accelerator. It provided beams for CERN's first experiments in particle and nuclear physics, where the accelerated particles could reach energies up to 600 MeV. The foundation stone of CERN was laid at the site of Synchro-Cyclotron by the first director general of CERN, Felix Bloch. After its remarkably long thirty-three years of service time, the Synchro-Cyclotron (SC) was decommissioned in 1990, and nowadays it accepts visitors as an exhibition area in CERN.

A Synchro-Cyclotron (as a general idea) was invented by Edwin McMillan in the year 1945. Its main purpose is to accelerate charged particles like protons. The machine consists of two D-shaped hollow metal electrodes (called Dees) with a gap between them, connected to a radio frequency (RF) alternating voltage source. These dees are placed on a plane in a way that their openings on the flat sides look at each other. The particles inside the Synchro-Cyclotron can be accelerated from one dee to the other by the force produced by the electrical field between dees. The particles accelerated between dees with this method are rotated by the magnetic field created by two large magnets placed below and above the structure.

The machine continues to accelerate particles by alternating the direction of the electrical field until they reach the maximum radius and then extracts them via a beam tube and sends them toward a target or another machine. Throughout the process, the frequency is being decreased to compensate relativistic mass increase due to the speed of the particles approaching the speed of light. In late 1951, a UNESCO meeting about a new European Organization for Nuclear Research was held in Paris. In the meeting, the Synchro-Cyclotron was proposed as an ideal solution for a medium-energy accelerator to use until they built a much more powerful accelerator.

Later in May 1952, in the first council meeting of the proposed organization, Cornelis Bakker was appointed as director of the Synchro-Cyclotron Study Group. After a month, in a report called Provisional Program of Synchro-Cyclotron Study Group, the group decided that they would need a design that could provide 600 MeV protons. The initial objective of this group stated as indicating the scope of the work to be done and studying and/or designing the necessary items. After preliminary studies, the first meeting of the SC study group was held in Copenhagen in mid-June. Decisions made in the meeting included several trips to see similar machines around the world, making contacts to find appropriate companies that can build necessary pieces, and preparing basic drawings of the machine. After a second meeting at Amsterdam in August, a progress report dated October 1, 1952, was prepared to be presented in the meeting of the European Council for Nuclear Research, which was going to be held in Amsterdam in October.

According to the report, the group aimed to finish its work in a year and a complete report to be presented to the European Council for Nuclear Research. A preliminary design drawing of the SC was attached to the report, which stated that the work of the group was progressing "satisfactorily" and they were cooperating "adequately."

In the year 1953, after a mere year of research, meetings, and reports alike, the design of the Synchro-Cyclotron started. The construction of the machine began in 1954 on the site at Meyrin, with the parts coming from all over Western Europe. In late 1955, Wolfgang Gentner became the director of the Synchro-Cyclotron

Study Group, as former director Cornelis Bakker became the director general of CERN. The research program for the Synchro-Cyclotron started to be planned to be able to start experiments as soon as possible. The SC was ready to produce its first beam in August 1957, practically on the date foreseen.

A press release by CERN on August 16, 1957, stated that the SC, as the third largest accelerator of its type in the world, has started to work at its full energy. In late 1958, the Synchro-Cyclotron made its first important contribution to nuclear physics by the discovery of the rare electron decay of the pion particle. This discovery helped theorists a lot by proving that this decay really occurs. The Synchro-Cyclotron was used for an average of 135 hours per week during 1961; it ran continuously every day of the week except Mondays, which were reserved for maintenance. The Synchro-Cyclotron was accelerating a jet of protons fifty-four times a second, up to a speed approximately 240,000 kilometers per second (80 percent of the speed of light).

In May 1960, plans for an isotope separator were published in Vienna. The isotope separator was built by CERN's Nuclear Chemical Group (NCG) and used in measurements of production rates of radionuclides produced in the Synchro-Cyclotron. High production rates observed during these measurements proved that the SC was the ideal machine for experiments for online production of rare isotopes. In April 1963, a group of physicists met at CERN to discuss for the isotope-separator project. In late 1964, a formal proposal was submitted for the project and accepted by the CERN director general. In the same year, the Synchro-Cyclotron started to concentrate on nuclear physics alone, leaving particle physics to a more powerful accelerator built in 1959, the Proton Synchrotron. In May 1966, the Synchro-Cyclotron was shut down for major modifications. Until mid-July, the capacity of the Synchro-Cyclotron and its associated facilities were improved. Also, a new tunnel was constructed for an external proton beamline to the new underground hall for the new isotope separator. In 1967, it started supplying beams for the dedicated radioactive-ion-beam facility called ISOLDE, which still carries out research ranging from pure nuclear physics to astrophysics and medical physics.

In 1969, preparations started to increase the beam intensity and improve the beam extraction efficiency of the (SC) Synchro-Cyclotron, which was shut down in June of 1973 for modifications. The highly improved machine started working again for physical research with its new name, SC2, in January 1975. In 1990, ISOLDE was transferred to the Proton Synchro-Cyclotron Booster, and the SC finally closed down after 33 years of service. Now it serves as an exhibition for area visitors. The exhibition includes a video about the birth of CERN and the Synchro-Cyclotron.

Using projection mapping technology, it displays simulations of the accelerating particles on the SC and demonstrates parts of it. Some objects and tools which were used at the time the SC was started are also in the hall for visitors to see. The 600 MeV Synchro-Cyclotron (SC) was built in 1957, was CERN's first accelerator. It provided beams for CERN's first experiments in particle and nuclear physics. In 1964, this machine started to really concentrate on nuclear physics alone, leaving particle physics to the newer and even more powerful Proton Synchro-Cyclotron. The SC became a remarkably long-lived machine. In 1967, it started supplying beams for a dedicated radioactive-ion-beam facility called ISOLDE, which still carries out research ranging from pure nuclear physics to astrophysics and medical physics. In 1990, ISOLDE was transferred to the Proton Synchro-Cyclotron Booster, and the SC closed down after thirty-three years of service.

The visit starts in a "time tunnel," taking visitors back from the present to the beginning of physics research at CERN, in 1954. Timelines displayed on side walls show the evolution of accelerators and technology used at CERN along with cultural milestones. Once in the accelerator room, visitors are shown a thirteen-minute video that shows the birth of CERN, then how and by who the Synchro-Cyclotron was used, using the latest projection-mapping technology. Finally, visitors are show various objects and tools that were used at the time the Synchro-Cyclotron was started. The video show is currently available in the following languages: Bulgarian, English,

French, German, Greek, Italian, Spanish, Polish, Portuguese, and Turkish.

The Proton Synchrotron (PS) is a particle accelerator at CERN. It is CERN's first synchrotron, beginning its operation in 1959. For a brief period, the PS was the world's highest-energy particle accelerator for the Intersecting Storage Rings (ISR) and the Super Proton Synchro-Cyclotron (SPS) and is currently part of the Large Hadron Collider (LHC) accelerator complex. In addition to protons, PS has accelerated alpha particles, oxygen, and sulfur nuclei, electrons, positrons, and antiprotons. Today the PS is part of CERN's accelerator complex. It accelerates protons for the LHC as well as a number of other experimental facilities at CERN. Using a proton source, the protons are first accelerated to the energy of 50 MeV in the linear accelerator Linac 2. The beam is then injected into the Proton Synchrotron Booster (PSB), which accelerates the protons to 1.4 GeV, followed by the PS, which pushes the beam to 25 GeV. The protons are then sent to the Super Proton Synchrotron and accelerated to 450 GeV before they are injected into the LHC. The PS also accelerates heavy ions from the Low Energy Ion Ring (LEIR) at an energy of 72 MeV, for collisions in the LHC.

In mathematics and physics, a scalar field associates a scalar value to every point in a space—possibly physical space. The scalar may either be a (dimensionless) mathematical number or a physical quantity. In a physical context, scalar fields are required to be independent of the choice of reference frame, meaning that any two observers using the same units will agree on the value of the scalar fields at the same absolute point in space (or space-time) regardless of their respective points of origin. Examples used in physics include the temperature distribution throughout space, the pressure distribution in a fluid, and spin zero quantum fields, such as the Higgs field. These fields are the subject of scalar field theory.

To define all this, mathematically, a scalar field on a region *U* is a real or complex-valued function or distribution of *U*. The region *U* may be a set in some Euclidean space, Minkowski space, or more generally, a subset of a manifold, and it is typical in mathematics to impose further conditions on the field, such that it be continuous or often continuously differentiable to some order. A scalar field is a tensor field of order zero, and the term *scalar field* may be used to distinguish a function of this kind with a more general tenor field, density, or differential form. Physically, a scalar field is additionally distinguished by having units of measurement associated with it.

In this context, a scalar field should also be independent of the coordinate system used to describe the physical system—that is, any two observers using the same units must agree on the numerical value of a scalar field at any given point of physical space. Scalar fields are contrasted with other physical quantities, such as vector fields, which associate a vector to every point of a region, as well as tensor fields and spin field. More subtly, scalar fields are often contrasted with pseudoscalar fields. In physics, scalar fields often describe the potential energy associated with a particular force. The force is a vector field, which can be obtained as a factor of the gradient of the potential energy scalar field.

Examples include thus:

- Potential fields, such as the Newtonian gravitational potential, or the electric potential in electrostatics, are scalar fields that describe the more familiar forces.
- A temperature, humidity, or pressure field, such as those used in meteorology.

Examples in quantum theory and relativity: In quantum field theory, a scalar field is associated with spin-0 particles. The scalar field may be real or complex valued. Complex scalar fields represent charged particles. These include the charge Higgs field of the standard model, as well as the charged pions mediating the strong nuclear interaction. In the standard model of elementary particles, a scalar Higgs field is used to give the leptons and massive vector bosons their mass, via a combination of the Yukawa interaction and the spontaneous symmetry breaking. This mechanism is known as the Higgs mechanism.

A candidate for the Higgs boson was first detected at CERN in 2012. In scalar theories of gravitation, scalar fields are used to describe the gravitational field. Scalar-tensor theories represent the gravitational interaction through both a tensor and a scalar. Such attempts are examples the Jordan theory as generalization of the Kaluza-Klein theory and the Brans-Dicke theory. Scalar fields like the Higgs field can be found within scalar-tensor theories, using as scalar field the Higgs field of the standard model. This field interacts gravitationally and Yukawa-like (short-ranged) with the particles that get mass through it. Vector fields associate a vector to every point in space. Some examples of vector fields include the electromagnetic field and the Newtonian gravitational field.

Another are tensor fields, which associate a tensor to every point in space. For examples, in general relativity, gravitation is associated with the tensor field called Einstein tensor. In Kaluza-Klein theory, space-time is extended to five dimensions, and its Riemann curvature tensor can be separated out into ordinary four-dimensional gravitation plus an extra set, which is equivalent to Maxwell's equations for the electromagnetic field, plus an extra scalar field known as the dilaton. The dilaton scalar is also found among the massless bosonic field in string theory.

The Higgs boson is an elementary particle in the standard model of particle physics produced by the quantum excitation of the Higgs field, one of the fields in particle physics theory. It is named after physicist Peter Higgs, who, in 1964, along with five other scientists, proposed the Higgs mechanism to explain why particles have mass. This mechanism implies the existence of the Higgs boson. The boson's existence was confirmed in 2012 by the ATLAS and CMS collaborations based on collisions in the LHC at CERN. On December 10, 2013, two of the physicists, Peter Higgs and Francois Englert, were awarded the Nobel Prize in Physics for their theoretical predictions. Although the Higgs name has come to be associated with this theory (the Higgs mechanism), several researchers between about 1960 and 1972 independently developed different parts of it.

In mainstream media, the Higgs boson has often been called the God particle, from a 1993 book on the topic, although the nickname is strongly disliked by many physicists, including Higgs himself, who regard it as sensationalism. Physicists explain the properties of forces between elementary particles in terms of the standard model—a widely accepted framework for understanding almost everything in physics in the known universe, other than gravity. (A separate theory, general relativity, is used for gravity.) In this model, the fundamental forces in nature arise from properties of our universe, called gauge invariance and symmetries. The forces are transmitted by particles known as gauge bosons.

In the standard model, the Higgs particle is boson with spin zero, no electronic charge, and no color charge. It is also very unstable, decaying into other particles almost immediately. The Higgs field is a scalar field, with two neutral and two electrically charged components that form a complex doublet of the weak isospin SU(2) symmetry. The Higgs field has a "Mexican hat-shaped" potential. In its ground state, this causes the field to have a nonzero value everywhere (including otherwise-empty space), and as a result, below a very high energy, it breaks the weak isospin symmetry of the electroweak interaction. (Technically, the no-zero expectation value converts the Lagrangian's Yukawa coupling terms into mass terms.) When this happens, three components of the Higgs field are "absorbed" by the SU(2) and U(1) gauge bosons (the Higgs mechanism) to become the longitudinal component of the now-massive W and Z bosons of the weak force.

The remaining electrically neutral component either manifests as a Higgs particle or may couple separately to other particles known as fermions (via Yukawa couplings), causing these to acquire mass as well. Field theories had been used with great success in understanding the electromagnetic fields and the strong force, but by around 1960, all attempts to create a gauge invariant theory for the weak force (and its combination with fundamental force electromagnetism, the electroweak interaction) have consistently failed, with gauge theories thereby starting to fall into disrepute as a result.

The problem was that the symmetry requirements in gauge theory predicted that both electromagnetisms gauge boson (the photon) and the weak forces gauge bosons (W and Z) should have zero mass. Although the photon is indeed massless, experiments show that the weak forces bosons have mass. This meant that either gauge invariance was an incorrect approach, or something else—unknown—was giving these particles their mass, but all attempts to suggest a theory able to solve this problem just seemed to create new theoretical issues. By the late 1950s, physicists had not resolved these issues, which were significant obstacles to developing a full-fledged theory for particle physics.

If electroweak symmetry was somehow being broken, it might explain why electromagnetism's boson is massless, yet the weak force bosons have mass, and solve the problems. Shortly afterward, in 1963, this was shown to be theoretically possible, at least for some limited (nonrelativistic) cases. Following the 1962 and 1963 papers, three groups of researchers independently published the 1964 PRL symmetry breaking papers with similar conclusions and for all cases, not just some limited cases.

They showed that the conditions for electroweak symmetry would be "broken" if an unusual type of field existed throughout the universe and, indeed, some fundamental particles would acquire mass. The field required for this to happen (which was purely hypothetical at that time) became known as the Higgs field (after Peter Higgs, one of the researchers), and the mechanism by which it led to symmetry breaking as the Higgs mechanism. A key feature of the necessary field is that it would take less energy for the field to have a nonvalue than a zero value, unlike all other known fields; therefore, the Higgs field has a nonzero value (or vacuum expectation) everywhere. It was the first proposal capable of showing how the weak force gauge bosons could have mass despite their governing symmetry, within a gauge invariant theory.

Although these ideas did not gain much initial support or attention, by 1972 they had been developed into a comprehensive theory and proved capable of giving "sensible" results that accurately described particles known at that time and which, with exceptional accuracy, predicted several other particles discovered during the following years. During the 1970s, these theories rapidly became the standard model of particle physics. There was not yet any direct evidence that the Higgs field existed, but even without proof of the field, the accuracy of its predictions led scientists to believe the theory might be true.

By the 1980s, the question of whether or not the Higgs field existed, and therefore whether or not the entire standard model was correct, has come to be regarded as one of the most important unanswered questions in particle physics. According to the standard model, a field of the necessary kind (the Higgs field) exists throughout space and breaks certain symmetry laws of the electroweak interaction. Via the Higgs mechanism, this field causes the gauge bosons of the weak force to be massive at all temperatures below an extreme high value. When the weak force bosons acquire mass, this affects their range, which becomes very small. Furthermore, it was later realized that the same field would also explain, in a different way, why other fundamental constituents of matter (including electrons and quark) have mass.

For many decades, scientists have no way to determine whether or not the Higgs field existed, because the technology needed for its detection did not exist at that time. If the Higgs field existed, then it would be unlike any other known fundamental field, but it also was possible that these key ideas, or even the entire standard model, were somehow incorrect. Only discovering that the Higgs boson and therefore the Higgs field existed solved the problem. Unlike other known fields, such as the electromagnetic field, the Higgs field is scalar and has a nonzero constant value in vacuum.

The existence of the Higgs field became the last unverified part of the standard model of particle physics and, for several decades, was considered "the central problem in particle physics." The presence of the field, now confirmed by experimental investigation, explains why some fundamental particle have mass, despite the symmetries controlling their interactions implying that they should be massless. It also resolves several other longstanding puzzles, such as the reason for the extremely short range of the weak force. Although the Higgs field is nonzero everywhere and its effects are ubiquitous, proving its existence was far from easy. In principle, it can prove to exist by detecting its excitation, which manifest as Higgs particles (the Higgs boson), but these are extremely difficult to produce and detect.

The importance of this fundamental questions led to a forty-year search, and the construction of one of the world's most expensive and complex experimental facilities to date, CERN's Large Hadron Collider, in an attempt to create Higgs bosons and other particle with a mass between 125 and 137 GeV/c^2, was announced; physicists suspected that it was the Higgs boson. Since then, the particle has been shown to behave, interact, and decay in many of the ways predicted for Higgs particles by the standard model, as well as having even parity and zero spin, two fundamental attributes of a Higgs boson. This also means it is the first elementary scalar particle discovered in nature. As of 2018, in-depth research shows the particle continuing to behave in line with predictions for the standard model Higgs boson.

More studies are needed to verify with higher precision that the discovered particle has all the properties predicted or whether, as described by some theories, multiple Higgs bosons exist. The hypothesized Higgs mechanism made several accurate predictions; however, to confirm its existence, there was an extensive search for a matching particle associated with it—the Higgs boson. Detecting Higgs bosons was difficult due to the energy required to produce them and their very rare production even if the energy is sufficient. It was therefore several decades before the first evidence of the Higgs boson was found. Particle colliders, detectors, and computer capable of looking for Higgs bosons took more than thirty years (c. 1980–2010) to develop.

By March 2013, the existence of the Higgs boson was confirmed, and therefore, the concept of some type of Higgs field throughout space is strongly supported. The nature and properties of this field are now being investigated further, using mare data collected at the LHC. Various analogies have been used to describe the Higgs field and boson, including analogies with well-known symmetry-breaking effects, such as the rainbow and prism, electric field, ripples, and resistance of macro objects moving through media (such as people moving through crowds or some objects moving through syrup or molasses). Evidence of the Higgs field and its properties has been extremely significant for many reasons.

The importance of the Higgs boson is largely that it is able to be examined using existing knowledge and experimental technology, as a way to confirm and study the entire Higgs field theory. The Higgs boson validates the standard model through the mechanism of mass generation. As more precise measurements of its properties are made, more advanced extensions may be suggested or excluded. As experimental means to measure the field's behaviors and interactions are developed, this fundamental field may be better understood. If the Higgs field had not been discovered, the standard model would have needed to be modified or superseded.

Related to this, a belief generally exists among physicists that there is likely to be "new" physics beyond the standard model, and the standard model will, at some point, be extended or superseded. The Higgs discovery, as well as the many measured collisions occurring at the LHC, provide physicists a sensitive tool to parse data for where the standard model fails and could provide considerable evidence guiding researchers into future theoretical developments. When it comes to symmetry breaking of the electroweak interaction, below an extremely high temperature, electroweak symmetry breaking causes the electroweak interaction to manifest in part as the short-ranged weak force, which varies by massive gauge bosons.

This symmetry breaking is required for atoms and other structures to form, as well as for nuclear reactions in stars, such as our sun. This Higgs field is responsible for this symmetry breaking. This Higgs field is pivotal in generating the masses of quarks and charged leptons (through Yukawa coupling) and the W and Z gauge bosons (through the Higgs mechanism). It is worth noting that the Higgs field does not "create" mass out of nothing (which would violate the law of conservation of energy), nor is the Higgs field responsible for the mass of all particle. For example, approximately 99 percent of the mass of baryons (composite particle such as the proton and neutron) is due instead to quantum chromodynamic binding energy, which is the sum of the kinetic energies of quarks and the energies of the massless gluons mediating the strong interaction inside the baryons.

In Higgs-based theories, the property of "mass" is a manifestation of potential energy transferred to fundamental particles when they interact ("couple") with the Higgs field, which has contained the mass in the form of energy. The Higgs field is the only scalar (spin 0) field to be detected; all the other fields in the standard model are spin 1/2 fermions or spin 1 boson. According to Rolf-Dieter Heuer, director general of CERN when the Higgs boson was discovered, this existence proof of a scalar field is almost as important as the Higgs's role in determining the mass of other particles.

It suggests that the other hypothetical scalar field suggested by other theories, from the inflation to quintessence, could perhaps exist as well. There has been considerable scientific research on possible links between the Higgs field and the inflation—a hypothetical field suggested as the explanation for the expansion of space during the first fraction of a second of the universe (known as the "inflationary epoch"). Some theories suggest that a fundamental scalar field, and its existence, has led to papers analyzing whether it could also be the inflation responsible for this exponential expansion of the universe during the big bang.

Such theories are highly tentative and face significant problems related to unitarity but may be viable if combined with additional features, such as large nonminimal coupling, a Brans-Dicke scalar, or other "new" physics, and they have received treatments suggesting that Higgs inflation models are still of interest theoretically. In the standard model, there exists the possibility that the underlying state of our universe, known as the vacuum, is long-lived, but not completely stable. In this scenario, the universe as we know it could effectively be destroyed by collapsing into a more stable vacuum state. This was sometimes misreported as the Higgs boson "ending" the universe.

If the masses of the Higgs boson and top quark are known more precisely and the standard model provides an accurate description of particle physics up to extreme energies of the Planck scale, then it is possible to calculate whether the vacuum is stable or merely long-lived. A 125–127 GeV Higgs mass seems to be extremely close to the boundary for stability, but a definitive answer requires much more precise measurements of the pole mass of the top quark. New physics can change this picture.

If measurements of the Higgs boson suggest that our universe lies within a false vacuum of this kind, then it would imply—more than likely in many billions of years—that the universe's forces, particles, and structures could cease to exist as we know them (and be replaced by different ones), if a true vacuum happened to nucleate. It also suggests that the Higgs's self-coupling and its function could be very close to zero at the Planck scale, with "intriguing" implications, including theories of gravity and Higgs-based inflation. A future electron-positron collider would be able to provide the precise measurements of the top quark needed for such calculations.

When talking about "vacuum energy," more speculatively, the Higgs field has also been proposed as the energy of the vacuum, which at the extreme energies of the first moment of the big bang caused the universe to be a kind of featureless symmetry of undifferentiated, extremely high energy. In this kind of speculation, the single unified field of a grand unified theory is identified as (modelled upon) the Higgs field, and it is through successive symmetry breakings of the Higgs field, or some similar field, at phase transitions that the presently known forces and fields of the universe arise. The relationship (if any) between the Higgs field and the presently observed vacuum energy density of the universe has also come under scientific study.

As observed, the present vacuum energy density is extremely close to zero, but the energy density expected from the Higgs field, supersymmetry, and other current theories are typically many orders of magnitude larger. It is unclear how these should be reconciled. This cosmological constant problem remains a further major unanswered problem in physics.

Could there be a practical or technological impact? As yet, there are no known immediate technological benefits of finding the Higgs particle. However, a common pattern for fundamental discoveries is for practical applications to follow later and, once the discovery has been explored further, perhaps becoming the basis for new technologies of importance to society.

The challenges in particle physics have furthered major technological progress of widespread importance. For example, the World Wide Web began as a project to improve CERN's communication system. CERN's requirement to process massive amounts of data produced by the Large Hadron Collider also led to contributions to the fields of distributed and cloud computing.

CHAPTER 39

Particle physicists study matter made from fundamental particles whose interactions are mediated by exchange particles—gauge bosons—acting as force carriers. At the beginning of the 1960s, a number of these particles had been discovered or proposed, along with theories suggesting how they relate to one another, some of which had already been reformulated as field theories in which the objects of study are not particles and forces but quantum fields and their symmetries. However, attempts to produce quantum field models for two of the four known fundamental forces—the electromagnetic force and the weak nuclear force—and then to unify these interactions were still unsuccessful.

One known problem was that gauge invariant approaches, including nonabelian models such as Yang-Mills theory (1954), which held great promise for unified theories, also seemed to predict a known massive particle as massless. Goldstone's theorem, relating to continuous symmetries within some theories, also appeared to rule out many obvious solutions, since it appeared to show that zero-mass particles also would have to exist that simply were "not seen." According to Guralnik, physicists had "no understanding" how these problems could be overcome. Particle physicist and mathematician Peter Woit summarized the state of research at that time:

Yang and Mills work on non-abelian gauge theory had one huge problem: in perturbation theory it has massless particles which don't correspond to anything we see. One way of getting rid of this problem is not fairly well understood, the phenomenon of confinement realized in QCD, where the strong interactions get rid of the massless "gluon" states at long distances. By the very early sixties, people had begun to understand another source of massless particle: spontaneous symmetry breaking of a continuous symmetry. What Philip Anderson realized and worked out in the summer of 1962 was that, when you both gauge symmetry and spontaneous symmetry breaking, the Nambu-Goldstone massless mode can combine with the massless gauge field modes to produce a physical massive vector field. This is what happens in superconductivity, a subject about which Anderson was (and is) one of the leading experts.

The Higgs mechanism is a process by which vector bosons can acquire rest mass without explicitly breaking gauge invariance, as a byproduct of spontaneous symmetry breaking. Initially, the mathematical theory behind spontaneous symmetry breaking was conceived and published within particle physics by Yoichiro Nambu in 1960, and the concept that such a mechanism could offer a possible solution for the "mass problem" was originally suggested in 1962 by Philip Anderson, who had previously written papers on broken symmetry and its outcomes in superconductivity. Anderson concluded in his 1963 paper on the Yang-Mills theory that "considering the superconducting analog, these two types of bosons seem capable of canceling each other out, leaving finite mass bosons."

In March 1964, Abraham Klein and Benjamin Lee showed that Goldstone's theorem could be avoided this way in at least some nonrelativistic cases and speculated it might be possible in truly relativistic cases. These approaches were quickly developed into a full relativistic model, independently and almost simultaneously, by three groups of physicists: by Francois Englert and Robert Brout in August 1964, by Peter Higgs in October 1964, and by Gerald Guralnik, Carl Hagen, and Tom Kibble (GHK) in November 1964. Higgs also wrote a short but important response published in September 1964 to an objection by Gilbert, which showed that if calculating within the radiation gauge, Goldstone's theorem and Gilbert's objection would become inapplicable. (Higgs later described Gilbert's objection as prompting his own paper.)

Properties of the model were further considered by Guralnik in 1965, by Higgs in 1966, by Kibble in 1967, and further by GHK in 1967. The original three 1964 papers demonstrated that when a gauge theory is combined with an additional field that spontaneously breaks the symmetry, the gauge bosons may consistently acquire a finite mass. In 1967, Steven Weinberg and Abdus Salam independently showed how a Higgs mechanism could be used to break the electroweak symmetry of Sheldon Glashow's unified model for the weak and electromagnetic interactions (itself an extension of work by Schwinger), forming what became the standard model of particle physics.

Weinberg was the first to observe that this would also provide mass terms for the fermions. At first, these seminal papers on spontaneous breaking of gauge symmetries were largely ignored, because it was widely believed that the (nonabelian gauge) theories in question were a dead-end and, in particular, that they could not be renormalized. In 1971–1972, Martinus Veltman and Gerard't Hooft proved renormalization of Yang-Mills was possible in two papers covering massless, and then massive, fields. Their contribution, and the work of others on the renormalization group—including "substantial" theoretical work by Russian physicists Ludvig Faddeev, Andrei Slavnov, Efim Fradkin, and Igor Tyutin—was eventually "enormously profound and influential," but even with all key elements of the eventual theory published, there was still almost no wider interest.

For example, Coleman found in a study that "essentially no one paid any attention" to Weinberg's paper prior to 1971 and discussed by David Politzer in his 2004 Nobel speech—now the most cited in particle physics—and even in 1970, according to Politzer, Glashow's teaching of the weak interaction contained no mention of Weinberg's, Salam's, or Glashow's own work. In practice, Politzer states, almost everyone learned of the theory due to physicist Benjamin Lee, who combined the work of Veltman and Hooft with insights by other and popularized the completed theory.

In this way, from 1971, interest and acceptance "exploded" and the ideas were quickly absorbed in the mainstream. The resulting electroweak theory and standard model have accurately predicted (among other things) weak neutral currents, three bosons, the top and charm quarks, and with great precision, the mass and other properties of some of these. Many of those involved eventually won Nobel Prizes or other renowned awards. A 1974 paper and comprehensive review in *Reviews of Modern Physics* commented that "while no one doubted the [mathematical] correctness of these arguments, no one quite believed that nature was diabolically clever enough to take advantage of them," adding that the theory has so far produced accurate answers that accorded with experiment, but it was known whether the theory was fundamentally correct.

By 1986 and again in the 1990s, it became possible to write that understanding and proving the Higgs sector of the standard model was "the central problem today in particle physics."

On the summary and an impact of the PRL papers, the three papers written in 1964 were each recognized as milestone papers during *Physical Review Letters*'s fiftieth anniversary celebration. Their six authors were also awarded in 2010 J. J. Sakurai Prize for theoretical Particle Physics for this work. (A controversy also arose the same year, because in the event of Nobel Prize, only up to three scientists could be recognized, with six being credited for the papers.)

Two of the three PRL papers (by Higgs and by GHK) contained questions for the hypothetical quantum, the Higgs boson. Higgs's subsequent 1966 paper showed the decay mechanism of the boson; only a massive boson can decay, and the decay can prove the mechanism. In the paper by Higgs, the boson is massive, and in closing a sentence, Higgs writes that "an essential feature" of the theory "is the prediction of incomplete multiplets of scalar and vector bosons." (Frank Close comments that the 1960s gauge theorists were focused on the problem of massless vector bosons, and the implied existence of a massive scalar boson was not seen as important; only Higgs directly addressed it.)

In the paper by GHK, the boson is massless and decoupled from the massive states. In reviews dated 2009 and 2001, Guralnik states that in the GHK model, the boson is massless only in a lowest-order approximation, but it is not subject to any constraint and acquires mass at higher order, and adds that the GHK paper was only one to show that there are not massless Goldstone bosons in the model and to give a complete analysis of the general Higgs mechanism. All three reached similar conclusions, despite their very different approaches: Higgs's paper essentially used classical techniques, Englert and Brouts's involved calculating vacuum polarization in perturbation theory around an assumed symmetry-breaking vacuum state, and GHK's used operator formalism and conversation laws to explore in depth the ways in which Goldstone's theorem may be worked around. Some versions of the theory predicted more than one kind of Higgs fields and bosons, and alternative "Higgsless" models were considered until the discovery of the Higgs boson.

To produce Higgs bosons, two beams of particles are accelerated to very high energies and allowed to collide within a particle detector. Occasionally, although rarely, a Higgs boson will be created fleetingly as part of the collision byproducts. Because the Higgs boson decays very quickly, particle detectors cannot detect it directly. Instead, the detectors register all the decay products (the decay signature), and from the data the decay process is reconstructed.

If the observed decay products match a possible decay process (known as a decay channel) of a Higgs boson, this indicates that a Higgs boson may have been created. In practice, many processes may produce similar decay signatures. Fortunately, the standard model precisely predicts the likelihood of each of these, and each known process, occurring. So if the detector detects more decay signatures consistently matching a Higgs boson than would otherwise be expected if Higgs bosons did not exist, then this would be strong evidence that the Higgs boson exists. Because Higgs boson production in a particle collision is likely to be very rare (1 in 10 billion at the LHC), and many other possible collision events can have similar decay signatures, the data of hundreds of trillions of collisions needs to be analyzed and must "show the same picture" before a conclusion about the existence of the Higgs boson can be reached.

To conclude that a new particle has been found, particle physicists require that the statistical analysis of two independent particle detectors each indicate that there is lesser than one-in-a-million chance that the observed decay signatures are due to just background random standard model events—i.e., that the observed number of events is more than five standard deviations (sigma) different from that expected if there was no new particle. More collision data allows better confirmation of the physical properties of any new particle observed and allows physicists to decide whether it is indeed a Higgs boson as described by the standard model or some other hypothetical new particle.

To find the Higgs boson, a powerful particle accelerator was needed, because the Higgs bosons might not be seen in lower-energy experiments. The collider needed to have a high luminosity in order to ensure enough collisions were seen for conclusions to be drawn. Finally, advanced computing facilities were needed to process the vast amount of data (twenty-five petabytes per year as of 2012) produced by the collisions. For the announcement of July 4, 2012, a new collider known as the Large Hadron Collider (LHC) was constructed at CERN with a planned eventual collision energy of 14 TeV—over seven times any previous collider—and over 300 trillion ($3x10^{14}$) LHC proton-proton collisions were analyzed by LHC Computing Grid, the world's largest computing grid (as of the year 2012), comprising over 170 computing facilities in a worldwide network across thirty-six countries.

The first extensive search for the great Higgs boson was conducted at the Large Electron-Positron Collider (LEP) at CERN in the 1990s. At the end of its service in 2000, LEP had found no conclusive evidence for the Higgs. This implied that if the Higgs boson were to exist, it would have to be heavier than 114.4 GeV/c^2.

The search continued at Fermilab in the United States, where the Tevatron—the collider that discovered the top quark in 1995—had been upgraded for this purpose. There was no guarantee the Tevatron would be able to find the Higgs, but it was the only supercollider that was operational since the Large Hadron Collider (LHC) was still under construction and the planned Superconducting Super Collider had been canceled in 1993 and never completed. The Tevatron was only able to exclude further ranges for the Higgs mass and was shut down on September 30, 2011, because it no longer could keep up with the LHC. The final analysis of the data excluded the possibility of a Higgs boson with a mass between 147 GeV/c^2 and 180 GeV/c^2. In addition, there was a small (but not significant) excess of events possibly indicating a Higgs boson with a mass between 115 GeV/c^2 and 140 GeV/c^2. The Large Hadron Collider (LHC) at CERN in Switzerland was designed specifically to be able to either confirm or exclude the existence of the Higgs boson. Built in a twenty-seven-kilometer tunnel under the ground near Geneva originally inhabited by LEP, it was really a design to simply collide two beams of protons.

Theory suggested that if the Higgs boson existed, collisions at these energy levels should be able to reveal it. As one of the most complicated scientific instruments ever built, its operational readiness was delayed for fourteen months by a magnet quench event nine days after its inaugural tests, caused by a faulty electrical connection that damaged over fifty superconducting magnets and contaminated the vacuum system.

Data collection was finally commenced in March 2010. By December 2011, the two main particle detectors at the LHC, ATLAS and CMS, had narrowed down the mass range where the Higgs could exist to around 116–130 GeV (ATLAS) and 115–127 GeV (CMS). There had also already been a number of promising event excesses that had "evaporated" and proven to be nothing but random fluctuations. However, from around May 2011, both experiments had seen among their results the slow emergence of a small yet consistent excess of gamma and 4-lepton decay signatures and several other particle decays, all hinting at a new particle at a mass around 125 GeV. By around November 2011, the anomalous data at 125 GeV was becoming "too large to ignore" (although still far from conclusive), and the team leaders at both ATLAS and CMS each privately suspected they might have found the Higgs. Another important date was on November 28 of 2011, when at an internal meeting of the two team leaders and the director general of CERN the latest analyses were discussed outside their teams for the first time, suggesting both ATLAS and CMS might be converging on a possible shared result at 125 GeV, and initial preparations commenced in case of a success finding.

The truth is, this information was not known publicly at that time. The narrowing of the possible Higgs range to around 115 to 130 GeV and the repeated observation of small but consistent event excesses across multiple channels at both ATLAS and CMS in the 124 to 126 GeV region were public knowledge with "a whole lot of interest." It was therefore widely anticipated around the end of 2011 that the LHC (Large Hadron Collider) would provide sufficient data to either exclude or positively confirm the finding of a "real Higgs boson" by the end of 2012, and this was when their 2012 collision data (with slightly higher 8 TeV collision energy) had been examined.

CHAPTER 40

On June 22, 2012, CERN announced an upcoming seminar covering tentative findings for 2012, and shortly afterward (from around July 1, 2012), according to an analysis of the spreading rumor in social media, rumors began to spread that this would include a major announcement, but it was unclear whether this would be a stronger signal or a formal discovery. Speculation escalated to a "fevered" pitch when reports emerged that Peter Higgs, who proposed the particle, was to be attending the seminar and that "five leading physicists" had been invited, generally believed to signify the five living 1964 authors, with Higgs, Englert, Guralnik, Hagen attending and Kibble confirming his invitation (Brout having died in 2011).

The date was July 4, 2012, and both of the CERN experiments announced they had independently made the same discovery: CMS of a previously unknown boson with mass 125.3 +/- 0.6 GeV/c^2 and ATLAS of a boson with a mass 126.0+/- 0.6 GeV/c^2. Using the combined analysis of two interaction types (known as channels), both experiments independently reached a local significance of 5 sigma, implying that the probability of getting at least as strong a result by chance alone is less than 1 in 3 million. When additional channels were taken into account, the CMS significance was reduced to 4.9 sigma. The two teams had been working "blinded" from each other from around late 2011 or early 2011 or early 2012—meaning, they did not discuss their results with each other, providing additional certainty that any common finding was genuine validation of a particle.

This level of evidence has been confirmed by two separate teams and experiments and meets the formal level of proof required to announce a confirmed discovery. One date is very important relating to all this; it is July 31, 2012, when the ATLAS collaboration presented additional data analysis on the observation of a new particle, including data from a third channel, which improved the significance to 5.9 sigma (1 in 588 million chance of obtaining at least as strong evidence by random background effects alone) and mass 126.0 +/- 0.4 (stat) +/- (sys) GeV/c^2, and CMS improved the significance to 5 sigma and mass 125.3 +/- 0.4 (stat) +/- 0.5 (sys) GeV/c^2.

The new particle was tested as a Higgs boson. Following the 2012 discovery, it was still unconfirmed whether or not the 125 GeV/c particle was a Higgs boson.

On one hand, observations remained consistent with the observed particle being the standard model Higgs boson, and the particle decayed into at least some of the predicted channels. Moreover, the production rates and branching ratios for the observed channels broadly matched the predictions by the standard model within the experimental uncertainties. However, the experimental uncertainties currently still left room for alternative explanations; meaning, an announcement of the discovery of a Higgs boson would have been premature. To allow more opportunity for data collection, the LHC's proposed 2012 shutdown and 2013–2014 upgrade were postponed by seven weeks into the year 2013.

In November 2012, in a conference in Kyoto, researchers said evidence gathered since July was falling into line with basic standard model more than its alternatives, with a range of results for several interactions matching that theory's predictions. Physicist Matt Strassler highlighted "considerable" evidence that the new particle is not a pseudoscalar negative-parity particle (consistent with this required finding for a Higgs boson), "evaporation" or lack of increased significance for previous hints of nonstandard model findings, expected standard model interactions with W and Z bosons, absence of "significant new implications" for or against supersymmetry, and in general, no significant deviations to date from the results expected of a standard model boson.

However, some kinds of extensions to the standard model would also show very similar results, so commentators noted that based on other particles that are still being understood long after their discovery, it may take years to be sure and decades to fully understand the particle that has been found. These findings meant that as of January 2013, scientists were very sure they had found an unknown particle of mass ~125 GeV/c^2 and had not been misled by experimental error or a chance result. They were also sure, from initial observations, that the new particle was some kind of boson. The behaviors and properties of the particle, so far as examined since July 2012, also seemed quite close to the behaviors expected of a Higgs boson.

Even so, it could still have been a Higgs boson or some other unknown boson, since future tests could show behaviors that do not match Higgs boson. As of December 2012, CERN still only stated that the new particle was "consistent with" the Higgs boson, and scientists did not yet positively say it was the Higgs boson. Despite this, in late 2012, widespread media reports announced (incorrectly) that a Higgs boson had been confirmed during the year. In January 2013, CERN director general Rolf-Dieter Heuer stated that based on data analysis to date, an answer could be possible *toward* mid-2013, and the deputy chair of physics at Brookhaven National Laboratory stated in February 2013 that a "definitive" answer might require "another few years after the collider's 2015 restart."

In early March 2013, CERN research director Sergio Bertalucci stated that confirming spin-0 was the major remaining requirement to determine whether the particle is at least some kind of Higgs boson. On the fourteenth of March 2013, CERN confirmed that "CMS and ATLAS have compared a number of options for the spin-parity of this particle, and these all refer no spin and even parity [two fundamental criteria of a Higgs boson consistent with the standard model]. This coupled with the measured interactions of the new particle with other particles, strongly indicates that it is a Higgs boson." This also makes the particle the first elementary scalar particle to be discovered in nature.

There are examples of tests used to validate that the discovered particle is the Higgs boson.

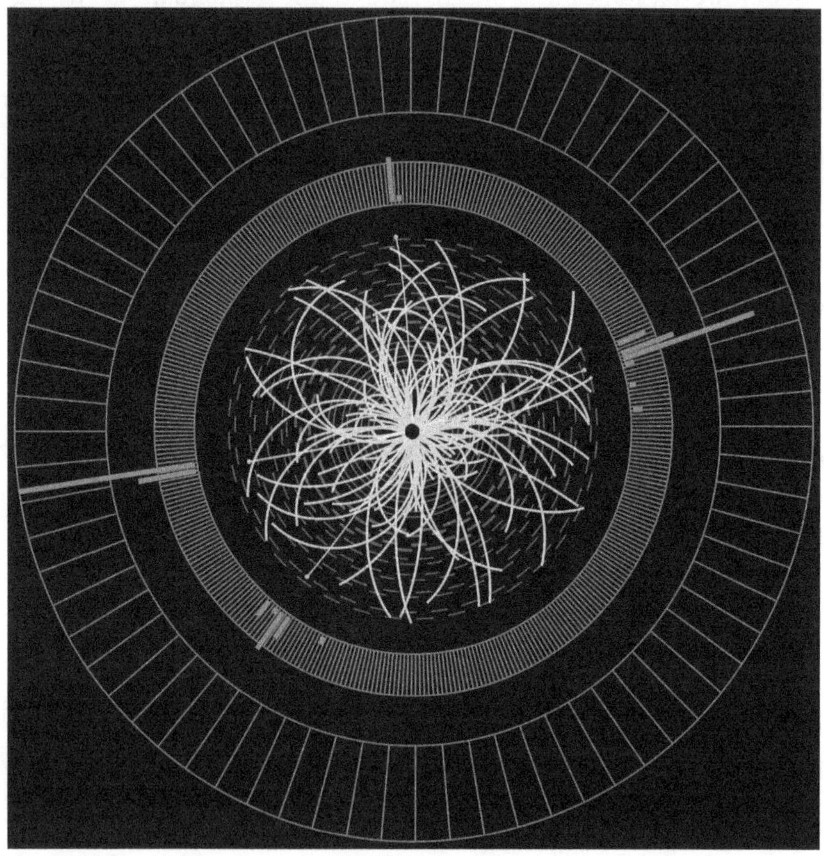

HIGGS BOSON

In July 2017, CERN confirmed that all measurements still agree with the predictions of the standard model and called the discovered particle simply the Higgs boson. As of 2019, the Large Hadron Collider has continued to produce finding that confirm the 2013 understanding of the Higgs field and particle. The LHC's experimental work since restarting in 2015 has included probing the Higgs field and boson to a greater level of detail and confirming whether or not less common predictions were correct. In particular, exploration since 2015 had provided strong evidence of the predicted direct decay into fermions, such as pairs of bottom quarks—described as an "important milestone" in understanding its short lifetime and other rare decays—and also to confirm decay into pairs of tau leptons.

This was described by CERN as being "of paramount importance to establishing the coupling of the Higgs boson to leptons and represents an important step towards measuring its couplings to third generation fermions, the very heavy copies the electrons and quarks, whose role in nature is a profound mystery." Published results as of March 19, 2018, at 13 TeV for ATLAS and CMS had their measurements of the Higgs mass at 124.98 +/- 0.28 GeV and 125.26 +/- 0.21 GeV respectively. In July 2018, the ATLAS and CMS experiments reported observing the Higgs boson decay into a pair of bottom quarks, which make up approximately 60 percent of all its decays. Some believe there is a theoretical need for the great Higgs boson.

Gauge invariance is an important property of modern particle theories, such as the standard model, partly due to its success in other areas of fundamental physics, such as electromagnetism and the strong interaction (quantum chromodynamics). However, there were great difficulties in developing gauge theories for the weak nuclear force or a possible unified electroweak interaction. Fermions with a mass term would violate gauge symmetry and therefore cannot be gauge invariant. (This can be seen examining the Dirac Lagrangian for a fermion in terms of left- and right-handed components; we find none of the spin-half particles could ever flip helicity as required for mass, so they must be massless.)

W and Z bosons are observed to have mass, but a boson mass term contains the combination, which clearly depend on the choice of gauge, and therefore these masses, too, cannot be gauge invariant. It seems that none of the standard model fermions or bosons could "begin" with mass as an inbuilt property except by abandoning gauge invariance. If gauge invariance were to be retained, then these particles had to be acquiring their mass by some other mechanism or interaction. Additionally, whatever was giving these particles their mass has to not "break" gauge invariance as the basis for other parts of the theories where it worked well and has to not require or predict unexpected massless particles or long-range forces (seemingly an inevitable consequence of Goldstone's theorem) that did not actually seem to exist in nature.

A solution to all these overlapping problems came from the discovery of a previously unnoticed borderline case hidden in the mathematics of Goldstone's theorem, that under certain conditions it might theoretically be possible for a symmetry to be broken without disrupting gauge invariance and without any new massless particles or forces and having "sensible" (renormalizable) results mathematically. This became known as the Higgs mechanism. The standard model hypothesizes a field that is responsible for this effect, called the Higgs field, which has the unusual property of a nonzero amplitude in its ground state—i.e., a nonzero vacuum expectation value. It can have this effect because of its unusual "Mexican hat-shaped" potential, whose lowest "point" is not at its "center." In simple terms, unlike all other known fields, the Higgs field requires less energy to have a nonzero value than a zero value, so it ends up having a nonzero value everywhere.

Below a certain extremely high energy level, the existence of this nonzero vacuum expectation spontaneously breaks electroweak gauge symmetry, which in turn gives rise to the Higgs mechanism and triggers the acquisition of mass by those particles interacting with the field. This effect occurs because scalar field components of the Higgs field are "absorbed" by the massive bosons as degrees of freedom and couple to the fermions via Yukawa coupling, thereby producing the expected mass terms. When symmetry breaks under these conditions, the Goldstone bosons that arise interact with the Higgs field (and with other particles capable of interacting with the Higgs field) instead of becoming new massless particles.

The intractable problems of both underlying theories "neutralize" each other, and the residual outcome is that elementary particles acquire a consistent mass based on how strongly they interact with the Higgs field. It is the simplest known process capable of giving mass to the gauge bosons while remaining compatible with gauge theories. Its quantum would be a scalar boson, known as the Higgs boson.

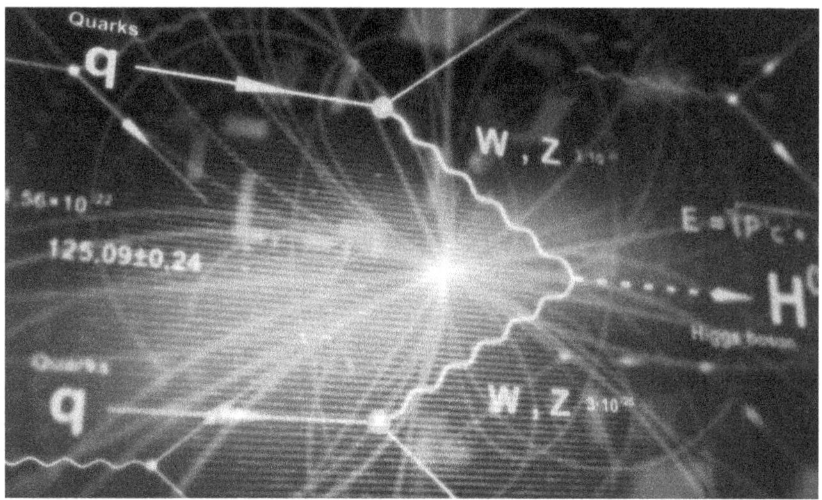

Let's talk about properties of the Higgs field. In the standard model, the Higgs field is a scalar tachyonic field—*scalar* meaning it does not transform under Lorentz transformations, and *tachyonic* meaning the field (but not the particle) has imaginary mass and, in certain configurations, must undergo symmetry breaking. It consists of four components: two neutral ones and two charged component fields.

Both of the charged components and one of the neutral fields are Goldstone bosons, which act as the longitudinal third-polarization components of the massive W+, W-, and Z bosons. The quantum of the remaining neutral component corresponds to (and is theoretically realized as) the massive Higgs boson. This component can interact with fermions via Yukawa coupling to give them mass as well. Mathematically, the Higgs field has imaginary mass and is therefore a tachyonic field. While tachyons (particles that move faster than light) are a purely hypothetical concepts, fields with imaginary mass have come to play an important role in modern physics. Under no circumstances do any excitations ever propagate faster than light in such theories; the presence or absence of a tachyonic mass has no effect whatsoever on the maximum velocity of signals (there is no violation of causality).

Instead of faster-than-light particles, the imaginary mass creates an instability: Any configuration in which one or more field excitations are tachyonic must spontaneously decay, and the resulting configuration contains no physical tachyons. This process is known as tachyon condensation and is now believed to be the explanation for how the Higgs mechanism itself arises in nature, and therefore the reason behind electroweak symmetry breaking. Although the notion of imaginary mass might seem troubling, it is only the field, and not the mass itself, that is quantized.

Therefore, the field operators at spacelike separated points still commute (or anticommute), and information and particles still do not propagate faster than light. Tachyon condensation drives a physical system that has reached a local limit—and might naively be expected to produce physical tachyons—to an alternate stable state where no physical tachyons exist. Once a tachyonic field such as the Higgs field reaches the minimum of the potential, its quanta are not tachyons anymore but rather are ordinary particle, such as the Higgs boson.

CHAPTER 41

The standard model does not predict the mass of the Higgs boson. If mass is between 115 and 180 GeV/c^2 (consistent with empirical observations of 125 GeV/c^2), then the standard model can be valid at energy scales all the way up to the Planck scale (10^{19} GeV). Many theorists expect new physics beyond the standard model to emerge at the TeV-scale, based on unsatisfactory properties of the standard model. The highest possible mass scale allowed for the Higgs boson (or some other electroweak symmetry breaking mechanism) is 1.4 TeV; beyond this point, the standard model becomes inconsistent without such a mechanism, because unitarity is violated in certain scattering processes.

It is also possible, although experimentally difficult, to estimate the mass of the Higgs boson indirectly. In the standard model, the Higgs boson has a number of indirect effects; most notably, Higgs loops result in tin corrections to masses of W and Z bosons. Precision measurements of electroweak parameters, such as the Fermi constant and masses of W/Z bosons, can be used to calculate constraints of the mass of the Higgs. As of July 2011, the precision electroweak measurements tell us that the mass of the Higgs boson is likely to be less than about 161 GeV/c^2 at 95 percent confidence level (this upper limit would increase to 185 GeV/c^2 if the lower bound of 114.4 GeV/c^2 from the LEP-2 direct search is allowed for).

These indirect constraints rely on the assumption that the standard model is correct. It may still be possible to discover a Higgs boson above these masses if it is accompanied by other particles beyond those predicted by the standard model. Everyday matter is composed of atoms, once presumed to be matter's elementary particles—*atom* meaning "unable to cut" in Greek—although the atom's existence remained controversial until about 1910, as some leading physicists regarded molecules as mathematical illusions, and matter as ultimately composed of energy. Soon, subatomic constituents of the atom were identified. As the 1930s opened, the electron and the proton had been discovered, along with the photon, the particle of electromagnetic radiation.

At that time, the recent advent of quantum mechanics was radically altering the conception of particles, as a single particle could seemingly span a field as would a wave, a paradox still eluding satisfactory explanation. Via quantum theory, protons and neutrons were found to contain quarks—up quarks and down quarks—now considered elementary particles. Within a molecule, the electron's three degrees of freedom (charge, spin, orbital) can separate via the wave function into three quasiparticles (holon, spinon, orbiton). Yet a free electron, which is not orbiting an atomic nucleus and lacks orbital motion, appears unsplittable and remains regarded as an elementary particle.

Around 1980, an elementary particle's status as indeed elementary—an ultimate constituent of substance—was mostly discarded for a more practical outlook, embodied in particle physics' standard model, what's known as science's most experimentally successful theory. Many elaborations upon and theories beyond the standard model, including the popular supersymmetry, double the number of elementary particles by hypothesizing that each known particle associates with a "shadow" partner far more massive, although all such superpartners remain undiscovered. Meanwhile, an elementary boson mediating gravitation—the graviton—remains hypothetical.

According to the current models of big bang nucleosynthesis, the primordial composition of visible matter of the universe should be about 75 percent hydrogen and 25 percent helium-4 (in mass). Neutrons are made up of one up and two down quarks, while protons are made of two up and one down quark. Since the other common elementary particles (such as electrons, neutrinos, or weak bosons) are so light or so rare when compared to atomic nuclei, we can neglect their mass contribution to the observable universe's total mass. Therefore, one can conclude that most of the visible mass of the universe consists of protons and neutrons, which, like all baryons, in turn consist of up quarks and down quarks.

Some estimates imply that there are roughly 10^{80} baryons (almost entirely protons and neutrons) in the observable universe. The number of protons in the observable universe is called the Eddington number. In a term of number of particles, some estimates imply that nearly all matter, excluding dark matter, occurs in neutrinos, which constitute the majority of the roughly 10^{86} elementary particles of matter that exist in the visible universe. Other estimates imply that roughly 10^{97} elementary particles exist in the visible universe (not including dark matter), mostly photons and other massless force carriers.

The standard model of particle physics contains twelve flavors of elementary fermions, plus their corresponding antiparticles, as well as elementary bosons that mediate the forces and the Higgs boson, which was reported on July 4, 2012, as having been likely detected by the two main experiments at the Large Hadron Collider (ATLAS and CMS). However, the standard model is widely considered to be a provisional theory rather than a truly fundamental one, since it is not known if it is compatible with Einstein's general relativity. There may be hypothetical elementary particles not described by the standard model, such as the graviton, the particle that would carry the gravitational force, and sparticles, supersymmetric partners of the ordinary particles.

CHAPTER 42

The future circular collider (FCC) is a conceptual study that aims to develop designs for a post-LHC particle accelerator with an energy significantly above that of previous circular collider (SPS, Tevatron, LCH). After injection at 3.3 TeV, each beam would have a total energy of 560 MJ. At a collision energy of 100 TeV, this increases to 16.7 GJ. These total energy values exceed the present LHC by nearly a factor of 30. The FCC study explores the feasibility of different particle collider scenarios with the aim of significantly increasing the energy and luminosity compared to existing colliders. It aims to complement existing technical designs for linear electron/positron colliders (ILC and CLIC).

The study explores the potential of hadron and lepton circular colliders, performing an analysis of infrastructure and operation concepts and considering the technology research and development programs that are required to build and operate a future circular collider. A conceptual design report was published in early 2019, in time for the next update of the European Strategy for Particle Physics. The study hosted by CERN has been initiated as a direct response to the high-priority recommendation of the updated European Strategy for Particle Physics, published in 2013, which asked that "CERN should undertake design studies for accelerator projects in a global context, with emphasis on proton-proton and electron-positron high-energy frontier machines. These design studies should be coupled to a vigorous accelerator R&D program, including high-field magnets and high-gradient accelerating structures, in collaboration with national institutes, laboratories, and universities worldwide." The goal was to inform the next Update of the European Strategy for Particle Physics (2019–2020) and the wider physics community for the feasibility of circular colliders complementing previous studies for linear colliders as well as other proposal for particle physics experiments. The launch of the FCC study was also in line with the recommendations of the United States Particle Physics Project Prioritization Panel (P5) and of the International Committee for Future Accelerators (ICFA).

The discovery of the Higgs boson at the LHC, together with the absence so far of any phenomena beyond the standard model in collisions at center of mass energies up to 8 TeV, has triggered an interest in future circular colliders to push the energy and precision frontiers complementing studies for future linear machines. The discovery of a "light" Higgs boson with a mass of 125 GeV revamped the discussion for a circular lepton collider that would allow detailed studies and precise measurement of this new particle. With the study of a new eighty- to one-hundred-kilometer-circumference tunnel (see also VLHC) that would fit in the Geneva region, it was realized that a future circular lepton collider could offer collision energies up to 400 GeV (thus allowing for the production of top quarks) at unprecedented luminosities.

The design of FCC-ee was combining the experience gained by LEP2 and the latest B factories. Two main limitations to circular accelerator performance are energy loss due to synchrotron radiation and the maximum value of magnetic fields that can be obtained in bending magnets to keep the energetic beams in a circular trajectory. Synchrotron radiation is of particular importance in the design and optimization of a circular lepton collider and limits the maximum energy reach that can be reached as the phenomenon depends on the mass of the accelerated particle. To address these issues, a sophisticated machine design along with the advancement of technologies like accelerating RF cavities and high-field magnets are needed.

Future "intensity and luminosity frontier" lepton colliders like those considered by the FCC study would enable the study with very high precision of the properties of the Higgs boson, the W and Z bosons, and the top quark, pinning down their interactions with an accuracy at least in order of magnitude better than today. The FCC-ee could collect 10^{12} Z boson, 10^8 W pairs, 10^6 Higgs bosons, and $4x10^5$ top-quark pair per years.

As a second step, an "energy frontier" collider at 100 TeV (FCC-hh) could be a "discovery machine" offering an eightfold increase compared to the current energy reach of the LHC. The FCC integrated project, combining FCC-ee and FCC-hh, would rely on a shared and cost-effective technical and organizational infrastructure, as was the case with LEP followed by LHC. This approach improves by several orders the sensitivity to elusive phenomena at low mass and, by an order of magnitude, the discovery reach for new particles at the highest masses. This will allow to uniquely map the properties of the Higgs boson and electroweak sector and broaden the exploration for different dark matter candidate particles complementing other approaches with neutrino beams, noncollider experiments, and astrophysics experiments.

The LHC has greatly advanced our understanding of matter and the standard model (SM). The discovery of the Higgs boson completed the particle content of the standard model of particle physics, the theory that describes the laws governing most of the known universe. Yet the standard model cannot explain several observations, such as evidence for dark matter, prevalence of matter over antimatter, and the neutrino masses.

The LHC has inaugurated a new phase of detailed studies of the properties of the Higgs boson and the way in which it interacts with the other SM particles. Future colliders with a higher energy and collision rate will largely contribute in performing these measurements, deepening our understanding of the standard model processes, test its limits, and search for possible deviations or new phenomena that could provide hints for new physics. The future circular collider (FCC) study develops options for potential high-energy frontier circular colliders at CERN for the post-LHC ear. Among other things, it plans to look for dark matter particles, which account for approximately 25 percent of the energy in the observable universe. Through new experiments, a collider can probe the full range of dark matter (DM) masses allowed by astrophysical observations. There is a very broad class of models for weakly interacting massive particle (WIMS) in the GeV-10s of TeV mass scale, which could be in the range of the FCC.

FCC could also lead the progress in precision measurements of electroweak precision observables (EWPO). The measurements played a key role in the consolidation of the standard model and can guide future theoretical developments. Moreover, results from the measurements can inform data from astrophysical/cosmological observations. The improved precision offered by the FCC integrated program increases the discovery potential for new physics.

Moreover, FCC-hh will enable the continuation of the research program in ultrarelativistic heavy-ion collisions from RHIC and LHC. The higher energies and luminosities offered by FCC-hh when operating with heavy ions will open new avenues in the study of the collective properties of quarks and gluons. The FCC study also foresees an interaction point for electrons with protons (FCC-eh). These deep inelastic scattering measurements will resolve the parton structure with very high accuracy providing a per-mile accurate measurement of the strong coupling constant. These results are essential for a program of precision measurements and will further improve the sensitivity of search for new phenomena, particularly at higher masses.

The FCC study originally put an emphasis on proton-proton (hadron or heavy ion) higher-energy collider that could also house an electron-positron (ee) high-intensity frontier collider as a first step. However, after assessing the readiness of the different technologies and the physics motivation, the FCC collaboration came up with the so-called FCC integrated program foreseen as a first-step FCC-ee with an operation time of about ten years at different energy ranges from 90 GeV to 350 GeV, followed by FCC-hh with an operation time of about fifteen years.

The FCC collaboration has identified the technological advancements required for reaching the planned energy and intensity and performs technology feasibility assessments for critical elements of future circular colliders (i.e., high-field magnets superconductors, radio frequency cavities cryogenic and vacuum system, power systems, beam screen system, a.o.). The project needs to advance these technologies to meet the requirements of a post-LHC machine but also to ensure the large-scale applicability of these technologies that could lead to their further industrialization. The study also provides an analysis of the infrastructure and operational cost that could ensure the efficient and reliable operation of a future larger-scale research infrastructure.

Strategic R&D identified in the CDR over the coming years will concentrate on minimizing construction costs and energy consumption while maximizing the socioeconomic impact with a focus on benefits for industry and training. Scientists and engineers are also working on the detector concepts needed to address the physics questions in each of the scenario (hh, ee, he). The work program includes experiment and detector concept studies to allow new physics to be explored. Detector technologies will be based on experiment concepts, the projected collider performance, and the physics cases.

New technologies have to be developed in diverse fields, such a cryogenic, superconductivity, material science, and computer science, including new data processing and data management concepts. A lepton collider with center-of-mass collision energies between 9 and 350 GeV is considered a potential intermediate step toward the realization of the hadron facility. Clean experimental conditions have given e^+e^- storages rings a strong record both for measuring known particles with the highest precision and for exploring the unknown. More specifically, high luminosity and improved handling of lepton beams would create the opportunity to measure the properties of the Z, W, Higgs, and top particles, as well as the strong interaction, with increased accuracy.

It can search for new particles coupling to the Higgs and electroweak bosons up to scales of $\Lambda = 7$ and 100 TeV. Moreover, measurements of invisible or exotic decays of the Higgs and Z bosons would offer discovery potential for dark matter or heavy neutrinos with masses below 70 GeV. In effect, the FCC-ee could enable profound investigations of electroweak symmetry breaking and open a broad indirect search for new physics over several orders of magnitude in energy of couplings. Realization of an intensity-frontier lepton collider, FCC-ee, as a first step requires a preparatory phase of nearly eight years, followed by the construction phase (also civil and technical infrastructure, machines, and detector, including commissioning) lasting ten years.

A duration of fifteen years is projected for the subsequent operation of the FCC-ee facility, to complete the currently envisaged physics program. This makes a total of nearly thirty-five years for construction and operation of FCC-ee. A future energy-frontier hadron collider will be able to discover force carriers of new interactions up to masses of around 30 TeV if they exist. The higher collision energy extends the search range for dark matter particles well beyond the TeV region, while supersymmetric partners of quarks and gluons can be searched for at masses up to 15–20 TeV, and the search for a possible substructure inside quarks can be extended down to distance scales of 10^{-21} meters.

Due to the higher energy and collision rate, billions of Higgs bosons and trillions of top quarks will be produced, creating new opportunities for the study of rare decays and flavor physics. A high-energy hadron collider housed in the same tunnel but using new FCC-hh class 16T dipole magnets could extend the current energy frontier by almost a factor 2 (27 TeV collision energy) and delivers an integrated luminosity of at least a factor of 3 larger than the HL-LHC. This machine could offer a first measurement of the Higgs self-coupling and directly produce particles at significant rates at scales up to 12 TeV—almost doubling the HL-LHC discovery reach for new physics. The project reuses the existing LHC underground infrastructure and large parts of the injector chain at CERN.

It is assumed that HE-LHC will accommodate two high-luminosity interaction points (IPs) 1 and 5, at the locations of the present ATLAS and CMS experiments, while it could host two secondary experiments combined with injection as for the present LHC. The HE-LHC could succeed the HL-LHC directly and provide a research program of about twenty years beyond the middle of twenty-first century. As the development of a next-generation particle accelerator requires new technology, the FCC study has studied the equipment and machines that are needed for the realization of the project, taking into account the experience from past and present accelerator projects.

The foundations for these advancements are being laid in a focused R&D programs:

- A 16-tesla high-field accelerator magnet and related superconductor research
- A 100 MW radio frequency acceleration system that can efficiently transfer power from the electricity grid to the beams
- A highly efficient large-scale cryogenics infrastructure to cool down superconducting accelerator components and the accompanying refrigeration systems

Numerous other technologies from various fields (accelerator physics, high-field magnets, cryogenics, vacuum engineering, material science, superconductors) are needed for reliable, sustainable, and efficient operation.

High-field superconducting magnets are a key enabling technology for a frontier hadron collider. To steer a 50 TeV beam over a one-hundred-kilometer tunnel, 16-Tesla dipoles will be necessary, twice the strength of the magnetic field of the LHC. The main objectives of a R&D on 16 T Nb3Sn dipole magnets for a large particle accelerator are to prove that these types of magnets are feasible in accelerator quality and to ensure an adequate performance at an affordable cost. Therefore, the goals is to push the conductor performance beyond present limits, to reduce the required "margin on the load line" with consequent reduction of conductor use and magnets size, and the elaboration of an optimized magnet design maximizing performance with respect to cost.

The magnet R&D aims to extend the range of operation of accelerator magnets based on low-temperature superconductors (LTS) up to 16 T and explore the technological challenges inherent to the use of high-temperature superconductors (HTS) for accelerator magnets in the 20 T range.

Let's talk about superconducting radio frequency cavities. The beams that move in a circular accelerator lose a percentage of their energy due to synchrotron radiation: up to 5 percent every turn for electrons and positrons, much less for protons and heavy ions. To maintain their energy, a system of radio frequency cavities constantly provides up to 50 MW to each beam.

FCC study has launched dedicated R&D lines on novel superconducting tin-film coating technology that will allow RF cavities to be operated at higher temperature (CERN, Courier, April 2018), thereby lowering the electrical requirement for cryogenics, and reduce the required number of cavities thanks to an increase in the accelerating gradient. An ongoing R&D activity, carried out in close cooperation with the linear collider community, aims at raising the peak efficiency of klystrons from 65 percent to above 80 percent. Higher-temperature, high-gradient Nb/Cu accelerating cavities and highly efficient RF power sources would find numerous applications in other fields.

Liquefaction of gas is a power-intensive operation of cryogenic technology. The future lepton and the hadron colliders would make intensive use of low-temperature superconducting devices, operated at 4.5 K and 1.8 K, requiring very large-scale distribution, recovery, and storage of cryogenic fluids. As a result, the cryogenic systems that have to be developed correspond to two to four times the presently deployed systems and require increased availability and maximum energy efficiency. Any further improvements in cryogenics are expected to find wide applications in medical imaging techniques. The cryogenic beam vacuum system for an energy-frontier hadron collider must absorb an energy of 50 W per meter at cryogenic temperatures.

CHAPTER 43

To protect the magnet cold bore from the head load, the vacuum system needs to be resistant against electron cloud effects, highly robust, and stable under superconducting quench conditions. It should also allow fast feedback in presence of impedance effects. New composite materials have to be developed to achieve these unique thermomechanics and electric properties for collimation systems. Such materials could also be complemented with the ongoing exploration of thin-film NEG coating that is used in the internal surface of the copper vacuum chambers. A 100 TeV hadron collider requires efficient and robust collimators, as 100 kW of hadronic background is expected at the interaction points.

Moreover, fast, self-adapting control systems with submillimeter collimation gaps are necessary to prevent irreversible damage of the machine and manage the 8.3 GJ stored in each beam. To address these challenges, the FCC study searches for designs that can withstand the large energy loads with acceptable transient deformation and no permanent damage. Novel composites with improved thermomechanical and electric properties will be investigated in cooperation with the FP7 HiLumi LHC DS and EuCARD2 programs. The Large Hadron Collider at CERN with its high-luminosity upgrade is the world's primary instrument, and with its high-luminosity upgrade, it is foreseen to operate until 2036.

A number of different proposals for a post-LHC research infrastructure in particle physics have been launched, including both linear and circular machines. The FCC study explores scenarios for different circular particle colliders housed in a new one-hundred-kilometer-circumference tunnel building on the tradition of the LEP and LHC both housed in the same twenty-seven-kilometer-circumference tunnel. A time frame for thirty years is appropriate for the design and construction of a large accelerator complex and particle detector. The experience from the operation of LEP and LHC and the opportunity to test novel technologies in the high-luminosity LHC provide a basis for assessing the feasibility of a post-LHC particle accelerator.

The FCC collaboration published in 2018 the four volumes of a Conceptual Design Report (CDR) as input to the next European Strategy for Particle Physics. The four volumes focus on: (a) Volume 1, Physics Opportunities, (b) Volume 2, FCC-ee: The Lepton Collider, (c) Volume 3, FCC-hh: The Hadron Collider, and (d) Volume 4, The High-Energy LHC. The FCC study, hosted by CERN, is an international collaboration of 135 research institutes and universities and twenty-five industrial partners from all over the world. The FCC study was launched following a response to the recommendation made in the Update of the European Strategy for Particle Physics 2013, adopted by CERN's council. The study is governed by three bodies: The International Collaboration Board (ICB), the International Steering Committee (ISC), and the International Advisory Committee (IAC).

The ICB reviews the resource needs of the study and finds matches within the collaboration. It so channels the contributions from the participants of the collaboration, aiming at geographically well-balanced and topically complementary network of contributions. The ISC is the supervisory and main governing body for the execution of the study and acts on behalf of the collaboration. The ISC is responsible for the proper execution and implementation of the decisions of the ICB, deriving and formulating the strategic scope, individual goals, and work program of the study. Its work is facilitated by the Coordination Group, the main executive body of the project, which coordinates the individual work packages and performs the day-to-day management of the study.

Finally, the IAC reviews the scientific and technical progress of the study and shall submit scientific and technical recommendations to the International Steering Committee to assist and facilitate major technical decisions.

CERN and criticism? The FCC proposed particle accelerator has been criticized for costs, with the cost for the energy-frontier hadron collider (FCC-hh) variant of this project projected to be over twenty billion US dollars. Its potential to make new discoveries has also been questioned by physicists.

Theoretical physicist Sabine Hossenfelder criticized a relevant promotional video for outlining a wide range of open problems in physics, despite the fact that the accelerator will likely only have the potential to resolve a small part of them. She noted that (as of 2019) there is "no reason that the new physical effects, like particles making up dark matter, must be accessible at the next larger collider." Response to this criticism came both from the physics community as well as philosophers and historians of science who emphasized the exploratory potential of any future large-scale collider. A detailed physics discussion is included in the first volume of the FCC Conceptual Design Report. Gian Giudice, head of CERN's physics department, wrote a paper on the "future of high-energy colliders," while other commentary came from Jeremy Bernstein, Lisa Randall, Harry Cliff, and Tommaso Dorigo among others.

In a recent interview, theorist for the CERN courier, Nima Arkani-Hamed, described the concrete experimental goal for the post-LHC collider. "While there is absolutely no guarantee we will produce new particles, we will definitely stress test out existing laws in the most extreme environments we have ever probed. Measuring the properties of the Higgs, however, is guaranteed to answer some burning questions....A Higgs factory will decisively answer this question via precision measurements of the coupling of the Higgs to a slew of other particles in a very clean experimental environment."

Moreover, there has been some philosophical responses to this debate, most notably from Michela Massimi, who emphasized the exploratory potential of future colliders: "High-energy physics beautifully exemplifies a different way of thinking about progress, where progress is measured by ruling out live possibilities, by excluding with high confidence level (95 percent) certain physically conceivable scenarios and mapping in this way the pace of what might be objectively possible in nature. 99.9 percent of the time this is how physics progresses and in the remaining time someone gets a Nobel Prize for discovering a new particle."

A high-luminosity upgrade of the LHC (LH-LHC) has been approved to extend its operation lifetime into the mid-2030s. The upgrade will facilitate the detection of rare processes and improve statistical measurements. The future circular collider study complements previous studies for linear colliders. The Compact Linear Collider (CLIC) was launched in 1985 at CERN. CLIC examines the feasibility of a high-energy (up to 3 TeV), high-luminosity lepton (electron/positron) collider. The International Linear Collider is similar to CLIC project, planned to have a collision energy of 500 GeV. It presented its technical design report in 2013. In 2013, the two studies formed an organizational partnership, the Linear Collider Collaboration (LCC), to coordinate and advance the global development work for a linear collider.

ABOUT THE AUTHOR

Nick Huntley was born and raised in Fort Wayne, Indiana. He has always been fascinated with science, Einstein, Tesla, time travel, and everything that makes up the universe. He grew up in the early 1970s, back before color television, computers, the internet, and the almighty cell phone. This energetic young man began working and making money at Kroger, bagging groceries, and washing dishes at a popular Italian restaurant at the tender age of just thirteen, in places like Arlington, Texas, and Fort Wayne, Indiana. Not ashamed of a hard day's work, Nick left those jobs to begin studies in the sciences. Nick received a degree in electronics engineering technology and worked mostly as a reliability engineer while raising a family and running his own security systems business in the evening hours to provide additional income for his growing family.

Nick's firsthand experience in the electronics engineering field and a deep passion for science lend him credibility in his genre of the complex concepts related to the universe, accelerators, detectors, colliders, and the great Higgs boson.

CPSIA information can be obtained
at www.ICGtesting.com
Printed in the USA
BVHW070251091121
621087BV00021B/124

9 781647 015169